BITTEN
SHIFTER

AN URBAN FANTASY
STAND-ALONE

BITTEN
SHIFTER

THE BITTEN CHRONICLES

BROGAN THOMAS

BITTEN SHIFTER - THE BITTEN CHRONICLES
WWW.BROGANTHOMAS.COM

Copyright © 2025 by Brogan Thomas

Ebook ASIN: B0DFC87MHN
Paperback ISBN: 978-1-915946-55-3
Hardcover ISBN: 978-1-915946-56-0

Edited by M.D. Bowling and proofread by Sam Everard
Cover design by Melony Paradise of Paradise Cover Design

For my hubby

Chapter One

Their cars block the driveway, so I grab a free space further down the street without a second thought. I finished the freelance project early; it's mid-morning, and Paul isn't expecting me home.

I bet they are watching a film.

They have always been such good friends. Lately, Paul has been helping Dove more around her house, taking on the heavier, more physical tasks. I'm so proud of him—proud of how generous and kind he is, helping my sister for me. He's thoughtful like that.

I hope they have got popcorn.

As I step through the door, something shifts in the air. A feeling of unease curls in my stomach, and the cutesy tune I'm humming catches in my throat.

Music. Sexy music.

Clothes lie haphazardly scattered across the floor—his and hers.

Still, like the absolute numpty I am, I convince myself there must be a straightforward explanation because there's always a logical explanation. Right?

Instincts, which I ignore, scream at me to leave. *Get back in the car, Lark, drive away, and come back later at your usual time!*

But no. I ignore that little voice of reason. I don't even know why I go upstairs.

I... need to see, I guess—silly me.

The door to the bedroom is wide open. I frown and tilt my head, hoping what is happening before me will magically change. If I view the scene from a different angle, it might be less obscene.

Less real.

Dove is vigorously riding my husband on our marital bed as if she is trying to break that sucker off.

My hand trembles as I pull out my phone. It takes two attempts to fish it out of my pocket, and my breath catches as I hit record.

I wince at her over-the-top screams.

I'm not a perv. This isn't about voyeurism. I need evidence.

Evidence of the end of my marriage. If I don't record it, he will gaslight me later. He will tell me it didn't happen—that I misunderstood or imagined it all.

He can't.

I might have a soft heart, but I'm no weak-willed ninny.

I only manage to film a few more seconds. I can't stand here any longer. I'm sure I've recorded enough to make my point. Any more of this, and I will have to bleach my eyeballs.

With the loud music covering my retreat, on leaden legs, I back up, turn and go downstairs. Instinctively, I head to the furthest room in the house without stepping outside: the kitchen.

As soon as I lay eyes on the sink, bile rushes up my throat. The porcelain is cold under my sweaty palms as I silently throw up.

When my stomach is empty, I wonder what to do now. I imagine sitting on the sofa, waiting for them to finish their little romp and come downstairs. I picture myself, vomit dripping from my lips and bile burning my tongue, trying to look dignified as I yell, *"Surprise!"* Or maybe go with a classic: *"Did you kids have fun?"*

What do other people do in this situation? Do they rant? Scream? Break things?

I wipe my mouth with the back of my hand, tuck loose strands of brown hair behind my ears with shaky fingers, and blink back tears.

My eyes fall to the drawer where I keep the knives.

Deep inside, I feel the urge to do something dramatic and bloody.

But that's not me. I'm not that person.

I've always been the peacemaker.

The pacifier.

The doormat.

I'm a practical person.

I get socially anxious and fret about saying the wrong thing, second-guessing every word that comes out of my mouth. In every situation, I never quite know what to do with my hands—they are strange, floppy, awkward things.

And I'm happiest curled up on the sofa with a book or buried in lines of monotonous code at work.

I've had training—if I hurt them, I will be the one locked up.

I'm not made for prison.

I can't touch them, even if I have every right to feel angry and betrayed. I can't ruin my life.

What life?

Our twenty-seven-year marriage is gone. The wreckage sits heavy on my chest, weighing me down. I feel broken, sad, and so bloody stupid.

It's ridiculous. What a waste.

What a waste of a lifetime spent with someone who never really loved me. Because if Paul loved me, he wouldn't be upstairs screwing my sister.

When we met, he was twenty-six, and I was a fresh-faced nineteen. So young. So naïve. And now? Now I'm a silly, middle-aged woman huddled in her kitchen while the two most important people in my life enjoy each other upstairs.

No, wait. Hold on.

I'm not even middle-aged, am I?

What is the average human lifespan these days? Eighty, if you are lucky? But last I checked, scientifically speaking, it's closer to seventy-three—if you don't end up a chew toy for a shifter or a vampire, that is. So, if you think about it, middle age is thirty-six and a half.

Thirty-six and a half.

Shit.

That's so young. And by that measure, I'm eleven years past middle age. I'm already well into dipping my toes into being useless to society.

I never thought I'd be useless to him—or that my sister would be a better fit. What a cliché. My sister. Paul had to do this with my beautiful, gregarious older sister.

At least it isn't a secretary—that I know of. I shake my head, my chin dropping as a pain-filled sigh rattles through my chest.

He is a weak-willed sisterfucker.

And Dove? She took the man I'd spent twenty-eight years of my life with... because she could.

After everything I've done for her. I've been her rock, made sacrifices, and there was nothing—*nothing*—I wouldn't have done for my sister.

If she called me to help bury a body, I'd show up with a shovel and gloves, no questions asked. Dove? She wouldn't ring for help if I were on fire. No, she'd warm her hands and complain about the smell of burning skin.

I loved them.

I trusted them.

What a mug I am.

I groan and bury my face in my hands. At least we never had kids. We were both selected for forced sterilisation as teenagers—a gift for the not-so-perfect specimens of the pure human population.

We were perfect together.

He was my person. I gave everything to our marriage. I would've done anything for Paul, the one I loved

5

beyond measure. I've always been a do-or-die kind of girl. Loyal.

I'm done.

I'm so done.

A whining sound, full of pain, bubbles up from my chest. Even as I hear it, I can't seem to stop—it's the sound of a tortured dog.

There's a thump upstairs, followed by laughter.

The horrid noise I'm making cuts off as my lips curl in disgust. I stare at the ceiling, my fingers flexing toward the knife drawer as though possessed.

I am not safe. Wow. That's such a weird, honest thought. *They aren't safe with me here.*

Now I understand why good people snap and go on a rampage. The crazy wants to burst out of my chest, clawing its way free like some alien creature.

I drag my hand away from the knife drawer again, the limb flopping to my thigh like dead weight.

I don't know how this happened.

There were no signs. No hidden phone calls. No suspicious behaviour. Or maybe there were, but I was too blind to see them. Even if there had been, I wouldn't have believed they could betray me like this.

My rose-coloured glasses don't go this shade of messed up.

I don't know how long it's been going on. Maybe it started today, or it could've been years.

Do I even want to know?

Does it matter?

There's no going back for me. Not now.

What do I do? What the heck do I do? I could wait

right here and confront them when they come downstairs. Scream. Cry. Wail. Listen to their lies as they twist everything until I don't know which way is up or down.

I could give Paul a chance to explain. But I already know what he will do. He will try to convince me to forgive him.

Forgiveness.

When I refuse, it will turn nasty. Paul won't be able to help himself. The blame game will start, and somehow, all of this will end up being my fault. And then what?

Now that I've uncovered their affair, what if they decide to chuck me out?

I can almost hear Dove's voice, dripping with faux sincerity: *"We're in love, Lark, and this is our house now."*

The thought hits me like a punch, and I rock back a step, slapping a hand over my mouth to stifle the manic cry clawing its way up my throat.

I'm expendable.

The realisation burns through my chest, sharp and unrelenting.

What if they don't care? What if they have no regrets? My heart, my ego, my sense of self—none of it will survive if they end up together. If Dove takes over my life.

I stand there, staring into space, while my inner voice screams at me to leave. *Run. Get out.*

But I'm frozen.

All I know is that I cannot—will not—be here when they come downstairs.

What the heck do I do? I don't want to be the cheated-on spouse. The sad, pathetic woman left behind. This is not my life. It can't be. It can't.

This is not my life!

Fate dealt me these cards through some cruel alignment of tiny circumstances—a perfect storm that led to me arriving home early. But you know what? I'm not bloody playing.

Fate can get stuffed.

I can't just abandon my life and disappear without a word...

Can I?

It would be a knee-jerk reaction born from pain. Immature. Petty.

And yet...

I never want to see either of them again. The idea of walking away without saying a single thing is so appealing. To not stick around for the inevitable circus: the screaming matches, the endless back-and-forth, the splitting of lives and memories into neat little transactional pieces—the rigmarole of tearing each other apart.

Ghosting Paul will drive him mad.

He loves the sound of his own voice and loves getting the last word. Why should I give him closure?

He'd never expect me to vanish, to drop off the face of the earth. And by doing the unexpected, he will be forced to experience the full impact of what he has done without it being cushioned by our relationship slowly fading.

It's an emotional bomb he isn't expecting.

My sister? Oh, Dove will be in for a treat. An angry, frustrated Paul isn't exactly attractive.

I don't care what happens next. I only hope it's torturous for both of them.

I gather my essential documents from the bottom kitchen drawer and head for the front door.

For the last time, I take in the home we built together—the life we built—now littered with their clothes scattered across the floor like rubbish.

What is left of our marriage? Lies, false memories, and stuff.

He can have it all—every last piece. Stuff can be replaced. Let Dove have my twenty-year-old knickers and my useless, cheating husband. If she wants Paul and my life so badly, she can have the entire package.

I grab my computer from the sofa, where I'd dumped it when I came home. Next to it is a client's thank-you gift—a bag and a beautiful bouquet of lilies, carnations, roses, and baby's breath.

My gaze lingers on the flowers.

Why shouldn't I let them know I've been here?

A deranged smile twitches my lips as the idea takes hold. I pick up the flowers and tuck the gift bag under my arm. Inside is a handwritten thank-you card and a bottle of champagne.

Conscious that I'm running out of time, I pluck the heads off the roses with aggressive snaps of my fingers. *A shame they aren't red*, I think, holding up the pink petals. But they will do.

I rip all the petals from the stems and scatter them at the bottom of the stairs, mingling them with the petals from the carnations. They form a winding path between the discarded clothing, leading toward the kitchen.

It's petty. It's theatrical. It's perfect.

In the kitchen, I remove my engagement, wedding, and

9

eternity rings and place them on the counter. Next, I add two long-stemmed glasses, the unopened bottle of champagne, the lilies, and a handful of baby's breath.

I tilt my head and appraise my work. Not bad. I hope it freaks them out.

The arrangement is elegant. Subtle. It says everything without me needing to leave a note or explanation.

Paul's a big boy. I'm sure he will figure it out.

Chapter Two

My shoulder clips the door frame as I stumble out, barely registering the twinge of pain. I softly close the front door behind me, shuffle down the garden path, and step onto the street. Rows of identical cookie-cutter houses stretch in both directions, prim and proper under the bright spring light.

I never liked this house. I never liked this street.

The gated housing estate where you are expected to wash your car every Sunday, keep your lawn trimmed to regulation height, and ensure the grass stays the right shade of green—hours of care for something that will inevitably grow back.

And if you didn't conform? The gossipy neighbours would make it their mission to let you know. The sneers. The passive-aggressive remarks. It always felt suffocating.

I glance around the pristine, silent street and feel the most overwhelming urge to shout: *"Paul, at number seven, is smashing the granny out of his wife's sister!"*

Now that would give them something to gossip about.

But I don't. Barely.

Instead, I clamp my mouth shut, scuttle down the road, and unlock the car. I drag my numb, emotionally drained body into the driver's seat. The door closes with a heavy thud that reverberates through me. I lean back with a groan.

I still need to do things before I can get the heck out of here. The last thing I want is to stay on this street a second longer, but these tasks won't wait. I pull my laptop from the passenger seat and open it.

First stop: the home security system.

"Dumbarse," I mutter when I see it's been switched to privacy mode. Of course, Paul forgot that I designed the damn thing. It records everything outside the house—cars, doors, the lot. I'd set it up after a string of local break-ins. Privacy mode shunts those recordings into a separate folder. A few quick clicks later, I locate and download the files. I don't look at them—the dozens of files. I don't need to. Just knowing they are there is enough for now.

Next: the bank accounts.

I log into our joint accounts and transfer half the savings to my personal account.

"I will find a solicitor tomorrow," I murmur, closing the laptop and setting it aside.

Last stop: my phone.

I hesitate for a moment. I'd chuck the whole thing in the nearest bin if I didn't need it for work. But I do—I'm self-employed. To avoid being driven mad by the cheater's incoming calls, I block all personal numbers. It does not take long—my friendship circle is embarrassingly small. Paul never liked any of my friends.

I slip the phone into the centre console, put on my glasses, and start the car. My hands shake as I grip the steering wheel. I take a deep, shuddering breath, but it does not help.

My skin crawls. All I can smell is them. Their coupling. They had sex in my bed. The evidence of their betrayal feels ingrained in my nose, clinging to my skin, hair, and clothes.

I want to shower. I want to scrub myself raw.

Rapid breaths whine through my tight throat. My internal temperature swings wildly between boiling hot and frigid cold. My head is spinning. I need to get a grip.

"Lark," I whisper, "you can do this."

I clench the wheel tighter, willing my hands to stop trembling. I can't lose it now—not when I'm about to drive. I've kept my cool until now.

Well, mostly. My lips twitch with a bitter laugh as I think about the flower display in the kitchen. At least they will know I left of my own volition and haven't gone missing, sparing them the need to call the police.

"I'm too old for this shit," I grumble, leaning back and letting my head thud softly against the headrest. I trace the bright blue sky with dry, unblinking eyes.

It's a beautiful day.

How dare it be beautiful?

It should be raining, at least. Thunder. Lightning. Some sign from the universe to mark the wreckage of my life.

A wild idea bubbles up in my mind. I let it simmer,

swirling around with the rest of my chaotic thoughts. Calmer now, I check my mirrors, glance over my blind spots, and slip the car into first gear. Robotically, I drive away from the shitshow that was my life.

The town fades behind me, its familiarity blurring into insignificance. Before I know it, I'm on the motorway, heading north toward the Sector Border.

I never thought I'd willingly drive toward the shifters.

Part of me—the broken, miserable part—wants to pull over, crawl under the nearest bridge, and wrap myself in a blanket of cardboard boxes. To give up. To just... stop.

But another part of me, the enraged, determined part, burns hotter. It wants to succeed. To thrive, if only to shove it in their faces. To scream, *"I don't need you, so eff off!"*

Bitter pain, I realise, is one heck of a motivator.

I drive for hours, the road blurring into a monotonous ribbon beneath my tyres. I force my mind to stay blank, refusing to pick apart my life with Paul. There's too much to untangle, too much pain clawing at the edges of my thoughts. Sobbing uncontrollably while behind the wheel isn't exactly safe.

So I focus on the engine's hum and the blur of signs flashing by. For now, that's all I can manage. The miles roll by as I stop only for fuel and cheap essentials: a few changes of clothes and toiletries—just enough to last until I'm settled somewhere.

And then I see it.

The Sector Border.

It looms in the distance, crawling up the horizon like a jagged scar cutting the sky. An impenetrable wall of magic, concrete, and electrified fencing spans the width of the

land, dividing the shifters from the rest of the country—
and the other human derivatives.

Derivative is the term people use.

Our DNA is still human—just with a twist. A splash of
extra junk DNA that works differently, making some of us
stronger.

Different.

Fangs, claws, and magic.

Vampires, shifters, magic users, and the rare, prized
pure humans—we all fall somewhere along a spectrum of
strength, with some unlucky individuals carrying a mix of
DNA that cancels itself out, leaving them next to useless.

Some say derivatives are a natural evolution. Others
spin tales of alien intervention. Supposedly, elf-like beings
tweaked our genome—probably the same theorists who
think aliens built our ancient ruins.

Science has not pinned down the origins of derivatives,
and most theories are quietly dismissed. Maybe the governments know more, but if they do, they are not talking.

Considering we don't even know all the species
lurking in the deep ocean, it's not a stretch to imagine
there's more about our genome that science has yet to
figure out.

Forty years ago, everything came to a head. Xenophobia
reached its peak, and society ripped itself apart.

We were killing each other. Pure humans, delicate in
comparison, teetered on the edge of extinction. Death rates
spiked. Birth rates plummeted.

For the derivatives—especially the blood drinkers—this
wasn't sustainable. They needed pure humans to survive.

The government had no choice. They passed laws that

changed everything: the derivatives would govern themselves.

Sectors were drawn up, dividing the country into pieces. Each species ruled its own.

And the fragile peace began.

Geographically, the shifters reign in the north, where the environment is harsh, wild, and staggeringly beautiful.

I glance again at the horizon-stealing barrier. It's a monstrosity, and the sight of it sends a shiver of apprehension down my spine. The shifters are territorial, and their borders reflect that.

They don't just guard their borders—they fortify them.

They maintain two borders: the internal one that leads into the heart of their empire, where only those with the correct DNA can enter, and the external one, the one looming through my car window.

This barrier separates the Human Sector from no-man's-land, a five-mile-wide, ninety-three-mile-long strip of neutral ground known as the Enterprise Zone. The area hosts national businesses where shifters coexist with other derivatives. Despite its collaborative nature, the security here is nothing short of airtight.

Entry into their territory isn't casual—it demands either a valid work visa or the explicit backing of a shifter sponsor.

Before I can even consider crossing into their sector, I will need to secure a qualifying job first.

Pure humans, vampires, and magic users aren't as rigidly separated as the shifters. The borders exist, but they are far from the military-grade fortresses the shifters have erected.

The tightly controlled Human Sector is in the centre of the country.

Below us, in the southeast, the vampires dominate the financial and political heart. Vampires, of course, are different. Their borders barely feel like boundaries. They want humans to visit—for dinner, if you catch my drift. Their sector borders feel more like invitations, with flashy buildings, vibrant nightclubs, and an entertainment culture designed to lure you in.

Magic users—mages, witches, and wizards—inhabit the southwest, where the air hums with latent power.

What everyone calls magic has a scientific explanation: it's a form of energy manipulation.

Pure humans perceive only a narrow slice of reality. Their senses are limited—six million receptor sites in the nose compared to more than a hundred million in a dog. And that's just smell.

Something unique in a magic user's brain allows us to manipulate the invisible forces of the world, such as magnetic fields, dark matter, and the substructures of reality. In essence, we manipulate gravity, mass, and molecular vibrations, using what humans can't see and what science has yet to fully understand to create incredible things.

As my vision wavers and exhaustion claws at me, I know I'm done for the day. I pull into the car park of a popular chain hotel. The sky is darkening, and I don't want to be on the streets after nightfall.

A yawn cracks my jaw, and booking a room feels like a chore. I power up my laptop, clicking through the motions to avoid having to talk to anyone more than absolutely necessary. If I can walk in, flash my ID, and get a key without speaking, that'll be perfect.

I don't have the energy for small talk. Tonight, the entire world can get lost.

While waiting for the hotel's booking system to update, I stare at the dusky sky, tapping my fingers on the keyboard's edge.

This is it.

It's time to put my shaky plan into action.

As a freelancer, I've worked with shifter businesses on and off for years. I'm not a superstar, but I'm good at my job, and people know I get things done.

Ten days ago, I received a job offer from the Shifter Ministry to help develop and implement a new defence system. It's an incredible opportunity—a once-in-a-lifetime kind of role.

But I dismissed it immediately, certain Paul wouldn't want me working for the shifters, let alone for their government.

I didn't even tell Paul about the offer.

He has never been good with the other derivatives, and the contract would require relocation. Even if his record was squeaky clean, he wouldn't have moved with me, no matter the prestige or benefits.

Paul won't admit it, but I know him too well. It's in his eyes, in the way he tenses when derivatives are mentioned. Like most pure humans, he is scared—scared of our differences, scared of our perceived weaknesses. That's why we lived smack bang in the middle of the Human Sector, on a gated estate where everything was controlled and contained.

The real kicker?

Both Dove and Paul are members of Human First, an anti-supernatural group. Idiots.

The Ministry undoubtedly has them on a watch list. I always steered clear of their nonsense, favouring tolerance and common sense. My job requires the highest security clearance.

Poking the supes is asking for trouble. I told them countless times not to mess with them; some of the stronger vampires can read your thoughts.

I glance down at the email I've pulled up. It's time to implement the first part of my plan. I never officially turned down the shifter job—life had been too hectic, especially with the big project I wrapped up today. Writing the rejection email was on my to-do list for tomorrow morning.

How fortuitous.

Now there's nothing stopping me.

I've got nothing better to do, nowhere else to go, and it's not like things can get any worse.

This job will give me more than a salary. It will give me a home, a fresh start, and an adventure. I rub the pale, empty skin of my ring finger, the absence of my wedding band achingly obvious.

It's a chance to go somewhere the past can't follow.

I read through the details of the offer again, the words blurring slightly in the dim light of the car and the harsh brightness of the screen. Then, quickly and decisively, I type out my acceptance, including the hotel's address so they can send over the paperwork.

If they are still interested, they will contact me.

I exit the car, smoothing down my trousers as I gather

my things. Chin up, shoulders back, I walk toward the hotel entrance.

The automatic doors slide open, and I'm greeted by a blast of sickly warm air that follows me into the lobby.

The hotel is standard—clean, efficient, and utterly forgettable, just like every other chain hotel. The air is tinged with the faint scent of freshly brewed coffee from the restaurant in the corner, mingling unpleasantly with the sharp pine scent of the floor cleaner.

I nod hello to the receptionist and give him my booking confirmation number. Moments later, I'm holding a keycard and heading to the lift.

I scan the card, hit the button for the fourth floor, and lean back against the cold, brushed steel wall. There's no mirror, but the black strip above the buttons reflects my face.

"Huh."

I look exactly as I did when I left work this afternoon. Not a hair out of place, not a hint of the turmoil churning inside me. It's impressive, really, how much of the pain I feel is invisible, etched nowhere but within.

The lift pings, and the doors slide open. I quickly find the room, and when the door clicks shut behind me, the dull, safe uniformity of four solid walls settles something inside me.

It feels as though I've finally stopped running.

I drop the shopping bags onto the suitcase holder next to the wardrobe, kick off my shoes, and strip out of my clothes.

The shower beckons.

Hot water pounds against my shoulders, runs down my

face, and pools at my feet. I scrub at my skin until it's bright pink, hoping to wash away the smell, the betrayal, the day.

But no matter how hard I scrub, it's still there.

I'm surprised I don't cry now that I'm safe and alone. I thought I would. I thought tears would come rushing out of me like a dam breaking, but instead, there's... nothing.

The numbness settles over me like a second skin, wrapping me in an emotional lockdown I can't break through. Somewhere in my mind, a little voice screams, *What the heck is wrong with you? Why aren't you more upset?*

I just feel hollow.

Chapter Three

Two days later, I receive a response from human resources. The email is short and to the point: a courier will deliver the contract to the hotel lobby at ten o'clock.

Shifters are old-fashioned about certain things; they don't trust electronic systems with top-level security documentation. Everything important is hand-delivered, with no exceptions.

When it's time to leave my room, I hesitate.

My hand lingers on the handle, muscles locked in a silent standoff with my confidence. It takes a monumental effort—mentally muttering and persuading myself—before I force the door open, step out, and join real life.

By the time I reach the tail end of breakfast, I've already lost most of my appetite.

The industrial toast maker is my first challenge. After a half-hearted battle—during which I seriously consider hitting the damn thing with my shoe—I settle for two slices, one burnt to a crisp and the other basically warm bread.

I smear them with strawberry jam, stuff the oddly textured slices into my mouth, and wash them down with two cups of bitter coffee. It does not help much.

At least I've killed some time.

With ten minutes left before the courier is due to arrive, I drift into the small lounge area and sink into a sofa facing the main doors. I set my laptop beside me and cross my arms, trying not to feel like a weirdo sitting here without a phone.

To my left, a wide column stretches to the ceiling, decorated with a tall fake palm in a pot that's seen better days. To my right, three vending machines hum mechanically, adding to the low murmur of conversation and the occasional clatter of a suitcase being dragged across the tiled floor.

I should have brought my phone.

But no—it's turned off, buried at the bottom of one of the plastic bags I shoved into the wardrobe. The past few days have been technical torture, with the nasty little voice in my head urging me to pick up the phone to check the missed and blocked calls.

I feel like an addict going cold turkey. It's not drugs, magic, or blood. It's a relationship.

Every memory has Paul at its centre, and that frightens me. Who am I without him? Our relationship didn't set the world on fire, but I thought we fit. I've spent so many years shrinking myself, compromising for the sake of 'us.' Maybe I compromised too much.

I made us work.

It's hard to let that go, harder still to shake the overwhelming sense of failure. I failed to see what was happening. I failed to protect myself.

When did he change? When did he decide I wasn't enough?

And how could Dove do this to me?

The questions loop endlessly in my head, making me feel sick. If there were a pill to forget, I'd take it in a heartbeat.

Maybe it wasn't just him. Perhaps it was the monotony of life—a day-in, day-out cycle of being a good worker and a good wife. Get up, make breakfast, go to work, come home, cook dinner, and spend quiet evenings together. It's what I thought he wanted. It's what I thought we both wanted.

Now, I hate the person I became.

I used to be a rebel who swore she'd never bow to anyone. My younger self would be appalled at this version of me. And yet here I am, looking back and wondering when I stopped fighting.

I grew up in a world where girls were told to be seen and not heard, where smiling through harassment was expected, and where a woman's right to her body was never her own.

I learned to be polite, to say thank you, to please everyone but myself.

To never rock the boat.

Even now, I admire women who speak their minds without fear. But that's not who I am. I'm always frightened of saying the wrong thing. I don't want to come across as mean or cruel.

I don't want to be alone.

I still want someone to love me, to be my person—someone who stands in the front row of my life, cheering me on, celebrating my triumphs, and catching me when I fall. I've spent so long cheering for others, but no one ever cheers for me.

Paul was never that person, was he?

I want to be angry and hate him, but he is not a monster, and he could have been worse. Even though he betrayed me, I still see the kind, funny man I married. I can't regret the twenty-eight years we shared, even if they led here. But I can never go back.

I'm not ready to call in a solicitor. I want to bury my head in the sand for a little while longer and let Paul suffer.

If I can sort out this new life first, build something stable before dealing with the wreckage of the old one, that would be perfect. It's not like the problem's going anywhere, but I will face it when I'm stronger—on my terms.

The only way forward is through, and I will get there.

Slowly, piece by piece, I will rebuild myself. I will start by being kinder to me. Because if there's one thing I've learned, it's that my cheerleader, my person, and my witness to this life is *me*—not anyone else.

I still can hardly believe I might be working on the other side of the border.

The shifters are a world unto themselves. Their leader, the Alpha Prime—what a name—rules his shifters with a grip tighter than steel. One wrong move, one significant mistake, and you are dead. Justice, if you can call it that, is brutal and absolute in the shifter world.

The thought briefly distracts me, as it always does. Alpha Prime. Every time I hear it, my inner child whispers *"Optimus Prime."* The Transformers fan in me won't let it go. Of course, the Alpha Prime isn't a giant robot fighting for freedom and humanity. He is the ruthless leader of an entire people, with the authority to decide life or death with a single word.

Shrouded in secrecy and speculation, knowledge about shifters has always been limited to a need-to-know basis. The shifter world shares only what it must. I remember learning in school that only alphas—the leaders—retain full control when they are in their animal form. Maybe that's why shifters enforce such strict security measures and maintain two impenetrable borders.

The idea of losing control and waking up with human skin between your teeth sends a shiver down my spine. I wrinkle my nose in revulsion. Nobody wants to channel their inner Hannibal Lecter.

At ten o'clock on the dot, the automatic glass doors glide open with a soft hiss, letting in a burst of damp air. My eyes flick up out of habit, and for a split second, I assume he is just another guest. But no—he's unlike anyone I've ever seen, let alone a courier.

He looks absolutely lethal.

Standing over six feet tall, he is dressed in a flawlessly tailored deep navy suit with a matching tie that probably costs more than my car. The glimpse of a crisp white shirt beneath only emphasises the broad width of his shoulders. His build is a classic inverted triangle—muscular and imposing—suggesting he is no stranger to physical training. His close-cropped dark hair, military sharp, and clean-shaven face do little to soften his features.

If anything, they highlight the hard lines of his jaw, high cheekbones, and the seriousness etched into his expression as he scans the lobby.

Only then, with the angle of his face, do I notice the faint, otherworldly glow of his eyes as they catch the light.

He is a shifter.

I've never understood why shifter's eyes glow like that. They call it 'beast shine,' which is both apt and rude. It's as if someone switched on their high beams. I've always wondered if they can turn it off—glowing eyes don't exactly scream stealth. Maybe it's different when they are in animal form.

It's been years since I last saw a shifter in person—not since childhood. Conference calls don't count. Most hotel guests seem unfazed, except for a pair of girls nearby who stop dead, their mouths hanging open as they gawk at him like he has walked off the cover of a billionaire romance novel. Maybe it's because we're near the sector border and shifters are less of a novelty here. Or perhaps he simply has that effect on people.

I shake my head, forcing my gaze away. None of this is my business. He's not breaking any rules, and the Human Sector does not mind the occasional shifter passing through —as long as they stay in human form.

Only the Shifter Ministry enforces the really restrictive laws.

Despite myself, I steal another glance at the man. Yeah, he is breathtakingly handsome—ridiculously so. His features are sharp and symmetrical, a perfection that does not seem real, like something out of Greek mythology. His strong nose and firm, unsmiling mouth give him a severity that demands attention. He's the sort of man you can't help but notice, whether you want to or not.

Stop it, Lark.

I huff, suppressing an absurd, creeping guilt of a married woman who's just cheated on her husband in thought. There's no reason to feel bad—I know that. It's not like I'm doing anything wrong. But when was the last time I looked at a man like this?

No, *ogled* a man.

Not that I'd touch this younger, handsome shifter with a ten-foot barge pole. Honestly, I'd be impressed if I ever went near another man again, given the state of my love life.

For a fleeting second, I imagine what being with someone like him would even look like. A tiny, cartoonish version of him appears in my head, all polished charm and perfect teeth. He winks and grins at me. *"Hey, baby."*

I snort at the absurdity of it. Almost immediately, I picture a horde of gorgeous women stampeding over me to get to him, as if I don't even exist. With a mental flick, I send the little figment flying out of my head.

Straight into the male danger zone.

I've made a lot of mistakes in my life. A pretty, unattainable man in a beautiful suit isn't one of them. You would need raging, uncontrollable hormones to even think about touching that one.

Not that the gorgeous shifter would give me a second glance. I look down at my sleeves, adjusting them unnecessarily. I'm not ugly—objectively, I'm attractive. But let's be real it's been years since I dressed for anything resembling seduction.

I wouldn't even know where to start.

I like my clothes comfortable, and my so-called beauty routine involves a quick slap of sunscreen, a dab of moisturiser, and battling the occasional rogue chin hair. If I'm honest, more than the occasional. Let's say I've become quite adept with wax strips.

I can't help it—I give him one last surreptitious lookover and to my absolute horror, the hottie shifter finishes scanning the lobby and... stalks towards me.

Well, isn't this interesting?

I shake my head in disbelief. Is *this* guy seriously the courier? *Really?* Because of course a Ministry courier would look like James Bond.

Is this my life now?

I wouldn't be in this situation if the Paul-and-Dove disaster hadn't happened. Meeting shifters and working with them will be part of my snazzy new government job—if I get it. I'd better get used to this sort of thing fast.

As he closes the distance between us, an odd, instinctive urge sweeps over me to hunch forward and protect my middle. It's primal and annoying, as though he is projecting alpha vibes at me from twenty feet away.

Nope. Not happening.

Feeling a tad reckless, I drop my arms, press my spine into the sofa, and lift my chin. I'm forty-seven years old. I've survived worse than one intimidating shifter.

I make direct eye contact and hold it.

His eyes—icy blue with a dark navy ring, sharp and arresting, reminiscent of a husky's—widen slightly. Blink, and I'd have missed it. A single sweep of his long lashes erases his surprise, leaving behind a cool, impassive stare.

I don't drop my gaze. His alpha vibes can get lost.

The part of me that would have shied away? That submissive part broke three days ago, and what remains lies somewhere in the hallway, scattered outside my bedroom door with the last scraps of my dignity. I've got nothing left to fear.

No fear. No joy. No hope...

Just rage.

A burning, unrelenting rage.

Chapter Four

LARK, what the heck are you doing? The thought cuts through me like ice water, jolting me out of my fury. My pulse stumbles, and shame quickly overtakes the anger. What was I thinking? Even among pure humans, direct eye contact like this can be considered aggressive.

Am I really trying to pick a fight with a shifter?

Suicidal?

I'm acting like a complete psycho.

I force myself to calm down. He has not done anything wrong. He can't help being male, ridiculously tall, and absurdly handsome.

My lips quirk into a self-deprecating smile. He is probably used to clueless humans. The last thing I want is for him to think I'm rude—or worse, a bigot. The only thing I have left is work, and I can't afford to mess this opportunity up by getting my head metaphorically—or literally—ripped off.

By now, he is standing before me, holding a hefty-looking envelope. Crap. I've missed my window to stand. If I do it now, we will be uncomfortably close. Instead, I stay seated and tilt my head up.

His nostrils flare and—wait—did he just sniff me?

I sit rigidly, pretending not to notice how deliberately he scents the air. Please, please let him be the courier and not some random guy who thinks sniffing humans in hotel lobbies is normal behaviour.

"Mrs Emerson," he says, his voice low and formal.

I nod, relieved. "Yes, that's me." I keep my tone polite and professional. Since he is delivering documents, I mentally dub him *Mr First Class*. "Are you the courier for the Ministry?"

"Something like that."

I wince internally. Not a courier, then. Great. Of course he is not, not in that suit. Probably some Ministry bigwig, and I've already managed to screw this up. *Come on, Lark, try to have some semblance of professionalism.*

"May I see some identification?" he asks.

"Yeah, sure." Awkwardly, I lift my hips and dig into the deep pocket of the cheap jogging bottoms I picked up in Tesco. After some fumbling, I retrieve my ID and hand it to him.

Careful not to touch my fingers, he takes the plastic card with a precision that feels deliberate. He studies it for what feels like an eternity, his thumb brushing over my name in an almost absentminded way. His jaw tightens slightly before he flicks the card between his fingers and hands it back.

I accept it and, with a polite smile, also take the package he extends to me. My arms sag slightly under its unexpected weight, and I balance it on my knees. "Okay, well, thank you."

He does not move.

I tilt my head and give him a small wave, encouraging him to move on like a lost lamb. "Thank you for coming and dropping this off."

"No, Mrs Emerson," he says, his tone patient but firm. "I must wait for you to review the documents and, if necessary, sign them."

"Oh." My eyebrows shoot up. "I thought it was just paperwork for me to look over." I glance down at the package, and its heft suddenly feels more significant. "That's... unconventional."

I glance around, the awkwardness pressing in. Should I do this here in the middle of the lobby? It's not like I can invite him up to my room. "It might take some time," I warn, trying to gauge his reaction. "Would you like to take a seat?"

He scans the area briefly, then shakes his head. "No, I'm fine." He settles into what I can only describe as parade rest, hands clasped behind his back, looking completely at ease.

"Right, okay." I try not to dwell on his unnerving stillness. I tug at the hem of my cheap Primark jumper, adjust my posture, and do my best to focus. Flipping the package over, I notice the flap is sealed with a blob of dark red wax stamped with a wolf. *Very fancy.*

I hum softly and carefully break the seal without

damaging the wax, then slide my fingers inside, wiggling the documents free.

As soon as I touch the paper, my fingertips tingle faintly. A prickle of nervous energy skates up my arms, and I can't stop myself from licking my lips.

The contract is saturated with magic—so much so that I can feel it zapping through my bones. *Magical paper. Of course it is.*

The spell woven into it is likely analysing me already, its tendrils poking around in my head, peeling back my thoughts and intentions.

My secrets.

Not freaky at all.

This kind of thing tends to make people squirm. The paper mages behind this type of parchment have a reputation, and it isn't a friendly one. If you have got skeletons in your cupboard, you don't want to touch their paper.

I take a slow breath, reassuring myself. It shouldn't be a problem. The magic isn't strong enough to pick up on my magical abilities.

At least, I hope not.

I turn the first page, and a sharp sting shoots through my fingertips. "Ouch! Stop that," I hiss, shaking the paper vigorously as though it will teach it a lesson. Bloody thing.

Mr First Class makes a slight muffled noise. When I glance up, his lips are pressed tightly together. His gaze is fixed on the doors outside, his face a perfect mask of polite indifference.

Oh no. He is going to think I'm not right in the head— who in their right mind talks to paperwork?

I spy red, embarrassed blotches blooming on my chest. Grimacing, I hunch over the document.

Apart from the creepy, finger-burning paper magic, everything seems in order. The role, however, is more military-adjacent than I'd expected, with a security focus that differs significantly from my usual work. A heaviness settles in my stomach as I reread the description.

Shifter Defence Digital
Defence Digital is part of Strategic Command and has a vital role within the Shifter Ministry in the age of information warfare.

This is important—high-stakes important. No wonder Mr First Class showed up instead of a regular courier. I blow out my cheeks, trying to shove down a sudden surge of doubt.

What am I getting myself into?

I skim the terms and conditions again, forcing myself to go slower this time. The eighteen-month timeframe is reasonable, the compensation is impressive, and the included apartment... well, the apartment is something else entirely.

I pause on the page detailing the accommodations and study the pictures. The Greenholm Ironworks is a beautifully restored historic site, originally built in 1790. The warm, golden brickwork and grand windows radiate charm. The complex includes detached and semi-detached homes, terraced houses, and luxurious apartments. There's even an indoor community pool, gym, and spa.

A pool! The idea of lounging by the water sparks a

smile, then I think about my hairy legs. Paul would have laughed and said I'd need a hedge trimmer to shave before daring to wear a swimming costume in public.

My smile dies as fast as it comes, a sharp pang striking my chest. The page crinkles under my grip, and I take a few steadying breaths.

It's okay. I'm okay.

I smooth out the paper and force myself to focus on the apartment details. It looks... perfect. I double-check everything for hidden pitfalls but find nothing to make me hesitate.

Without giving myself time to overthink, I reach into my bag and pull out a faithful old Biro. The end is so chewed it's a wonder it has not fallen apart, but it gets the job done. I sign my name with a decisive flourish.

Setting my copies aside, I tuck the signed documents back into the envelope and press it closed. Clearing my throat, I catch Mr First Class's attention. His piercing blue eyes snap to mine, and for a moment, I feel as though he is weighing me on an unseen scale.

I push the envelope toward him and force a confident smile. "You will find everything's in order," I say, keeping my tone calm and professional. "Thank you for waiting. I appreciate your time."

He takes the envelope with a single nod, his fingers brushing mine for the briefest moment. Then, just like that, he is back to his perfectly composed, slightly intimidating self.

"What did you do? Are you cheating on me?"

A woman's voice echoes across the lobby, raw with

disbelief. I glance up, startled, and spot the source immediately.

Her auburn hair gleams like a signal fire, and her pale face is a portrait of shock and fury. "With her? You did this with her? I can't believe you!"

The horrified man, the object of her wrath, steps out of the lift. He looks as if he's just been smacked in the face by reality. His panicked gaze darts to the blonde woman lingering behind him, then back to the redhead. He raises his hands in a futile display of innocence. "It's not what it looks like!"

"Yeah, sure, buddy," I mumble, sliding my signed documents into my laptop bag.

"It's a business meeting!" he insists, his voice rising as he edges closer.

She lets out a bitter laugh. "A business meeting that lasted all night? Do I look stupid to you?" Her voice cracks, but she holds her ground, shaking her head like she's trying to clear the betrayal from her mind. She takes a step back as though his presence physically repels her.

Desperate now, he lowers his voice and leans toward her. "Dayna, you're making a scene. Let's go home and talk about this. Please."

"No!" she snaps, jerking away from him. Her finger jabs into his chest with each word. "You are a liar. A cheater. I saw the messages. I know everything." She whirls to point at the blonde woman by the lift. "And you! You're a whore!"

The blonde woman's lips curl in a smirk. She steps forward, her hips swaying in a way that feels calculated, tucking a strand of hair behind her ear. Her chin tilts up, the picture of smug confidence.

My stomach twists. It's probably my own scars talking, but I despise her on sight.

"Dayna, stop," the man growls, trying to grab her wrist again.

She yanks her arm away with a glare that could melt steel. "No. Do not touch me. And don't come back home. I will have your bags ready for you to pick up. We're done. I want a divorce."

The lobby falls silent, save for the hum of the vending machines. People have stopped to stare; some whisper, while others pull out their phones to film. My hands grip my bag's strap like it's the only thing anchoring me.

"Where's the damn hotel security?" I mutter, casting a look towards the reception desk. A staff member is on the phone, talking frantically.

Watching this unfold makes me feel sick. Is the entire world cheating? I fidget with the strap of my bag, torn between wanting to scream, *Leave him! Leave him!* and rushing over to hug the poor woman, telling her she will survive this—that it will hurt, but she will get through.

Even though I know that's not always true.

The blonde wraps herself around the man's arm, pressing her body to his. Her voice turns syrupy and mocking. "Darling, what's all this about? Who's this woman?"

Dayna's expression is pure rage. "I'm his *wife.*"

The blonde lets out a theatrical gasp, her hand fluttering to her chest. "Oh, the ex-wife. The mad one, right?"

"Is that what you told her?" Dayna's voice trembles with rage and heartbreak. "That I'm crazy? What about our kids? Are they crazy too?" Her face crumples as reality crushes her, and her voice drops to a whisper. "Oh God, what am I going to tell the girls?"

Kids. Oh no. My chest aches for her, for them, for everything they are about to go through.

"Kids?" The blonde smirks, her tone laced with mockery.

She knows. She bloody well knows, and it only cements how much I hate people.

"Yes," Dayna snaps. "Our three children. Three little girls. We have been married for ten years—happily, I thought. But I guess now I'm your ex." A sad laugh cuts through the air like a blade. "Fine. You can have him. *She* can have you." She turns sharply, ready to leave.

But the blonde chuckles, low and mean. "You're right. She is mad. Come on, darling, let's go back to bed."

"Shut up, Jennifer," the man growls, trying to shake her off.

The redhead freezes mid-step, then spins back, her eyes brimming with tears and fury. Anger radiates off her like heat from a bonfire. "*Let's go back to bed*," she snarls, venom dripping from every word.

Uh oh.

Her trembling hand dives into her coat pocket and pulls out a sleek, six-inch wand of polished dark wood. My stomach drops.

She's a mage.

Oh no.

Jennifer also whips out a wand.

Foreign words tumble from Dayna's lips, sharp and guttural. The incantation crescendos with a flick of her wrist, and a thunderous crack splits the air.

BOOM.

The pressure in the lobby shifts violently, as if the atmosphere has imploded. Pain explodes in my ears, so intense I fear they are bleeding. Behind her, the hotel's glass doors and the floor-to-ceiling windows shatter in an instant, raining glittering shards across the pavement and car park.

The spell's shockwave sends everything loose flying. A rogue suitcase hurtles toward my head; I barely have time to gasp and throw my arms up.

Before it makes contact, a blue blur fills my vision.

Mr First Class moves faster than I can process, intercepting the impact of the luggage with his shoulder like it weighs nothing. Without missing a beat, he yanks a cushion from the sofa and deflects an errant spell. The cushion explodes into a cloud of stuffing and shredded fabric.

Then I'm airborne.

He scoops me up like I weigh nothing, dragging me over the back of the chair, my feet scraping against it. My back slams against the nearby column, and he pins me there, shielding me with his body.

His arms are steel bands as he tucks my head against his chest, muffling the chaos around us. His suit is soft against my cheek, and he smells clean and expensive—like cedarwood and leather. Even so, I'm trembling. The air around us plummets at least ten degrees, biting through my clothes as the ozone tang of wild magic saturates the hotel.

Another explosion erupts, this one even closer. I flinch when the fake plant beside us disintegrates in a shower of pottery shards, pelting my calves.

A heavy hand strokes my hair. "It's okay," Mr First

Class murmurs, his voice calm and steady. "I've got you. My security team is on the way."

His words barely register, drowned out by the chaos. Sparks fly as one of the vending machines takes a direct hit. It sputters in protest, spewing cans, which skitter, bounce and burst, drenching the floor—and our feet—in sticky liquid.

For a fleeting moment, silence falls. I risk a peek from the safety of his arms, spotting the two women shrieking and clawing at each other like feral cats. Security guards finally rush in and wrestle the two mages apart.

I exhale shakily, my heart pounding. My eyes follow the redhead as she's dragged away; she looks devastated, her face pale and blotchy with tears.

I hope she will be okay.

The shifter's eyes meet mine, and for a heartbeat, the chaos around us fades. It's unsettling, this electric sense of connection, as though he sees something hidden inside me —something I never knew existed, something Paul never tried to uncover.

Then, almost reluctantly, he lets me go. His severe expression snaps back into place, leaving me feeling both exposed and oddly small. Without breaking eye contact, he presses his hands against the wall above my head, does a clean, almost graceful push-up away from me, and takes a measured step back. His gaze sweeps over me, appraising.

Whatever test I'm apparently taking, I must pass, because he nods.

Gosh, he really is beautiful. It's not fair.

"Thank you," I say, my voice wavering a little. I shuffle

past him, brushing dust from my sleeves. "I hope your suit is all right."

He does not respond, his attention returning to the destroyed lobby. Spotting my computer still perched on the sofa, I hurry over. Plaster, dust, and shimmering bits of glass cling to it. I swipe at the mess with my sleeve, but the debris sticks. *I will have to get a wet cloth.*

As I fumble, I sense him move closer.

"If you collect your things, we can depart."

"Pardon?" I blink up at him, thrown by the sudden declaration. "Depart? Why are we going anywhere?"

"You can't stay here, Mrs Emerson. It isn't safe."

"It's perfectly saf—" I trail off, taking in the wreckage around us. Shattered glass, twisted metal, and toppled furniture. The sharp smell of ozone still lingers. *Oh no, he's right.* My voice drops to a whisper. "I... I haven't got anywhere else to go."

He studies me for a long moment, his jaw tightening slightly, then speaks with crisp efficiency. "I will arrange everything while you collect your belongings from your room. I will also handle your checkout." He adjusts his cuffs with practised finesse and strides off to the reception desk.

He does not bother waiting for my reply.

I stare after him, my mouth hanging open. "Wow. Things are moving fast. Way too fast."

For a brief second, I consider chasing after him to protest, or at least to ask questions, but I hesitate. The truth is, there's no point arguing.

With a resigned sigh, I sling my bag over my shoulder

and hustle toward the stairs, avoiding the smoking wreck of the lift. I guess this is it—my new life, my new adventure.

Ready or not, it's starting now.

Chapter Five

It takes less than five minutes to clear out my hotel room, motivated, of course, by the newly appointed blond bodyguard who is shadowing my every move. The shifter waits stoically outside my door as I pack, and now he follows me like a silent sentry.

I frown at his looming presence. He is massive, as though carved from granite and then dressed in an expensive suit. His broad shoulders practically fill the doorway, and his blond hair is cropped short, giving him a sharp, no-nonsense look. His green eyes sweep the room with the precision of someone who's used to keeping others safe—or taking them down.

All of this feels... excessive.

Sure, this is a government job, but I'm not exactly a rock star in my field. I'm competent, yes, but I've gone out of my way not to stand out. Maybe this is some over-the-top shifter security protocol. Or perhaps they are not protecting me at all—maybe they are making sure I'm not a spy or a troublemaker.

Fine by me, as long as they don't hurt me. I just need to get through the sector border, and then they will no longer be my problem. I can slip into obscurity among all the other humans working for the Ministry.

The blond guard escorts me outside. Mr First Class is on the phone, pacing as though he owns the pavement. He has not noticed me yet, so I hesitate. I'm not sure what the protocol is when he is on the phone and a half-dozen shifter guards are scattered around. Do I walk up? Wait for instructions? Risk being tackled to the ground if I make a sudden move?

I decide to stand still and stare at the horizon. There's a curious comfort in watching the world stretch endlessly, unmoved by my personal drama.

If there's one thing I do know, it's that I'm done playing the mousy wife. Surrounded by these shifters—literal predators—I need to find that fire buried deep inside.

Mr First Class tucks his phone into his jacket, his sharp blue eyes snapping to me. He takes in my plastic bags and then scans behind me. "Is that everything?" he asks, his tone laced with disbelief.

The man is observant—*too* observant. His eyes flick briefly to my bare ring finger, the pale band of skin betraying what used to be there. I lift the bags higher, a pathetic shield against his penetrating stare. "Yep, this is everything. I will get more once I'm settled."

As soon as I say it, a knot of worry twists in my stomach. Do they even have shops in the Enterprise Zone? The shifters are so secretive—who knows?

He grunts, apparently unimpressed, and waves a hand. A sleek, dark grey car pulls up to the kerb as if conjured by his command. Without a word, he strides to the back door, opens it, and gestures for me to get inside.

I blink at him. "Oh, no, thank you. I've got my car. I will follow you." I nod towards my Fiat 500 parked a few spaces away. I can drive myself and would rather not get into a car with a group of strangers.

His lips press into a hard line. "That won't be necessary. You will need a border escort, and your car isn't registered."

My jaw drops. "Not registered? What do you think I am—a delinquent? Of course it's registered," I sputter, indignant.

His eyes narrow. "Not with us. Your car is only registered for use within the other sectors. Mrs Emerson, you will be living and working in our Enterprise Zone. We have rules, and private vehicles are prohibited for the general public."

I mentally groan, but I force a polite nod. "Of course. I'm sorry—I didn't realise."

Behind him, the big blond bodyguard sneers, as if my car offence is the most hilarious thing he's heard all day.

A flush of embarrassment creeps up my neck. I can't help but second-guess every decision that brought me here. Signing those documents felt like the right move, but now I'm standing here, stripped of basic freedoms, wondering if I've made a colossal mistake.

What was I thinking? I don't know the rules, I don't

know these people—and I definitely don't know what the heck I'm doing.

But then I remember why I'm here—to get out of the Human Sector and start over.

Mr First Class extends his hand, palm up, an unmistakable demand. "Your keys."

I clutch my bags tighter. "What are you going to do with my car?"

"It will be safely stored until you return to this side of the border. Don't worry," he says, in a calm, soothing tone, as though talking to a rather testy toddler. His hand remains outstretched. "Everything you need will be within walking distance, and deliveries will bring your shopping straight to your door. You won't miss it."

I sigh, letting the tension escape in a long exhale, and switch my plastic bags to my other hand, the rustle of plastic loud against the tense silence. "Okay, thank you." I dig out my keys, staring at them for a moment before reluctantly handing them over. *Please don't let this be a mistake.*

His lips twitch, barely hiding a smile. Then, with the same smooth gesture, he waves me toward the waiting car. "Thank you, Mrs Emerson. Please, get in."

Each time he calls me *Mrs Emerson*, I feel a tiny piece of my soul wither. I awkwardly adjust the straps of my bag. "If we're going to be spending time in each other's company, could you maybe... call me Lark?" I try to keep my tone neutral, but there's a thread of desperation I can't quite mask.

Those pale blue eyes meet mine again, assessing me. At last, the corners of his mouth lift in the faintest smile.

"Okay, Lark."

"And you are?" The words spill out before I can stop them. I can't keep calling him *Mr First Class* in my head—it's bound to slip out at the worst moment.

"Merrick." The name drops from his mouth like it's being pried out with a crowbar.

Merrick. Huh. "It's nice to meet you, Merrick."

He huffs, takes my plastic bags, and hands them off to another shifter, who stows them in the car's boot. I'm glad I hid my dirty underwear at the bottom.

Clutching my laptop bag like a lifeline, I nod and manoeuvre into the backseat. The big blond bodyguard takes the front passenger seat, while another shifter slides into the driver's position.

I glance around at the suited, silent men surrounding me and the car, wondering where the heck they were when the mages were tearing up the hotel lobby. Nothing like a group of suited and booted shifters to scare you straight.

I look back at Merrick, expecting him to join us, but he does not move. Instead, he stands there on the kerb, his expression unreadable, as if he is holding the weight of the world on his broad shoulders.

"Good luck, Mrs Emerson," he says, his voice steady and low.

I clear my throat and give him a playful glare.

"Lark," he corrects himself with a small, almost reluctant smile.

Then, in one sharp motion, he slams the car door and steps back.

I stare out the window at Merrick's retreating figure. He doesn't offer a wave; he simply lifts his phone to his ear and marches off with that no-nonsense stride. And just like that, he is gone.

Why does that hurt? I don't even know him.

I will have to unpack that later—this sudden clinginess towards a stranger.

Since the 'incident,' I've tried to self-medicate and fix my broken heart with chocolate and sugar, hoping to kick-start some dopamine and happy hormones into my blood-stream. Nothing has prepared me for this confusing blend of excitement and danger in his presence.

I'm forty-seven years old. My idea of danger is faulty wiring at work, and I've gone out of my way to avoid anything that makes my heart skip a beat. Yet for a moment —just one—I forgot about the shitshow of my life.

I snap my seat belt into place as the car pulls away. The two men in the front carry on their quiet conversation, ignoring me completely. My Fiat sits abandoned in the hotel car park as we merge onto the motorway. I try not to look back at that piece of my old life, disappearing in the rearview mirror.

The border looms ahead.

It's difficult to describe the magic-infused monstrosity of concrete. The wall's surface is smooth and unbroken, making me feel like an ant. It stretches to the left and right as far as I can see, rising so high it vanishes into the grey haze above, blocking the sunlight and casting everything in shadow.

We keep driving, the motorway curving to the right. Twenty minutes later, we take an exit ramp, where a massive sign looms overhead:

Warning: you are approaching shifter territory. Turn back if unauthorised.

Below it, smaller signs add: prepare documents for inspection. Strictly no entry without prior approval.

I frown and glance at the paperwork sticking out of my bag. I've got my job contract, but I don't have any official-looking forms—no visas, permits, or whatever else might be required to cross into shifter territory. Surely Merrick would've made sure these guys have everything in order?

Still, the uncertainty nags me. I'm not the kind of person who likes to wing it. I prefer knowing what is coming and being prepared for every possible scenario. Right now, I feel as unprepared as I've ever been, and the looming wall ahead does not help.

I tap my fingers, trying to settle the anxiety buzzing in my chest. Five minutes. That's all I would've needed to get my head straight. But no one asked, and here I am, hurtling toward the unknown with no time to catch my breath.

Ahead, a series of booths are set up like drive-thru windows—without the yummy burger at the end—each made of dull concrete and metal. A few cars are lined up in front of them. We inch forward, join the queue, wait for about five minutes, and then it's our turn.

The guard's window is small, barely large enough for the interaction. Because of the border's towering shadow, overhead lights cast a harsh white glare on everything. Behind the booths are rows of parking bays marked by faded yellow lines. Each bay has a number painted on the ground, and more signs direct drivers where to park and wait for further instructions.

A guard leans out of the window, hardly glancing at our driver. His eyes are dull and bored—just another car, another person he will forget in seconds.

"Documents?" he drones.

The driver hands over a stack of papers. The guard looks at everyone in the car and scowls when he sees me.

The human.

Then he waves us on, directing us to parking bay number three.

We pull into the assigned spot, and the driver kills the engine. Turning to me, he says, "Mrs Emerson, a member of border personnel will need to speak with you to confirm everything's in order. You must answer their questions truthfully, and we will be on our way in no time." He notices my apprehension and softens his tone. "It's fine; the Ministry has all your pre-approved documents."

"Okay. Thank you."

Gosh, this is awful. What the heck am I doing?

CHAPTER SIX

IT DOES NOT TAKE LONG before the guard—now wearing a bright yellow jacket—steps out of the booth and meets an official-looking woman, a shifter, in a matching hi-vis vest. They exchange a few words, then both head for the car.

The border guard opens my door and steps aside as the woman speaks. "Mrs Emerson, would you please come with me for processing?"

I force a polite smile. "Yes, of course."

As I go to leave my computer behind, she adds, "Please bring all your technology."

Oh no. That doesn't sound good. "Okay." I grab the laptop bag, relieved I've pocketed my phone so I don't have to rummage through my plastic bags in the car's boot.

I've never been in trouble with the law, nor have I

spoken to anyone in authority, so this entire situation is way out of my comfort zone. It's intimidating—not because of the border's size or its buildings, but because of what it represents. This is where people like me are pulled apart and inspected; every word, every document, every answer is weighed and judged.

Swallowing hard, I climb out of the car and shuffle behind her, my oversized blond bodyguard trailing behind like a silent shadow.

The border official strides confidently, her dark hair swinging in a high ponytail that bobs with each step. The sharp click of her heels on the pavement draws attention to her long, toned calves. I can't help envying her effortless grace. Heels hurt my feet—they get squished and sore—so I stick to flat shoes. I glance down at my trainers and wiggle my toes, grateful for their cheap but blissfully comfortable support.

She leads us to a building off to the side. It's basic and functional—a single-storey structure of the same grey concrete, with no decoration or sign of wear. The pavement leading to it is worn but clean, with weeds sprouting at the edges.

A single entrance looms ahead a heavy metal door with a plain sign reading MAIN OFFICES.

The guard stops at the door, nods curtly, and hurries back to his booth.

Inside, the building is as stark as the outside. Pale off-white walls, a thin grey carpet worn smooth in places but spotless, and fluorescent lights buzzing overhead. A receptionist sits behind a long counter, her gaze fixed on her monitor. She doesn't look up as we pass.

We round a corner with a digital display flashing red numbers corresponding to tickets clutched by fidgety people in stiff yellow-and-grey plastic chairs. We bypass them entirely and head straight to what must be the border official's office.

She shrugs off her yellow vest, hangs it neatly on a peg, and gestures at a chair. "Please, take a seat."

I do as instructed, perching on the edge of the chair she indicates. She moves with practised elegance, smoothing her skirt as she sits, pulling in her chair, and stacking the documents on her desk. She picks them up and flips through them with sharp efficiency.

"Let's have a look, shall we?"

I don't reply—it wasn't really a question.

A silence stretches on as she clicks her tongue every so often while flipping through the pages.

I tuck my hands under my thighs to keep them still. Without my wedding and eternity rings to fiddle with, I keep catching myself twisting at nothing—an invisible band of absence around my finger. Maybe I should buy a few cheap silver rings?

At last, the border official looks up, her eyes shrewd but not hostile. "Everything seems to be in order." She pushes back from the desk, swivels to her computer, and begins typing with quick precision. Each keystroke echoes like part of a private rhythm. "Your documents and passes should arrive shortly."

Leaning back in her chair, she folds her hands in her lap and smiles—a pleasant but meaningless expression, the kind perfected in customer service.

I give her a polite smile in return.

Then we wait.

Five awkward minutes tick by before a knock breaks the silence. Another woman enters, dressed practically in trousers and sensible shoes. She's human, carrying a folder of documents. Offering a polite smile, she hands them to the border official.

"Thank you. That'll be all," the official says.

The newcomer nods and slips out, shutting the door behind her.

The border official extracts a shiny blue metal card from the folder and sets it on the desk with a click. "Here we are. This is your new identification." With two fingers, she slides it across the table.

I glance down. My name and photo stare back at me— an unflattering but familiar shot from my national ID. Below that is an address I recognise from the apartment brochure. The Greenholm Ironworks.

"And this is for your new bank account." She places a sleek black metal bank card next to the ID, then an envelope. "Your account details are inside. A small deposit has been made for your initial expenses."

I blink at the card. I bet it's heavier than it looks. Fancy. My old debit card was flimsy plastic—this one looks capable of doubling as a weapon.

She flips through more papers, then meets my gaze. "Now, your electronics, please."

"My... electronics?" My voice rises despite myself.

She wiggles her perfectly manicured nails expectantly. "Yes, your phone. For privacy and security reasons, unapproved technology isn't permitted."

Oh. That's... concerning.

With a sinking feeling, I dig my phone out of my pocket, hesitating. What is it with shifters today wanting all my stuff? It does not matter. It's just a phone. I've already backed up my data. But handing it over still feels like a strange betrayal. Her outstretched hand leaves no room for argument.

I turn the phone off, gripping it one last time, then reluctantly place it in her hand. She examines it like it might explode, then tosses it into a bin behind her.

Gone.

Surprisingly, I feel relieved. I didn't expect it, but it's almost freeing. It's as if I've shed another weight tethering me to the past. I inhale deeply—the first truly unencumbered breath I've taken in days.

Letting go feels good.

"Now, your laptop," the border official says briskly, as if requesting my laptop is perfectly normal.

And that's where I draw the line. I clutch the bag's strap, my fingers gripping tight. "Absolutely not," I say, more sharply than intended. My cheeks heat, but I straighten my back. "I need my computer for work."

Her eyes narrow, and for a tense moment we stare at each other.

Eventually, she sighs and flips through the papers once more. "It really shouldn't be allowed. It's policy. You VIP guests take such liberties." She mutters the last part under her breath, then turns to her computer. Her fingers flit across the keyboard. "Let's see... Hmm. It appears you have been granted permission. However, your home internet will be disabled for security reasons. You will only have access to your monitored work system."

Her saccharine smile fails to hide the edge in her voice. "We take security very seriously, Mrs Emerson."

"Of course," I mutter, loosening my grip on the laptop strap.

I pocket the two heavy cards and slip the documents into my bag, nodding once.

She opens her bottom drawer and pulls out a small black clamshell phone—something straight out of the early 2000s. Sliding it across the desk, she says, "This will be your phone while you are here. It's preprogrammed for essential calls and texts only."

I fight back a grimace. So much for accessing the internet. "Thank you." I drop it into my bag without a second glance.

"Remember," she says, her voice cold and final, "no mistakes, no breaches."

I take that as my cue to leave. "Thank you for your time."

The big blond bodyguard holds the door for me. As I step out, I glance back at him, unable to hide my curiosity. "What did she mean by VIP?"

He gives me a blank look.

These shifters sure are a cheerful lot.

Normally, that would annoy me, but today I don't have the energy to care. I just want out of here.

Soon enough, we're back in the car, inching forward in another queue toward the heavily guarded road that leads through to the other side. The setup reminds me of a medieval drawbridge, with villagers nervously crossing under a raised portcullis toward a distant castle.

But beyond this wall, there are no knights—only shifters.

The guards come into view, dozens of them in slate-grey uniforms, radiating authority as they line the gates. They watch the cars roll past with unrelenting focus. Their every movement and subtle shift of stance speaks of controlled power. They are not just guards; they are predators, ready to act at the slightest provocation.

I know shifters are naturally strong, their bodies designed for combat. They already have claws, teeth, and muscles capable of tearing a person apart. Seeing them armed with military-grade rifles churns my stomach. These are the guns you see in action films, the ones capable of firing a hundred rounds a second.

It's beyond unsettling—it's overkill.

What really makes my skin crawl is the direction they are pointing. Every rifle faces us—towards the Human Sector—not the Enterprise Zone.

The wall's true purpose becomes chillingly clear. It's not just about keeping shifters in; it's about keeping humans out. Or, I realise, perhaps the real threat lies beyond, and they have another army on the inside. A shiver crawls up my spine.

The closer we get, the more oppressive the air becomes. The more I feel the suffocating magic saturating the wall. The little hairs on my neck stand on end. That biting spell woven into the Ministry's paperwork was unpleasant, but it's nothing compared to whatever's wrapped around this border.

I hiss involuntarily, my nails digging into my palms, and the big blond shifter in the front passenger seat finally turns to look at me. He smiles slowly, baring his teeth in a way that offers no comfort.

"It's okay, Mrs Emerson," he says, his tone almost amused. "It will only hurt a little bit."

A little bit? Well, that's all right if it only hurts a little bit. I roll my eyes.

Chapter Seven

The car inches forward, and I groan under my breath. Getting through the sector border is like running a gauntlet, and now I feel... strange. My gut twists, the pain intensifying until it feels as though I'm being pressed into the back seat.

No, not just pressed—*squeezed*. The magic wrapped around the border feels like it's trying to force every atom of my body through the leather upholstery and into the boot.

A whimper escapes me before I clamp my lips shut, determined to endure. What is a little more pain? After all, I've been drowning in psychological anguish these past few days; physical pain is just another layer of punishment.

Up ahead, the air shimmers like a mirage, and the oppressive pressure vanishes as the car crosses through. I slump back, panting with relief, and wipe the sweat from my face with my jumper sleeve. My muscles ache as if I've just run a marathon.

I'm not sure what I was expecting—perhaps a grand archway or some glowing magical door—but instead, we're in a tunnel. A proper tunnel. Bright lights flicker overhead as we glide along, the smooth passage seeming endless, though it's probably only forty metres. Just as I start to relax, another shimmer of magic appears.

Oh, marvellous.

The second wave of magic hits like a sandstorm, raking across every nerve. It's not as bad as the first, but I still tense, gritting my teeth as we emerge into a shocking brightness.

I throw an arm across my eyes, blinking furiously as they sting and water. I have no idea how the shifters are coping with their enhanced eyesight, but the driver does not miss a beat.

It takes a few seconds of rapid blinking before I can squint at my surroundings.

It's... not what I imagined—perhaps open plains? A lion perched on a rock or a pack of wolves running wild. Instead, it's a perfectly maintained road winding through long grass, alive with wildflowers. It's so beautiful and pristine that I blink again, half wondering if I'm hallucinating.

So much for animalistic stereotypes.

The roads back in the Human Sector are riddled with potholes deep enough to swallow a person. But here? This tarmac is smoother than my relationship with Paul ever was.

The only hint of wildness lies in the untamed verges flanking the road, where daisies, poppies, dandelions, and other flowers I can't name sway in the breeze.

After about forty minutes, the landscape shifts. The road bends left, and I catch my first glimpse of the Enterprise Zone.

It's... stunning.

If someone had dropped me here blindfolded, I'd have sworn we were in one of the Vampire Sector's fanciest boroughs.

Ornate eighteenth-century buildings blend seamlessly with sleek, modern designs, all surrounded by a sea of green. Trees line the streets, their canopies casting cool, dappled shade across broad, immaculate pedestrian walkways. Shrubs in bloom and thoughtfully placed benches dot the area.

Winding paths thread through wildflower meadows, linking hidden picnic spots and peaceful seating nooks.

The entire place feels like a vast, living park.

Cyclists whizz past along dedicated lanes, their bright helmets just a blur. A fleeting thought interrupts my admiration; *I can't remember the last time I rode a bike.* This idyllic setting, under a bright blue sky, might feel less enchanting when the inevitable rain arrives, so I will definitely need a decent waterproof coat.

I scan the area for shifted animals but see none. Perhaps there are designated spaces for that. It makes sense if control is an issue. I feel a twinge of guilt for my earlier assumptions. The shifters seem far more organised than I expected —better even than the vampires, which is saying something.

"You're living in Zone Two," the driver says, breaking my reverie. His voice is calm, yet there's unmistakable pride beneath it. "It's the most secure area. The Ministry's technological centre is coming up on the right."

He gestures to a massive oval glass structure with sleek, modern lines and dark reflective panels. It looks like it belongs on the cover of an architecture magazine. I swallow hard. *Shit. I'm entirely out of my depth.* That's where I will be working? Me, in a place like that? It makes my old office look like a leaky garden shed.

We pass more buildings, including what the driver points out as the shopping centre. "They also handle online deliveries," he adds as he signals and slows down.

Ahead, nestled behind a copse of trees, stands the Ironworks.

It's even more extravagant in person than in the brochure. Golden-hued bricks shimmer in the sunlight, offset by grand windows that mirror the surrounding greenery.

The car comes to a stop beside a gravel path. My door opens, and before I fully register it, the blond bodyguard hands me my bags and a set of keys. Now that he is free of me, his grin is cheerful, almost smug.

"Good luck," he says, his tone dripping with amusement, making me feel like I've stepped into *The Hunger Games*.

Wonderful. I force a polite smile. "Thank you both for your help."

The driver nods. The door slams shut, and the car pulls away, leaving me alone on the path.

I turn to face my new home, my heart thumping with nerves and anticipation. The Ironworks towers before me, more luxurious than I'd ever imagined.

This is it—the start of my new life.

Adjusting my grip on the plastic bags, I take my first step toward the building.

In my cheap outfit, I feel awkwardly out of place—underdressed and entirely out of my depth.

The chequered flooring in the entrance lobby immediately draws my eye—probably original, its elegant design lending an old-world charm to the space. There's a grand, formal atmosphere here, more reminiscent of an old bank than an industrial building.

The ceiling is breathtaking. A dark-blue masterpiece with intricate detailing, crowned by a massive chandelier that looks like it belongs in a stately home. Plush sofas are scattered around, each paired with a small side table.

"Mrs Emerson, welcome to the Greenholm Ironworks."

I let out a startled squeak as a suited shifter appears beside me, flashing a friendly smile. My heart pounds; I clutch the plastic bags a little tighter, resisting the impulse to smack him with one. "Thank you," I manage to say.

The man is shorter than I expected for a shifter—probably just under six feet tall—with short, dark hair and a boyish face that does not quite match his tailored suit. Yet his presence is confident, even authoritative. "You're on our executive third floor, apartment three-zero-seven. It's a fully furnished one-bedroom with a wraparound glass balcony overlooking the river. The Enterprise Zone rule book has been placed in your living room for your convenience and safety. Please take time to familiarise yourself with it."

A rule book. Fantastic.

"Do you need help with your bags?" His gaze flicks to the flimsy plastic in my hands, and the corners of his mouth twitch as though he is stifling a laugh.

I offer a half-smile and shrug, lifting the bags slightly. "I'm fine, thanks."

He frowns momentarily, as though I've broken some unspoken code, then recovers with a brisk nod. "We don't have a curfew, but we strongly advise humans against staying out after dusk."

"I understand." Not so different from the Human Sector, I suppose.

"We have vampire residents, and though hunting is strictly prohibited, accidents can happen. Rest assured, incidents are dealt with swiftly and carry severe penalties for the vampires involved. Still, a night-time stroll could be misconstrued as... an invitation." He gives me a knowing look. "To mitigate risk, we offer a complimentary human escort service for travelling after dark."

A human escort service? Like dog-walking for people? "Okay," I say, trying not to laugh. "Thank you."

He gestures towards the lift. "You will need this." He waves a metallic-grey card, handing it to me. "It functions like a hotel key card and will grant access to the building, the lift, and your apartment. If you require assistance, simply press zero on your apartment phone or use the intercom to reach security. We are staffed around the clock to ensure your safety."

I nod, feeling like I've just received a safety briefing for *Jurassic Park*. "Thank you, um..."

"Matthew," he offers, flashing another friendly smile. "Roger's on this evening, and Ray takes the early-morning shift."

"Thank you, Matthew. That's really helpful."

"Of course, Mrs Emerson." He escorts me to the lift

and scans the card. As the doors slide open with a soft hiss, he hands it back to me. "Have a lovely afternoon."

"I will. You too." I step into the lift, giving him a small wave as the doors close.

The executive floor feels like another world. Its plush carpet muffles my steps, each footfall leaving a faint imprint. I count the doors until I reach 307. Juggling my bags and the key card, I fumble with the lock, dropping the bags in my haste. With a sigh, I nudge them across the threshold with my foot before stepping inside.

The heavy door swings shut behind me with a solid click. I set down the last bag and place the keys and card in a sleek bowl on a nearby console table.

The apartment is beautiful.

To my left is the kitchen, sleek black cabinets and a granite worktop with silvery veins running through it. Overhead, a lantern-style skylight floods the area with natural light.

I kick off my trainers, wiggling my toes inside my panda-print socks. The warm wooden floor is an unexpected delight. Exposed beams stretch overhead—an homage to the building's industrial roots. I wander through the space, past the kitchen and bedroom, into the living room.

Floor-to-ceiling black-framed windows make the space feel vast. Sunlight pours in, illuminating modern furnishings. A pair of double doors leads to the wraparound balcony overlooking the river.

This is far more luxurious than I ever anticipated. I trail my fingers over the leather sofa, marvelling at its softness.

My gaze drifts to the coffee table, where the dreaded rule book lies, perfectly centred. I will deal with that later.

The bedroom continues the sophisticated theme, though here the wooden floors are replaced by plush, dark-grey carpet. Another set of glass doors opens onto the balcony.

The bed—a massive king-size—remains swathed in plastic, with fresh bedding and towels folded neatly beside it.

Everything is pristine, unused.

A walk-in wardrobe—or dressing room—awaits, and the bathroom is equally indulgent with massive grey tiles, a separate shower, and a freestanding copper bath.

I carry a chair out onto the balcony, sink into it with a weary sigh, and close my eyes. The breeze tousles my hair, tugging at my clothes, its chill biting through my socks. Somewhere beneath me, the river gurgles by, and in the distance I hear children laughing.

Now that I'm here, I expected to feel relief. Instead, I'm oddly out of sorts.

I thought putting distance—and a massive shifter border—between myself and my old life would bring closure. Instead, I'm left with the hollow realisation. I wasn't running from the wreck of my marriage.

I was running from myself.

Chapter Eight

"You aren't lost, you're just in an uncomfortable stage of your life where your old self is gone, but your new self isn't fully born yet. You're in the midst of transformation."
- Marcos Alvarado

WHEN I TRY to turn on the television for some background noise, the screen flashes: NO INTERNET CONNECTION.

I chuckle under my breath. "Well played, border official. Well played."

A familiar hum of magic sparks inside me, and with a subtle mental nudge, I bypass the network block, reactivating the disconnected Wi-Fi. "But you will have to do better than that." The TV flickers to life, a cheerful talk show filling the silence.

That's the thing—I'm a mage. A technomancer.

It must have come from my absent father's side of the family. Dove and I have different dads, and while she inherited perfect hair and charm, I got... this.

My technomancy surfaced when I was fifteen, likely triggered by the stress of the government-mandated sterilisation. Magic coursing through a body deemed 'imperfect' must have been fate's idea of a joke. It never felt funny to me.

Even back then, I knew the stakes. If anyone discovered the human government had unknowingly sterilised a mage —no matter how minor the power—it could have ignited a war. So I kept it quiet.

Even now, nobody knows—not Paul, not Dove, no one.

Technomancy is rare, which is how I slipped under the radar. My abilities aren't flashy or world-altering, but they were temperamental when I was young. Phones would short-circuit, lights would flicker, and electronics around me would fail if I didn't consciously control my magic. It took years, but I mastered it, incorporating my abilities into my work and passing them off as technical skill.

I've always told myself I'm not a 'real' mage. My powers feel more like a peculiar knack—an unusual talent, like being good at maths or singing. I'm human. I feel human. But moments like this remind me I'm... different.

I'm nothing like the mages from this morning.

The hotel lobby nightmare replays in my head: Merrick shielding me, the suitcase thudding into him, and then his ripping a sofa cushion to bat away spells. I've never witnessed anything like it.

Shaking off the memory, I turn up the TV volume and hum along to a '90s dance tune while I settle in.

I put my things away, load the washing machine, make the bed, and compile a list of essentials—nothing fancy, just toiletries, vitamins, and an entirely new wardrobe.

I skim the rule book before venturing outside; most of it is common sense, nothing alarming.

With a sigh, I grab my glasses. I've never liked wearing them, but they are indispensable for navigating the world these days with my ageing vision.

Matthew spots me as I leave the building. Perched in the lobby like a watchful hawk, he offers a polite nod. I wave back and stick to the path that follows the road we drove in on.

The day is crisp and bright, with a slight chill in the air.

Walking stirs something familiar in me. When I was younger, I used to run—part of the conditioning and martial arts training that kept me in top shape. Those days feel like a lifetime ago, but the steady rhythm of my steps now clears my head. For the first time in a while, I sense a glimmer of purpose sneaking back in, one footstep at a time.

One step at a time, Lark.

I recall a quote I once read, though I can't remember it exactly—something about how, when things are hard and you feel lost, it's because your old self is gone, and the discomfort is part of becoming something new.

A transformation.

Like a butterfly.

I huff a quiet laugh. I hardly feel like a butterfly; I'm

more like a hairy caterpillar hiding in a bush. Still, the sentiment fits.

My pace slows, and my eyes widen as I turn a corner and see the strangest property.

"Wow," I breathe, the word spilling out unbidden.

The house before me is like something plucked from a dream—or perhaps a fairytale nightmare. A magnificent Edwardian-style doll's house, but life-sized and impossibly pristine.

Placing my hands on my hips, I tilt my head to study it. The building seems out of place, as if dropped here by mistake. Every aspect of its architecture is flawless, so exact it's almost unsettling.

Then I feel it.

Magic.

At first it's subtle, a faint tug in my chest, but it grows stronger, wrapping itself around me in a gentle yet insistent grip. It does not hurt, but it feels... aware, as if the house is examining me, sizing me up.

My breath hitches, and I whisper, "What are you?"

Of course, the house does not answer, but the strange sensation lingers—a peculiar blend of wariness and curiosity.

"It's a wizard's house," I mutter, shaking my head. I've only ever heard about them—whispers that they exist. I've never seen one in person.

It's too perfect—unsettlingly so. The paint gleams like it was applied this morning, flawless and unmarked. The walls shimmer like they have never known a storm or the passage of time.

The windows are spotless, reflecting the sunlight with

an ethereal brilliance. The lawn is a uniform deep green, trimmed with surgical precision. Flowerbeds burst with vibrant pink, yellow, and blue blooms—so dazzlingly bright they seem unnatural.

My instincts prickle, and a warning blares in my head.

"I wouldn't go in there," a warm voice calls behind me, breaking my trance.

I spin around to see an elderly woman. She is human, with pale skin, bright blue eyes, and a head of fluffy white curls that remind me of a dandelion gone to seed.

Her smile is wide, kind, and utterly disarming. I can't help smiling back.

"It's a wizard's house," she says, nodding towards it. "Damn thing's got a mind of its own. I saw some poor fool try to go in once. He made it as far as the gate before the house blasted him clean across the path—knocked him straight into that big oak." She gestures to a towering tree nearby and chuckles. "Dumbest thing I ever saw. Nobody's ever lived there. It just... appeared about fifty years ago and has not moved since. Keeps itself updated, too. Looks like it's waiting for somebody."

Her voice drops conspiratorially. "They say a wizard's house requires a willing soul—a powerful magic user who puts their soul inside it."

My stomach lurches. "A soul?" I eye the house uneasily, my throat tight. "Really?"

She nods solemnly. "Oh, you know how magic users are. They will do anything to avoid dying like the rest of us. They stick their souls into all sorts of things—lamps, wands, even bloody teapots. Anything to keep themselves going."

She grins as though she has not just shocked me to my core. "I'm Jo."

"Hi. Lark."

"Lark? That's an unusual name—I like it." Jo's grin widens. "Nice to meet you. Are you new to the area?"

"Yes, I just moved in."

"Oh, lovely! At the Ironworks?" I nod. "How exciting! You must be bright to land a job with the Ministry." Her eyes sparkle with approval. "Ah, here she is. Sandra, come say hello to our new neighbour, Lark!"

A second figure steps forward. I notice the rich brown of her shifter eyes. Sandra is about my height—wiry and lean, with short, dark hair, deep brown skin, and a vibrant energy that makes her seem hardly twenty-five. She slides her arm around Jo's waist and leans in with a practised ease.

Sandra focuses on me. "Well, welcome to the neighbourhood, Lark. If you ever need anything, let us know."

I glance once more at the wizard's house, feeling its uncanny attention, and murmur, "Thanks. I think I will be needing it."

"Lark works for the Ministry in IT," Jo announces proudly.

I blink. I didn't tell her that.

Sandra catches my surprise and laughs, her voice low and amused. "Don't look so shocked. Jo here knows everything. She's the fountain of all local knowledge—and the biggest gossip you will ever meet. She even handles all the new arrivals shopping, so if you're missing anything, it's her fault."

Jo elbows Sandra in the side, mock-scolding. "Ignore

her. She's always like this. Fifty years together, and she still teases me."

Fifty years.

Understanding dawns as I glance between them, and everything suddenly makes sense. They are together—together.

It's the kind of relationship people whisper about. Mixed-species partnerships like theirs are often frowned upon—not always out of overt prejudice, though that's part of it, but because of the cruel toll time takes. Jo has aged like any human, while Sandra remains frozen in her prime.

If they had met when Jo was younger, she might have had the option of turning. But turning a human into a shifter is perilous after twenty-five. Even if you have the right DNA, the risk of death is high, and the transformation is brutal.

At around fifteen, we're all tested—not only to see if we're permitted to have children, but also to check for traces of shifter, magic, or vampire DNA. A few young adults might be eligible for turning, but competition is fierce. It's the world's oddest popularity contest, with the highest possible stakes.

Becoming a derivative if you are human is nearly impossible. Governments impose strict quotas, and the odds of being chosen for shifting, spellcasting, or sprouting fangs are worse than those of becoming an astronaut.

Most derivatives today are born into it. For the rest of us, if your genome contains even a hint of derivative DNA but you don't meet the criteria for turning, you are sterilised.

Just like I was.

If Jo and Sandra met when they were young, Jo must not have fit the criteria either. Yet Sandra stayed. Despite everything, she stayed. And here they are, fifty years on, still giggling and teasing, gazing at each other with such tenderness it feels tangible, as though you could reach out and touch it.

Sandra kisses Jo's head with a gentle affection that makes my chest ache. A lump rises in my throat, and I turn away, swallowing a surge of envy.

I'm woman enough to admit that I'm jealous.

I will need to steer clear of loved-up couples, romcoms, and romance novels for a while. From now on, I will stick to thrillers and zombie apocalypses—stories where random men get their insides eaten. Plenty of chomping. That feels about my speed right now.

"Uh oh, we have made her uncomfortable," Jo says playfully, snapping me back from my thoughts.

"We're sorry," Sandra echoes, sounding genuine.

"Oh no, no," I groan, waving my hand as if to wave away the notion. "It's not you—it's me." My hand drops, and I gesture to the pale line on my finger where my wedding rings once were. "I, uh, just left my husband. So... yeah." I wince, the words still raw even as I say them. "It's a bit fresh."

And it's a miracle I stop myself from saying more. Typically, this is when my anxiety kicks into high gear, and I start spouting random nonsense to fill the silence. My filter breaks, and before I know it, I'm spewing out verbal babble. But today, I manage to stay quiet before I go completely overboard and things spiral.

Go me.

The glint of excitement in Jo's eyes suggests I've already said enough to keep her busy for a while. At least I didn't mention Dove. That's progress, right?

No—that was the old me. The me who apologised for everything, including breathing. The me who bent over backwards to keep everyone happy. The me who was too kind, too patient, and too scared to say no.

That version of me is gone.

Dead.

The new me? She is a badarse. She looks out for herself, does what she wants when she wants—within reason. I'm not looking to hurt anyone. But if I fancy reading all night with every light burning, I can. If I want to eat burgers for breakfast or have chocolate and ice cream for dinner, I will. Because now, the only person I have to consider is me.

And honestly? It's refreshing.

"Oh, we're so sorry," Jo says, her grin betraying the sympathy in her words.

Fantastic. As Sandra did warn me Jo loves to gossip. By tomorrow, I will be Zone Two's hottest topic—the heartbroken woman who left her husband and moved into the Ironworks. I suppress a chuckle. *Small steps, Lark. At least it's not the worst thing they could be whispering about.*

"Well, we're here if you need anything," Sandra offers, sounding warm and sincere.

"Thank you. That's very kind."

"Are you off shopping?" Jo asks, curiosity unwavering. "Anything nice?"

"Just a few bits and bobs."

"Oh, you will love it here," Jo enthuses. "Shopping is

wonderful. But you'd better hurry—only about four hours until sunset. You did read the rule book, didn't you?"

"I did." Well, I skimmed it.

"Good, good." She nods, clearly pleased. I nod along with her.

Sandra gently steers Jo away, shooting me an apologetic smile. "Come on, Jo, leave her be."

"Sandra, you know what happens around here after dark. Be careful, Lark."

"Thanks, I will. It was lovely meeting you both."

We exchange waves, and I skirt around the creepy wizard's house, taking the path farthest from it while eyeing its too-perfect façade. Then I continue on towards the shopping centre.

Chapter Nine

First impressions matter. I smooth down my snazzy new suit jacket and take a steadying breath as I approach my new workplace. The Ministry's technological centre is even more impressive up close. I follow the signs toward the entrance and pause to observe the well-dressed man ahead of me. Odd. Instead of proceeding directly through the doors, he stands in front of them, arms outstretched in an X shape, feet apart.

A scanner hums, casting a pale blue light over him. Moments later, the doors slide open, granting him entry.

Fascinating.

When it's my turn, I position myself as the signs instruct, resisting the temptation to probe the system with my magic. This technology feels like something straight out of a sci-fi novel. The scanner sweeps over me from head to toe, its faint hum raising goosebumps on my skin. After a pause that feels unnervingly long, the doors slide open. Relief floods me—I didn't break anything.

Inside, the security measures are even more intense. Another set of scanners stands ready to inspect anyone leaving, ensuring nothing illicit is taken outside.

A uniformed shifter clears his throat, catching my attention.

"Please proceed," another voice barks.

"Sorry," I mumble, shuffling forward under his withering glare. "It's my first day."

He grunts, unimpressed.

The entire palaver makes me jittery, and I'm grateful I arrived early. The last thing I need is to be late on my first day.

I join a silent line of people waiting to pass through a series of glowing metal arches. Flickering runes etched into the frames send faint tingles over my skin as I walk through. It feels like static electricity—not painful, but unsettling enough to make me glance nervously at the others. No one else reacts; they all seem accustomed to it.

At the end of the line is an inner door. I press my palm against the glass panel, my fingers slick with sweat. A cold, monotone voice confirms my identity, and the door slides open with a soft hiss.

The lobby is a masterpiece of modern design. High ceilings and polished white floors—so clean they almost glow —reflect the natural light flooding through sleek glass walls. A spiral staircase of steel and glass coils elegantly up to the higher floors, while a bank of lifts sits discreetly to the left.

I resist the urge to gawk like a tourist, forcing myself to

walk purposefully to the reception desk. Within minutes, a cheerful receptionist directs me to a meeting room on the fourth floor.

The room feels cavernous and sterile. A massive oak table dominates the space, surrounded by thirty chairs. Sitting alone at such a large table feels strange. The setup is minimalist: a jug of water, a glass, a dish of mints, a notepad, and a pen. I fidget, spinning the pen between my fingers as I wait.

The door creaks open, and a man with a friendly face and a slightly dishevelled suit pokes his head in.

"Ah, Mrs Emerson! Or may I call you Lark?"

"Of course."

"Excellent! I'm Henry, one of your managers." He steps fully into the room, closing the door behind him. "You're the new DevOps Engineer, right?"

"Yes."

"Brilliant." He claps his hands together and rubs them with enthusiasm before swinging a bag from his shoulder onto the table. From it, he pulls out a laptop and begins setting it up.

"This is your induction software." He pulls a face and gestures to the empty chairs. "Normally, we'd have a whole group of new starters going through this together, but your onboarding was fast-tracked. So, it's just you."

"That's fine," I say, ignoring the unspoken question behind his words.

He nods and starts flipping rapidly through slides. "We will skip the introductions section—no point introducing yourself to yourself, eh?" He chuckles before pushing the laptop toward me.

"The basics: bathrooms are down the hall, emergency exits are clearly marked, and the fire alarm test is every Tuesday morning. If it goes off any other day, assume it's real and follow the flashing signs. Coffee stations are on every floor—award-winning coffee, if you can figure out how the machines work. Oh, and we have hotel-style accommodations available if you ever need to stay onsite late. The restaurant is open 24/7."

I glance at the screen. An endless list of PowerPoint slides stares back at me.

Death by PowerPoint. This is going to be a long week.

Chapter Ten

I SHOVE the documents away with a huff of disgust. So much for a break. I'd thought a bit of light reading about my divorce might be a good idea. Big mistake. Now I have a stress headache pounding in the middle of my forehead.

Of course, the Ministry did background checks on me when I was hired. On my second day, they offered me the services of their legal team. Unusual, sure, but one hell of a work perk. The solicitor they assigned to me is a scary son of a beast—thorough, efficient, and ruthless.

Over the past three months, we have tackled everything, ticking off boxes and navigating the process faster than I ever thought possible. I'd been willing to give Paul the majority of our assets just to bring it to an end, but of course, it couldn't be that simple.

It was all going so well.

I signed the forms, we submitted everything, and I dared to hope it would be quick and clean.

Hope was stupid.

I scowl at the stack of papers in front of me. Now Paul's insisting we talk. He won't sign the bloody thing unless we meet in person.

So I have to see him.

Shit. I don't know what I was thinking—somehow getting through this without facing him again? It was never going to happen. Even after all these months, the thought of seeing his face makes me want to puke.

The only saving grace is that our 'friendly chat' will be under the watchful eyes of our solicitors.

Despite his Human First political connections, Paul has permission to enter the Enterprise Zone. The solicitor assures me they will keep everything professional and on track. Still, one meeting, one conversation... it feels like climbing into a pit with a poisonous snake.

I groan and flop back in my chair. What I want—what I really want—is to bounce my forehead off my desk until both the headache and my divorce magically disappear.

It's already been a long, crappy day. Some ancient code decided to implode—legacy stuff from before my time. Not my fault, but I've seen the issue before, so I know how to fix it. Hours of running scripts, debugging, and tweaking lines of code later, the system finally begrudged me its cooperation.

The problem? I've worked past my hours. Now it's dark outside, and instead of heading home like a normal person, I'm debating whether to call for a security escort.

The human escort service.

Ugh.

I've got a change of clothes in my bag. Maybe I will grab a room and sleep off the darkness instead. That feels safer than braving the streets.

The shifters might have fancy protective walls, but they didn't exactly kick everyone out when they took over—not here, at least. Not like their shifter-only sector. I shudder. No, that was a bloodbath.

Here in the Enterprise Zone, they conceded, allowing other derivatives to live here as long as everyone followed their rules. The high walls and strict security clearance give the illusion of safety, but unvetted people still wander about. I know it's been forty years, but that's nothing to a vampire.

Even the vetted ones—the ones with all the proper identification—don't guarantee safety. Just because someone has the paperwork does not mean they are friendly or have curbed their nasty appetites.

Zone Two might have beautiful streets and the air of a tranquil park, but for a human like me, it's like being a deer dropped into the savannah with lions and tigers circling.

Maybe coffee will help clear my head. I groan, the sound echoing faintly in the empty glass corridor as I wander toward the nearest coffee station—what everyone calls the brew room.

These suspended offices feel like they are floating inside a glass shell. I glance at the far wall, which offers an unobstructed view of the atrium, the security area, and the visitor's lounge far below. It's an impressive sight, but I'm glad I don't have an issue with heights. For some, this setup would be pure vertigo-inducing hell.

With my anxiety gnawing at me, I consider working through the night instead. Sleep is overrated anyway, and at least in the quiet, I can get things done without a team of anxious developers hovering over my shoulder.

This late, the codebase is all mine. I can comb through it uninterrupted, troubleshooting in peace. My technomancy often detects issues lurking below the surface, sometimes highlighting problems before they happen. Depending on what I find, I can fix them quietly or submit a request.

I nudge the door open, and the lights flicker on automatically. Sleek black counters gleam under a white lowered ceiling and soft recessed lighting. A row of machines lines the wall, ready to dispense any hot or cold drink you want. There's a small refrigerator in the corner stocked with various milk options, and a cabinet with mugs arranged in neat, Ministry-approved rows.

I ignore the generic pod machines and head straight for the silver beast. I warm up my wrists, crack my knuckles, and give it a friendly pat. "Hello, Wee Beastie."

I'm all for giving inanimate objects a personality and a name, and this one feels like an old friend.

I'm chuffed I can use it—I think I'm the only one who can. When I was sixteen, I worked at an amusement park, learning to make doughnuts, candy floss, and the perfect Mr Whippy ice cream cone. I mastered the art of cappuccinos there too. That's where my love for good coffee began.

Having a commercial-grade machine at work feels like a personal triumph. The amount the Ministry spends on staff perks blows my mind. A machine like this in a human-sector job? Not a chance. But I'm not complaining.

I grind the beans, press a few buttons, and let the silver beast work its magic. A perfect mug of coffee emerges, rich and steaming. I know full well that caffeine this late in the day is a terrible idea, but let's face it—coffee isn't what is likely to kill me.

No, I'm far more likely to be eaten by a shifter—and not in the fun way.

I wipe down the machine and pick up my mug, the steam curling upward in warm, comforting spirals. Inhaling deeply, I savour the rich aroma before bringing the cup to my lips. It's hot, but my 'asbestos mouth' handles it just fine.

Then I hear it—a noise outside, sharp and sudden.

I ignore it, focusing on my first sip, but it happens again. Louder this time. A bang. Curiosity prickles at the edges of my caffeine-fuelled calm. I set the mug down and move toward the door, cracking it open just enough to peek outside.

What I see makes me gasp, step back, and oh-so-carefully close the door.

The security guards are down.

From this angle, I can't tell if they were shot or if the noise came from wands. Stupidly, I left my glasses in the server room. Either way, whoever's gotten into the building must be professional to get past our military-grade security.

Screams echo from below, interspersed with sharp bangs and barked orders.

"ON YOUR KNEES! HANDS WHERE I CAN SEE THEM! ON YOUR KNEES!"

Few people are left in the building at this hour, but the intruders are so loud they sound like a mob.

Breathe, Lark. Think.

I've trained in Judo for over three decades. While Dove twirled in ballet shoes, I was on the mat, learning throws and falls. Judo didn't merely teach me discipline—it gave me tools on how to control my magic and temper, how to stay balanced physically and emotionally, and how to remain calm under pressure.

But none of that feels useful right now.

What I miss most about Judo is the beauty of it—the precision of locking down joints, the satisfaction of putting some six-foot meathead on his arse and twisting him into a pretzel until he tapped out.

But the first lesson? The one drilled into me over and over?

Run.

You don't fight knives, guns, or derivatives bigger and badder than you.

My heart pounds and my entire body shakes as adrenaline floods my system. I take that training to heart and frantically search for a place to hide.

The glass corridors are too exposed, and the brew room offers no salvation. A few tiny cupboards, barely big enough to hide a cat, and nothing else. This modern building wasn't designed with hiding in mind.

I'm trapped.

I scan the room again, desperate. My gaze roams over every surface and corner until, for some reason, I look up.

The ceiling tiles.

For eff's sake, no. I shake my head. The idea is ridiculous.

But the voices and banging grow closer.

I spring into action. Dumping my coffee down the sink, I rinse the cup and squirt a generous dollop of bleach down the drain. The sharp chemical smell hits my nose, and I hope it will hide my scent—or at least confuse whoever might come sniffing.

Grabbing a chair from the small table, I step onto it, wobbling slightly. Then, with a reluctant glance at my beloved coffee machine, I climb onto the counter. The surface creaks ominously under my weight as my toes press against the edge of the machine, my heels dangling precariously.

The ceiling tiles are just within reach. I stretch upward, shoving at the white, spongy square until it slides off its metal lip and rests atop the tile next to it. The gap looks big enough for my shoulders. If they fit, the rest of me will follow—or so I tell myself.

Oh, bloody hell. I'm now head-height with the ceiling. There's no chance. I'm not some spry action hero who can hoist herself up with a single pull-up. This isn't a movie. Sarah Connor, I am not. I haven't done a chin-up in seven years.

I glance down at the sturdy coffee machine, grimace, and mentally cross my fingers. The counter groans again as I shift my weight. Carefully, I place one hand against the wall for balance and step onto the machine.

"Sorry, Wee Beastie," I whisper, as if apologising will make this any less insane. "Please don't break."

My head and shoulders disappear into the ceiling, and I crane my neck to get a better look. The thin metal frame of the tiles isn't built to support a person's weight. But to my left is salvation, a large, solid duct—part of the kitchen's ventilation system.

It's not ideal, but it's my only option.

I'm going to have to pull myself up.

Gripping the edge of the vent, I try to haul myself up. My arms tremble, and I hiss through clenched teeth.

What am I even doing?

I'm too old for this shit.

But I'm also too young to die.

I might dress frumpy when I'm off the clock, but I've kept myself in decent shape. I'm strong enough. Besides, the thought of intruders bursting through the door and finding my bum hanging out of the ceiling spurs me on—both mortifying and potentially fatal.

Summoning every ounce of strength, I channel my inner badarse. I pull, tug, and scrape my way through the gap, softly grunting like a woman possessed. The ceiling's metal frame tears into my stomach and thighs, sharp and unforgiving. Pain flares, but I grit my teeth and keep moving.

Almost there.

I wiggle forward, my breaths sharp and uneven. My chest burns, my arms ache, and I can already feel bruises forming. But somehow, I manage to pull myself into the ceiling.

The metal duct beneath me makes an unhappy *bong* with my weight, and every tiny movement draws an ominous groan from the structure. I nudge the roof tile back into place, doing my best to leave no trace. Then I flip open my phone, its weak light barely cutting through the gloom.

I squint, tracing where the vent connects to the wall. It's boxed in tight—no way forward, no escape route. Just me, stuck in this cramped, creaking space. And, of course, no phone signal.

Fantastic.

Slamming doors, pounding footsteps, and harsh voices grow louder. They are getting closer, not even trying to be quiet. I close my eyes and pray the bleach I dumped in the sink is enough to mask my scent.

Taking a shallow breath to avoid inhaling whatever metal shavings the construction team left behind, I shift into an uncomfortable cross-legged position. My legs ache, and my ankles feel seconds away from mutiny. Rolling my shoulders, I settle in, preparing to sit still and silent for as long as it takes.

"We need to clear every room on this level."

My breath hitches. They are below me.

"Oh, I could really do with a coffee," one of them drawls. "Shooting Ministry staff is thirsty work."

My stomach twists violently, a cold shudder racing down my spine. I clamp a hand over my mouth to keep my breathing quiet. There's nothing I can do for anyone else right now. I have to stay hidden and wait this out. For once, stuffing myself into the ceiling feels like the smartest decision I've ever made.

"You're a bloody lunatic," his companion snaps. "We don't have time for your crap. Do you think the Ministry won't notice we have raided the building? We're on a tight schedule, you idiot. We're only here for the Alpha Prime's mate."

The Alpha Prime's mate? My mind stumbles over the

90

words, trying to make sense of them. Is he even mated? I had no idea. Obviously, he must be if they are attacking the building.

Not that I'd know anything about it. I've been neck-deep in work all day, and VIPs like that are way above my pay grade.

Their voices move farther down the corridor, and the banging and smashing restart.

I can only hope the Ministry's people will get here soon.

Time crawls. Ten minutes, maybe more. The noises grow faint, and I begin to relax, my breathing evening out.

Until she screams.

I can't see her, but the voice is unmistakable—high-pitched and squeaky. It has to be Sophie. Sweet, smart Sophie. She is only twenty-two, a shifter intern who barely started her placement here.

A loud bang echoes down the corridor, the sound of a door slamming open, followed by something heavy being dragged. My stomach clenches. Are they dragging her?

A dull *thud* follows, and the crying woman's voice carries upward, muffled but clear enough to make my heart race. The distinctive click of the door closing sends a chill through me, followed by a chuckle so low and vile it makes my skin crawl.

It's the most evil sound I've ever heard.

"Please, please, I don't know anything. Let me go. I'm only an intern. Please, let me go!" Sophie's voice cracks with desperation.

I slap my hand over my mouth, choking back a gasp, and stare at the nearest ceiling tile in horror. My breath comes fast and shallow, my heart hammering against my ribs.

"Oh no, love," the man says, his voice dripping with malice. "You *will* answer my questions and tell me what I want to know."

There's a series of distinctive clicks. I picture him removing his weapons and placing them on the counter. All the while, Sophie begs and cries, her voice growing more hysterical.

"I'll show you a photo, and you will tell me where she is," he snarls. "If you don't, I'll cut out your tongue."

I can picture him holding a knife to her throat.

She is just a kid.

I can't bloody sit here, safe and hidden, while she is down there being interrogated and tortured. *Be the person you needed when you were younger, Lark.*

My breath catches as I lean forward, every movement deliberate, every muscle screaming at me to stop. Carefully, I grasp the edge of the ceiling tile, its spongy surface irritating my fingertips. Slowly, I slide it out of its metal track, the faint scrape sounding impossibly loud to my ears. The tile shifts, and I ease it across until I can see into the room.

Ah, shit.

This is going to hurt.

Chapter Eleven

I tip sideways, let gravity take over, and drop arse-first into the room. Luck—or maybe fate—is on my side as I land squarely on him, cushioning my rapid descent as we both crash to the floor.

Sophie is huddled in the corner, tears streaming down her face.

For a split second, he is stunned—too disoriented to react. That's all the time I need. Muscle memory kicks in, the product of countless drills over the years. I throw my weight onto his back and snake my arm around his neck, trapping him between my biceps and forearm. My other hand braces the hold as he begins to thrash.

"Go to sleep, you scumbag," I hiss through clenched teeth. "Go to sleep."

A properly applied blood choke does not require much

strength—just precision. If I compress the carotid arteries and jugular veins correctly, he will be out cold in ten to twenty seconds. But he's not making it easy.

With a guttural growl, he surges to his knees, the sudden movement jarring my hold. I lock my legs around his waist, clinging like a limpet as he staggers towards the table, trying to scrape me off. The impact sends a shock wave through my shoulder, but I grit my teeth and hold firm.

When that does not work, the slippery scumbag rolls like a crocodile.

My head slams into a cupboard with a sickening crack. Stars dance across my vision. Luckily, the cupboard door breaks instead of my skull. Pain shoots down my spine, and my arm twitches around his neck.

Focus, Lark. Hold on!

It feels like an eternity, but it's probably only another ten seconds before he shudders and slumps. He is out like a light. I hold the choke for three more seconds, just to be sure, then let him sag lifelessly in my arms.

Ouch. Ouch. Ouch.

Everything hurts. My head is ringing, and my shoulder screams in protest. I shove him off me with a grunt, disgust curling in my chest. A quick pat-down of his pockets yields nothing useful.

His phone screen is cracked, so even if I wanted to see who this 'mystery mate' is, I can't. Besides, someone's bound to notice he is missing soon, and I have no intention of hanging around when they do.

Annoyed, I yank off his belt and use it to secure his arms behind his back. Then I pull off one of his boots—

gagging at the smell—and shove a filthy sock into his mouth.

"I wish I had something better to tie him up," I mutter, then glance at Sophie. "Are you all right?"

She nods, though the tears keep streaming. "Where did you come from?"

"I hid in the ceiling," I reply, gesturing upwards.

She looks up. "Oh, wow. That was smart."

"Thanks. Not how I planned to make my entrance, but I'm glad he chose this room."

I scan the counter and spot a small collection of weapons: a knife, a pistol, and a dart gun. My stomach churns at the sight of the pistol. I've never fired a gun—never wanted to—but suddenly I regret not knowing how.

"Come on, up you get." I motion for Sophie to stand. "Here's the plan." I point to the chair. "Stand on the chair, then step onto the counter. Use the coffee machine to boost yourself up, then pop your head through the ceiling."

Sophie hesitates, glancing at me and then at the ceiling.

"You've got this," I reassure her, my voice steady despite my racing heart.

Nodding, Sophie takes a shaky breath and begins to climb.

"There's a vent right in front of you. Do you see it?"

"Yes," she says, her voice muffled from within the ceiling.

"Okay, you will have to lift yourself and crawl onto it. Wait one second..." I grab a thick tea towel from a drawer. "Here, cover the sharp edges so you don't scrape yourself. All right? In you go."

Sophie's movements are shaky, but she is surprisingly

agile, managing to shimmy into the tight space with minimal fuss.

"There's not a lot of room," she whispers once she's settled.

"Yeah, I know."

She blinks down at me, puffy red eyes wide with worry. Clumps of sweaty blonde hair stick to her face, making her look even younger. "But what about you?"

What about me?

I swallow hard, wincing at the thought of what might come next. Ah well. This is what playing the hero looks like, isn't it? I force a bright smile. "There's no room for both of us. See that loose ceiling tile? Yes, that one. Pull it across."

"But, Lark..." Her lips tremble. "What about you?"

"I will be fine, Sophie." The words taste bitter, but I manage to keep my tone light. "Stay quiet, and we will get through this."

Her chin wobbles. "Please. I can't leave you down there. We can find another way. I can shift—"

"No." My voice is firm, but I soften it with a small, reassuring smile. "I will be fine, I promise. Now, go on—close it up."

Her hands shake as she slides the tile back into place, her movements slow and reluctant.

"Don't come down until you are positive it's all clear, okay?" I whisper.

"Okay."

"All right. Silent now."

The faint scrape of the ceiling tile settling back into position is the last sound I hear before silence descends.

I exhale quietly, leaning against the counter. My gaze

drifts to the wannabe torturer at my feet. It takes everything I have not to boot him in the head. Instead, I grab the dart gun. It makes a satisfying *pfft* as I fire, a blue-tipped dart embedding itself in his arse.

I nod with grim satisfaction.

Dart gun in hand, I crack the door open and listen. I have no idea where to go next. The main stairs are glass and steel—too exposed. The rear fire exit stairwell is better but still risky. Or I could hunt down another coffee station and climb into another vent.

Yeah, that's the best option. People rarely look up.

Except these aren't regular people, are they? I groan and shove the nasty inner voice aside. I'd give anything for shifter senses right now.

The corridor seems clear—quiet enough, at least. Crouching low, I dash down the hall, keeping close to the wall.

As I round a corner, I nearly collide with two armed men.

They freeze.

I freeze.

"Where the hell did you come from?" one growls.

His voice snaps me out of my stupor. Without thinking, I raise the dart gun and fire, not even bothering to aim. The shot hisses. One of them collapses with a heavy *thud*.

"Oh, shit." I spin on my heel and bolt in the opposite direction. "Oh, shit. Oh, shit."

Behind me, the other man's voice crackles as he shouts into his radio for backup. My breath hitches. Without slowing, I fling my magic behind me, aiming for his earpiece.

I'm not a real mage—barely a magical toddler—but I

can disrupt a poxy signal. It's messy, crude work, but I hope it's enough to throw them off. Let's see how they like being unable to communicate.

My trainers squeal against the concrete as I burst through the emergency stairs door, nearly colliding with the wall. They will expect me to go down, so I go up.

When I'm one level higher, I force myself to stop. Sprinting headlong in blind panic won't help. I grip the stair rail, doing my best to pant silently.

My stomach churns, and my legs tremble. At least the sprint has worn off some of the stiffness in my body. I don't feel like roadkill anymore—just prey trying to outrun the predator on its tail.

Okay, Lark. You've got this. Just keep moving.

I take a deep breath, placing my next step as silently as possible. Futile, really—if shifters are after me, they will smell the sweat and fear oozing from my pores like a neon sign.

I just have to hold on until help arrives.

Behind me, the door below creaks open with a low, ominous groan. I tiptoe upward, every nerve on high alert. The hair on the back of my neck rises—an instinct I can't explain. My lizard brain screams danger even before the sound reaches me.

A low growl resonates through the stairwell.

Well, there's no running from that.

What an incredible way to see my first shifter in animal form—while being hunted.

I'm so terrified. I'm shocked I haven't wet myself. I think it's a wolf, though I'm no expert. The growl is low and guttural—more dog than cat.

Instead of bolting headlong into certain doom, I pause in the corner. Heart hammering, I drop to the floor, roll onto my belly, and wriggle into position. Flat on the ground, arms outstretched, the dart gun steady in my grip, I hover my finger over the trigger.

I've seen people do this on TV. It seems logical to keep the target small, stay on the ground, and keep out of reach.

I'm also higher than the shifter, which has to be a slight advantage. Right?

Ignoring the reality that I'm facing a killing machine with claws and teeth, I steady my breathing and focus.

The shifter below isn't running. It's hunting. Stealthy. Precise.

The soft *click, click* of nails on the concrete stairs reaches my ears—quiet but utterly terrifying.

I swallow hard, my mouth dry as bone.

Closing one eye, I sight down the barrel, using the little bump thingy—whatever it's called—to aim down the stairs.

I suppose I'm as ready as I will ever be.

All those hours playing *Duck Hunt* as a kid had better pay off. Thirty-eight years later, Mum, let's hope you were wrong and it wasn't all a waste of time. I keep my breathing even, picturing a quacking duck on a bright blue screen—maybe there was a tree or some grass? I can't remember.

Steady, Lark. Steady.

Another growl echoes, deeper this time. My breath catches as I spot sandy-brown fur shimmering under the emergency lights. Then I see his eyes—glowing amber, lock on me with predatory intent.

Ah, so they *do* glow when they hunt. Great. Unless he is doing it on purpose to scare the crap out of me.

Steady. Wait until you have more of his body in sight.

The wolf prowls around the corner, his chest coming into view—broad, powerful, muscles rippling beneath thick fur.

I squeeze the trigger.

The dart flies true, hitting centre mass.

He lets out a low whine, his body swaying before slumping, unconscious.

I blink, stunned. Wow. I got another one. New talent unlocked. Let's hope he is merely unconscious and not dead, dead, because I have no idea what is in these darts. Either way, it's him or me.

I shake my head, push myself onto my knees, and start to—

A weight crashes into me from above.

My luck has officially run out.

The wolf has backup.

The dart gun clatters from my hand, bouncing down the stairs. My breath rushes out in a panicked wheeze as I smash into the floor. Twisting, I scramble onto my back, forearms raised to shield my throat as thick white fur presses against them. The wolf's massive bulk pins me.

I kick wildly, my knees slamming into his underbelly, feet driving at his hind legs, but it's no use. He is too heavy. His back claws dig into my left leg, shredding muscle like knives. My vision blurs, and I grit my teeth, struggling to keep him at bay as my strength fades.

I'm trapped. I can't breathe.

All I see are teeth and white fur—snarling, snapping teeth. His breath washes over my face, hot and rancid, a nauseating mix of meat and raw aggression.

My skin crawls; every instinct screams for me to do something.

With no other choice, I drop my right arm and strike, aiming for his ear. The sharp smack echoes as my palm connects. Ear shots are the worst—enough to disorient anyone, human or shifter.

Please work. Please buy me time.

The blow does not disorient him—it enrages him.

He snaps his teeth, and I scream as they clamp down on my arm. Pain explodes, searing and immediate, as though he has torn muscle from bone.

The agony is excruciating, but it fuels me. Driven by desperation, I hammer my fist into his head, over and over, until my knuckles ache and my strength wanes. My blows are clumsy but relentless.

It must annoy him at least, because he shifts his weight, freeing my right side.

My heart leaps with a flicker of hope—then he strikes.

Before I can react, a massive paw cracks across my face. The sheer force sends my head snapping back, and my skull collides with the unforgiving concrete.

A blinding flash of pain explodes behind my eyes, and then—

Nothing.

The world goes black.

Chapter Twelve

THE ROUGH, guttural snarls echo off the concrete walls, reverberating down to where I'm slumped against the steps. Dizzy, bleeding, and barely hanging on, I force my eyes open with a soft groan. No shifter is chewing on my arm, though it certainly feels like it.

Instead, a battle rages in the stairwell above me.

Claws scrape, fur flies, and the white wolf lunges, its pale coat a blur. Jaws snapping, it aims for the larger dark-grey wolf blocking its path. The bigger wolf meets the attack head-on, their teeth clashing in a savage chorus.

The white wolf snaps again, lunging for the grey's throat.

The grey wolf twists, deflecting the attack, and counters with a powerful lunge. His teeth sink into the white wolf's side, driving it back up the stairs, away from me. A gash in the white wolf's shoulder spatters blood onto the wall. Their bodies slam into the metal railing, which creaks under their combined weight as they tear into each other.

I clutch my bitten arm, feeling blood seeping between my fingers—warm and sticky. Pain radiates in sharp pulses, but I can't take my eyes off the fight.

The grey wolf is steady and focused, using his sheer size to overpower the smaller, more frantic white wolf. His movements are controlled and deliberate. As he bites down again, blood spraying, his head turns slightly, and I glimpse his eyes—pale blue, like shards of ice catching the light.

Husky eyes.

My breath catches. *Merrick?*

No, I'm delirious. It can't be him. I haven't seen Mr First Class in months, not since I signed my contract. My head is fuzzy, my vision is hazy. The pain clouds everything, pulling me back to the reality of my mangled arm.

The sharp agony makes me wince. My poor forearm is a mess—bloody, torn, and barely functional. I can't bring myself to look at it. The sight alone would turn my stomach.

Lark, get your arse up. Move. You need to get away from those wolves.

I have no idea if the grey wolf is trying to save me or drive off competition for his next meal—a human snack.

Summoning every ounce of willpower, I struggle to pull my jumper over my head, leaving me in just my bra and work trousers. Modesty is the least of my worries. I wrap the blue fabric tightly around my arm, biting back a cry as the pressure sends fresh waves of pain shooting through me.

It's not ideal. It's not hygienic. But it's better than bleeding out on these cursed stairs.

Wobbling, I force myself upright. My legs are like jelly, and every movement feels monumental. On my toes, I carefully skirt around the darted wolf, placing my feet in the narrow gaps between its limp form and the edge of the treads. My good hand brushes the cold metal railing for balance. The last thing I need is a fast trip down these stairs, adding a broken neck to my growing list of problems.

A glint of metal and plastic catches my eye—the dart gun.

I crouch, barely holding myself steady, and scoop it up without passing out.

Three floors later, I stumble through the fire door at the back of the building. I'm out.

The night air hits me like a slap on my sweat-drenched skin—a chilling reminder of how exposed I am.

It's still pitch dark, and I know I shouldn't be out here. Leaving the building half-dressed and bleeding heavily is a suicide mission.

I lean against the smooth glass wall, smearing blood in messy streaks as I try to catch my breath. My head pounds in sync with my pulse, an unbearable pressure that muddles my thoughts, clouding my judgment.

I shouldn't be making any life-changing decisions right now, but... I need help.

Overriding everything is the gnawing fear that I'm not safe here.

Wolves are fighting on the stairs, and I don't know what other threats might be lurking around the building. I can't go to the front entrance—it's just as dangerous. There's nowhere safe. Nowhere I can be sure I won't run into gun-toting maniacs or another snarling shifter.

I can't be sure who's friend or foe.

The soft glow of the distant path lights twinkle like a cruel taunt. Do I stay and wait for whatever fresh hell is coming, or do I take my chances out there?

I'm in a no-win situation. My gut twists. There's no good option, but I can't just stand here waiting to be killed.

Every instinct tells me I need to get somewhere familiar, somewhere secure. I want to go home. At least there, I will have locked doors, my own space, and security guards who can help me get medical attention.

That thought drives me forward. The need to escape overwhelms the warning bells in my mind, and my flight instinct takes over.

One shaky step after another, I head towards the gravel path that'll lead me home. My steps sway, my vision wavers. After only a few minutes, I realise I've made a mistake.

I shouldn't have left.

The blow to my head has rattled my brain and knocked out all my common sense.

My left sock feels oddly wet, and my trainer squelches with every step. I must be bleeding where the white wolf dug his claws into my leg. Great. What a nightmare. My hand tightens on the gun's grip. If anything comes for me, it's not getting me without a fight.

My vision narrows, but I keep moving, propelled by sheer determination. Passing a large oak tree, I recognise it —I'm almost home. Just a couple more minutes, and I can get medical attention.

A lone wolf howls.

I misstep, trip over nothing, and crash into a wooden gate.

My weight makes the latch click, and the gate swings open. I lose my balance and fall. I brace myself for a hard landing, but instead, I hit soft grass where I expected gravel. It almost feels like the ground lifts to meet me, then gently sets me down.

"What the h...? Blood loss is making me nuts." I shake my head, trying to make sense of what just happened.

Pain pulses through my arm in time with my heartbeat as I lift my head to take in the familiar gate. My stomach drops as realisation dawns.

I've fallen headlong into the wizard's garden.

From the frying pan into the fire.

The wizard's house looms ahead. I try to push myself up, but my body refuses to cooperate.

Beyond the gate, the steady, rhythmic beat of shoes on gravel grows louder. A man sprints towards me, his pale face catching the flicker of park lights. His eyes—odd, glowing red—are locked on me with terrifying intent.

What the f—? Red eyes?

Vampire.

My heart pounds, deafening in my ears. The metallic tang of blood mingles with the acrid taste of fear on my tongue.

He springs, fingers clawed, fangs dripping with venom, his unblinking gaze fixed on my throat. I raise my arm pitifully to shield myself, but I know it's futile.

The magic surrounding the wizard's house activates in a sudden, blinding flash of white. The vampire is slammed backwards, his body twisting mid-air before landing softly on his feet, hissing like a feral cat. He shakes his head, his gaze sharp and calculating.

I glance down. My hand still grips the dart gun, miraculously steady despite my shaking body. I lift it and aim at his chest as he cautiously approaches the gate.

He crouches with an unnervingly casual air, dipping his fingers into something on the gravel path. When he brings them to his lips, they glisten red.

My blood.

"You taste divine," he murmurs, groaning as he licks his fingers clean.

I pull the trigger.

The dart whistles through the air, but faster than I can track, the vampire moves almost lazily to the side. The dart vanishes into the dark, and he chuckles—low and taunting.

"Fear. Pain. Such a perfect bouquet," he says, his voice a silken purr. "Don't make me stoop to licking your offering off the ground, girly. Be kind, won't you? Leave the garden. I will ignore the wolf spit and make it quick. No need to waste a drop." His tongue flicks out, with a flash of fang in the faint light.

"No, you're all right," I rasp, my voice barely above a whisper.

He tilts his head, trying to capture my gaze, but my vision is too hazy to focus. Vampires can trap your mind with a single look, but I'm too far gone for even that.

The world tilts, my strength drains, and the pain dulls into nothingness.

And then, within the grounds of the wizard's house

and under a hungry vampire's watchful eye, I do something incredibly stupid.

I pass out.

Again.

Chapter Thirteen

I BLINK AWAKE. Focusing takes a few seconds. Everything is hazy. I squint at the sunlight filtering through unfamiliar lace curtains, illuminating dust motes drifting lazily in the air. The bed beneath me feels ridiculously plush, like I'm floating on a cloud. The duvet smells of vanilla, its thick, warm fabric patterned with tiny embroidered flowers.

Where the heck am I?

I push myself up slightly and look around. The room feels like it's been plucked straight out of a storybook. The walls are covered in dainty floral-patterned wallpaper adorned with small frames holding intricate, hand-drawn portraits. In the corner stands an old-fashioned wardrobe, its dark wood polished to a shine, next to a small dressing table with an oval mirror.

"Hello?" I call, slipping out of bed. My bare feet sink into a warm rug. "Is anyone there? I'm awake."

Nothing. The house is silent.

My work outfit is gone. I'm squeaky clean, dressed in soft jogging bottoms and a long-sleeved jumper.

I also feel... fine. Too fine. Pushing up the sleeve of the jumper, I check my arm. The wound should still be gnarly, but it isn't. It looks years older than it should. Looping scars twist around my forearm. I rub it, my fingers tracing the ropy muscle. It's slightly dented, but there's no pain. I open and close my fist. Everything works perfectly.

When the bedroom door creaks open, my eyes snap to the widening gap. I wait, expecting someone to appear, but no one does. Could it have been the wind from an open window?

Gah. This entire situation is giving me the creeps.

How did I get here? Have I been asleep so long that I've healed?

I screw my eyes shut and rub my forehead vigorously. Come on, brain. Flashes of memory surface, hiding Sophie in the ceiling—I hope she is safe. The agony of teeth sinking into my arm. The white and grey wolves fighting. Bleeding as I walked home.

My stomach drops. "Shit. I'm in the wizard's house."

Gentle magic washes over me like a soft pat on the head, and the bedroom door swings wider—an invitation. Goose-bumps ripple across my skin. I glance back at the bed, then at the door.

Instead of crawling under the covers and pretending none of this is happening, I force myself to move.

I step into the hallway and head downstairs.

At the foot of the stairs, my black trainers—the same ones soaked in blood and muck last night—sit neatly on a shoe rack by the front door. I stop, unease prickling the back of my neck. They are spotless, gleaming as if they have just come out of the box. I reach to grab them, and the entire rack disappears into the wall.

"What the—" I step back, and the rack pops out again.

"Oh, so you don't want me to go? I can take a hint."

Down the hall, a door creaks open. My muscles ache as I shuffle over and peer inside. It's a dining room, and a single place is set at the far end of a long mahogany table. A high-backed chair slides out with a gentle scrape of wood on the carpet. Beside the plate, a fork performs a quick, playful twirl, then makes an oddly cute scooping motion before lying back down.

"What in the *Beauty and the Beast* is going on?"

This house has a soul. I've felt it ever since I stumbled into its garden last night, half dead and scared out of my mind. Whatever magic resides here—it's not malicious. If it wanted to hurt me, it could have done so while I lay unconscious. Instead, it healed my wounds, cleaned me, dressed me, and tucked me into bed.

Swallowing my fear, I square my shoulders and enter the dining room.

The chair is warm as I lower myself into it.

On the table are a glass of water, a tall glass of freshly squeezed orange juice, and a steaming cup of coffee. The rich, nutty aroma of the coffee makes me groan. I gulp the water first, soothing my parched throat, then lift the coffee to my lips.

My eyes flutter shut as the taste blooms across my

tongue. "Oh, wow," I murmur. It's delicious—better than anything the Wee Beastie could brew. "Thank you," I add softly, unsure if the house can hear me but needing to say it anyway.

My attention shifts to the breakfast before me—perfect golden toast, fluffy scrambled eggs, a small mountain of baked beans, and a neat row of eight crispy bacon rashers. I hesitate, glancing at the thankfully inert fork. I poke it once, just in case, then pick it up and take a cautious bite.

It's incredible.

My stomach growls, and suddenly I'm ravenous. I devour every bite, the meal's warmth chasing away the lingering cold in my bones. I can almost feel my blood sugar rising.

When I set down the fork, the plate disappears, whisked away as though by an unseen hand. In its place appears a bowl of fruit—perfectly sliced melon, juicy strawberries, crisp apple slices, and fragrant orange segments. I eat those too, savouring the burst of sweetness.

"I need to be going soon," I say, my voice tentative. "I have to report to the Ministry. They will want to know what happened, and I don't want them thinking I had anything to do with last night."

The house remains silent, but the air shifts. A faint, comforting warmth brushes my cheek, like an unseen hand offering reassurance.

I yawn, my body betraying me as fatigue creeps back in. My gaze falls to the white scar peeking out from under my sleeve. It's unsettling how clean and healed it looks, compared to the gory mess I was last night. By all rights, I should be dead. If not from blood loss, then from the vampire who would've gladly drained the rest of me if the wards hadn't stopped him.

"Thank you," I say softly, meaning it with every fibre of my being. "Thank you for saving my life."

I trace my fingers over the edge of the table, thinking. Healing magic is rare, usually performed by medical mages who chant wounds closed or fix broken bones. It's incredible—but also outrageously expensive. How did this house heal me? Could the soul inhabiting it have once belonged to a med mage?

The thought lingers as I glance around the room. "Thank you for the meal and for keeping me safe."

Another yawn escapes. It's getting hard to keep my eyes open. Eating, healing, and the weight of everything I've been through—it's too much. My chin dips to my chest, and the room blurs around me. Sleep pulls me under, and I don't resist.

CHAPTER FOURTEEN

MY EYES DRIFT SHUT for what feels like a second. When I open them with a sharp gasp, everything has changed.

I'm no longer in the dining room. I'm no longer in the wizard's house.

Instead, I'm back in my bedroom. The familiar beams on the ceiling stretch above me, the warm covers tucked snugly around me, my pillow perfectly fluffed beneath my head.

I blink, disoriented. "How did I get back here?" I whisper into the stillness. "Did I imagine all of it?"

For a moment, doubt creeps in. Maybe it was all some fever dream, a hallucination brought on by blood loss and adrenaline. But the lingering taste of freshly brewed coffee and ripe fruit on my tongue tells me otherwise. My stomach

—full, warm, and content—certainly does not feel imaginary.

The house zapped me back here.

It knew I was too tired to leave on my own, so it sent me home.

Wow.

A shrill ringing pierces the quiet. I groan, my hair a wild tangle, and push it away from my face. The sound grates at my ears, relentless and urgent.

The phone.

I stumble out of bed, legs shaky, and shuffle down the hallway. My black trainers are sitting neatly by the front door, side by side.

This is getting weird.

The phone keeps ringing, leading me toward the kitchen. When I reach the counter, I find my mobile beside a neatly folded pile of clean work clothes—the same clothes I wore last night, now spotless.

Before I can grab it, the ringing stops.

"Of course it stops," I mutter, rubbing my face with both hands. My hair is a disaster—a riot of dark waves that feels heavier, somehow fuller. "What is going on with my hair?"

The landline starts ringing—the dusty one hidden behind the sofa. It can only be work as no one else has the number.

My bladder, however, has other priorities, and it's not taking no for an answer. I do a ridiculous wee-shuffle-dance to the loo and take care of business. Afterwards, I wash my hands, glance up—and freeze.

There's a stranger in the mirror.

I lean forward so fast my forehead almost headbutts the glass. My breath fogs the surface as I study the face staring back.

No.

No, no, no.

"Oh my gosh, what did the magic of the house do?"

The woman in the mirror is me, but not me.

I tilt my head.

The stranger tilts hers back.

I stumble to the side, one hand darting blindly out the door into the hallway, slapping at the wall. It takes three tries to find the light switch, and when I finally flick it on, the bathroom fan kicks in with a low hum.

No amount of light helps. My skin is smoother, almost luminous, with a faint golden hue. I grip the sink as though it's the only thing keeping me upright. "What the heck is going on?"

As panic rises, something inside me growls.

Ooh, that's not a good sign.

CHAPTER FIFTEEN

SURELY A LITTLE SPIT from a shifter isn't enough to trigger a change at the DNA level. That can't be how humans turn—there's supposed to be a ceremony, magic, all sorts of steps. It can't be as simple as a bite. No, it does not make sense that one bite could flip a switch and cause this much change.

Humans don't just turn furry overnight.

The only other possibility is that the wizard's house triggered something inside me—or used powerful magic to save my life—and this transformation has nothing to do with the bite. Maybe it's just my imagination running wild, a trick of the mind.

I stare at the mirror.

That—right there—is not my imagination.

I run my hands over my hips, searching for the

comforting soft roll I'd always convinced myself was necessary cushioning. It's gone. I'm slimmer, my figure more proportionate—if that makes sense. My once long legs and short torso now seem balanced. There's more space between my hips and ribs, almost as if my body's been rearranged and I've been stretched out.

"This is... all so confusing."

My eyes aren't their warm, familiar brown anymore. Dark silver stares back, framed by thick lashes. Even if the expression is a tad feral, they are not glowing—at least, not as far as I can tell. Then again, perhaps you can't tell when you are looking at yourself?

My face is mine, but it's not. I've never looked like this, even on my best day. My nose is perfectly straight, a little narrower than before. My eyes are slightly wider apart, and my cheekbones... they are so defined.

I touch them. In the mirror, I see my skin pucker. I can feel my thumbs digging in.

It's real, not some elaborate prank.

My jaw is almost square but still feminine, and my hair is darker, triple its original thickness and weight. No wonder I was struggling with it.

I don't just look different; I look like someone else entirely—someone from another time. My great-grandmother's face stares back at me—her jaw, her nose, even those dark, intense eyes. The silver colour? That's new. It's as if my DNA got thrown into a cosmic blender, and the universe pulled out the best bits of my lineage to create this.

I open my mouth wide, shove trembling fingers inside, and prod teeth that are now perfectly straight, smooth, and blindingly white. My tongue and fingers search out the little bumps inside my lips and cheeks—remnants of years of absentminded biting.

Gone.

I can't even find the tiny scar between my eyes from when one of the twins at school threw a rock at me.

It's gone.

All of it is gone.

Every freckle, every blemish—erased. Apart from the white wolf's bites and claw marks, my skin is flawless. Do shifters have perfect skin? I can't recall. I never cared enough to check.

It's as though I've been... soul-snatched, my essence poured into this stranger's body. I can't decide if it's amazing or utterly horrifying.

Horrifying, I think. I liked being me. I enjoyed being forty-seven.

Now I look barely out of my teens.

Who in their right mind wants to be a teenager again? Living in that chaos once was more than enough. Not again. Please, not again. This—this is my worst nightmare. Sure, some women would kill to wake up younger, more vibrant, more perfect than ever before.

But me? I feel like I've been flung into a waking nightmare.

As you age, you fade into the background, and with that comes a fragile sense of safety, even if it's an illusion. I liked my face the way it was—familiar, lived-in. I wasn't drop-dead gorgeous. Not perfect, not stunning, but fine. It was mine.

This face, though—wide eyes, absurdly full lips. It's as if magic took the golden ratio as a personal dare and decided to show off. I don't want this. I don't want to be this person, to appear twenty-plus years younger, to be young again.

Everyone says youth and beauty are gifts, but to me, beauty is a trap.

The landline starts ringing again, relentlessly, followed by the mobile. Whoever's calling isn't giving up; they are seriously determined. The noise cuts through my thoughts, grounding me in the present. Grateful there are no more mirrors in the rest of the apartment, I slam the bathroom door behind me, shutting out my reflection.

I grab the mobile off the counter. The screen flashes NUMBER WITHHELD—a lump forms in my throat. I hate answering these kinds of calls, but I press the button anyway.

"Hello?"

"Mrs Emerson, where have you been?" growls a familiar voice.

Merrick.

How on earth do I recognise his voice? Goosebumps erupt along my arms. "Oh, hi. Have you got a parcel for me?"

"Answer the question. Where have you been? It's been two days."

"Two days?" I squeak, yanking the phone away to check the date. Oh crap. He is right—it has been two days. I suppose rearranging your face and body takes time. Clearing my throat, I try to sound casual. "Well, you see, I got bitten, and—"

"I know you got bitten. I was there when you bled all over the place."

My heart skips a beat. So, I was right. He was the one fighting the white wolf.

"Thank you—"

"Are you okay? Where have you been? There've been no reports at the medical centre of your admission. How are you still alive? How did you heal yourself, Mrs Emerson?"

I clamp my mouth shut, panic bubbling in my chest. How am I supposed to explain this?

"Is there some magic you brought through the sector border we're unaware of?" he presses.

"No," I mumble, my voice small. "No, the, you see—" I stop. Nothing I say is going to sound sane.

"Your blood trail ends at the wizard's house."

Anger flares, and I snarl, "Oh, if you already know the answer, why bother asking?" I fling my free hand up and pace the kitchen like a caged animal.

"I wanted to see if you were going to lie."

"You didn't give me a chance!" I snap, then, quieter, "I'm not going to lie."

Not that I could, given the evidence written all over my face. How exactly do I answer the door to greet him like this? With a bag over my head and call it a new fashion trend?

His growl reverberates through the phone, and something inside me stirs. I glance at my arm, almost expecting to see fur sprouting through my skin. Whatever's happening to me isn't just on the surface. It's deeper. It's much more than how I look.

He is still talking—ranting, really—but my head is buzzing, and I've completely tuned him out. "Merrick, I'm sorry," I cut in. "I'm not feeling well. I really need to go back to bed."

"Lark, did you at least get medical attention?"

"Yes. About that..." My words falter. How do I explain?

"I'm coming to your apartment," he declares.

"No, no, no, no, no, no," I squeak, then fake a loud, exaggerated yawn. "I, um, like I said, I'm not feeling well. And, um, I'm really tired. I need some rest."

"You are refusing to see me?" His tone is incredulous, like no one's ever dared tell him no before.

"Please, just give me a couple of days. I will call the Ministry to explain everything, so no one gets into trouble. Is Sophie okay? I put her in the—"

"She is fine," he snaps, cutting me off. "She told me you rescued her, then hid her in your hiding spot while you took on armed terrorists with a dart gun. You could have been killed."

"I'm fine," I say quickly. "I mean, I'm sort of fine. I will be okay."

Not lying to him is quickly becoming a full-blown challenge.

"You are human and easily damaged. What you did was a mistake," he growls. "I will give you a day, and then I'm coming for you."

Well, that's not ominous at all.

"Okay. All right. Um, do I need to call the Ministry, or—?"

"The Ministry is aware," he says curtly. Then he hangs up. No goodbye, no closing words—just silence.

Ooh, he was mad. I stare at the phone, then drop it

onto the counter and sink into a kitchen chair, my head in my hands.

What the heck am I going to do?

It's not like I can pack a bag and leave. Every piece of identification shows my old face—my real face, my actual age. No one will believe I'm the same person.

I can't run. I can't hide.

No. I need to woman up, avoid mirrors, and get used to this new normal. I've never been one to obsess over my reflection anyway. As long as there's nothing in my teeth, I'm good. It is what it is, and I have to deal with this. This... this face? It's just a surface, a façade. It's not who I am.

What people see does not reflect the mess happening inside. I'm still me, right? Just... wrapped differently. I can moan and cry all I want, but like the end of my marriage, it won't change a bloody thing.

This isn't something I can escape. The thought hits me. *Shifters are dangerous.*

What if this does not stop at my face? What if I turn into something else?

I feel some 'thing' within me. There's no guarantee I will become a wolf—or anything remotely manageable.

And a wolf? A wolf isn't a puppy.

I close my eyes, and the memory crashes in, swift and brutal. The sharp teeth sinking into my arm, the sheer weight of the wolf pinning me down, the sickening grind of bones under its bite.

"Oh no," I whisper, clutching my arm as if I can still feel the phantom pain. My stomach lurches; I slap a hand over my mouth as bile rises in my throat. I can't tell if I'm going to vomit or pass out.

Inside me, something whines—a soft, pitiful sound.

A keening moan escapes my lips, high-pitched and panicked. I slide to the floor, back against the kitchen cupboards, trembling.

I should've told Merrick to come immediately. I should've begged him to stay on the phone.

I'm an idiot. A bloody fool.

My breathing turns shallow, my chest heaving in quick, panicked bursts. What will happen to me? What are they going to do? Unregulated shifters are a threat.

They will kill me.

They are going to bloody kill me for being an unsanctioned shifter. I'm as good as dead.

CHAPTER SIXTEEN

I TOLD Merrick I was going back to bed, and I really didn't want to lie to him—not now. Almost childlike, I crawl under the covers, even though my mind is racing and my body feels anything but restful.

I lie there, staring at the ceiling, willing sleep to come. It takes longer than I'd care to admit, but eventually, despite my whirling thoughts, exhaustion wins and I drift off.

When I wake, I sit on the edge of the bed, breathing hard.

Everything feels... different.

The air smells like me—vanilla body cream, the chemical strawberry scent of my shampoo, faint perspiration clinging to the sheets, and the metallic tang of coins in the bowl by the front door. It's as though the apartment is steeped in every smell I've ever left behind. It's eerie how a room can capture so much of its occupant.

Outside, I hear a bike. I can even hear the rider's breathing and the crunch of tyres on gravel.

My ears twitch—wait, no, that can't be right! I slap a hand against my perfectly normal-shaped ear, shake my head, and try to clear it, but it's no use.

The faint ticking of the wall clock swells inside my head like a relentless metronome, *tick, tick, tick,* hammering against my skull.

I clench my teeth, and even that feels wrong.

"Oh no," I whisper, rubbing my temples. My voice sounds too loud.

I've changed again.

I don't feel human—not any more.

In the hallway, I see the jagged edge where the wooden floor meets the skirting board and the tiny scratches in the varnish. I can pick out every fibre of the duvet cover under my hand. It's startlingly crisp against my fingers, almost painful. Every thread, crease, and imperfection is suddenly vibrant beneath my touch.

It's as though my body no longer knows how to filter the world.

I stand, and the motion feels alien—too smooth, too deliberate. I prowl. My eyes widen, and a raw, frightened sound escapes me.

"Why is this happening to me?" I mutter, gripping the edge of the door.

The wood groans under my fingers, and somehow, I know that if I squeeze just a little more, it will crumble to dust.

"It's too much. Way too much."

Moving with bizarre, fluid grace, I head to the dressing room and grab the cotton wool balls I usually use to cleanse my face. I pull a couple apart and shove a generous wad up each nostril and into my ears.

The cotton wool muffles the world, muting the onslaught of these new sounds and scents. My heart rate finally slows, and I manage a deep, steady breath. I can still taste the smells on my tongue, but the cotton helps. At least I no longer hear footsteps outside anymore.

Short of blindfolding myself, I can't do much about my vision. For now, I will just try not to focus too hard on anything.

I check the time.

At least one thing is going my way—I haven't slept the day away. There are still hours left before I'm supposed to see Merrick tomorrow. I have time.

Time to figure this out.

I need to work on these overwhelming senses and learn how to control myself. I can't spend the rest of my life wandering around with wads of cotton wool shoved in my ears and nose. That's hardly a solution—it's barely a stopgap.

Whether I like it or not, I need an ally. I need Mr First Class's help. But he is not going to lift a finger for me if I turn up rocking in a corner, screaming about the ticking clock or the smell of loose change by the door. He wouldn't understand. How could he? He has lived with these senses all his life, learned to adapt, probably does not notice them any more. For him, this is normal.

If life has taught me one thing, it's that panic never

helps. Acting in panic only digs the hole deeper and makes things worse.

So I inhale deeply and plant my feet on the floor.

Positive thinking for the win. I can do this.

"Okay, let's see what this new body can do."

I'd normally go to the gym, but nobody needs to see me like this—the madwoman with cotton wool everywhere. Not yet. I'm not ready to leave the apartment, let alone the building.

I push the furniture aside to create space and stand barefoot in the middle of the living room.

Extending my arms, I study my hands, flexing my fingers before curling them into fists. They look familiar, but they are not the same. My nails feel sharper, and I can sense the currents of cool air sliding over each finger, as if the slightest movement stirs a breeze.

My balance also feels different—more centred, lower, and stable. I crouch, testing the muscles in my legs. They are tighter than I expected.

"Okay," I say, my voice sounding strange in my blocked ears.

I assume a basic Judo stance, one I've repeated thousands of times. This time, however, it's too easy. My body reacts before my mind can catch up, flowing into the movement. I shift my weight, testing a throw in slow motion, and nearly stumble when the force comes too strong, too fast.

"What the heck?" I pause, concentrating on my feet, rolling from heel to toe and feeling the floor beneath me. My steps are lighter and more precise.

I've lived with awkward, sometimes clumsy joints, but

suddenly everything fits. A grin spreads across my face before I can quell it. I'm terrified and exhilarated all at the same time. I'm faster, stronger, more agile than I ever imagined.

I spend the next couple of hours doing light gymnastics, footwork drills, and strength exercises to adjust to this new body.

After the first hour, I need to breathe properly, so I remove the cotton from my nose.

After two hours, I feel calmer. The exercise helps, and being immersed in my own scent grounds me. My vision is also less distracting, though sound remains a problem.

I've got a plan.

First, I go online and order some noise-cancelling headphones—the sort they say can block out everything short of an air raid siren. Then I add various strongly scented items to my cart: menthol, vanilla, and eucalyptus. Anything I can apply near my nostrils to blunt this overwhelming sense of smell. It might be ridiculous but I'm willing to experiment; I will try anything.

If I can mute these senses, even a little bit, I might stand a chance of feeling normal.

Next, I add a pair of sunglasses. Brightness isn't really the issue, but maybe wearing tinted lenses will trick my brain into thinking I've got a new prescription—a sort of mind-optical placebo. I don't know. It's worth a shot. Anything beats teetering on the brink of a sensory meltdown.

I fill my cart to meet the minimum delivery requirement and hit send. Relief fills me when the screen confirms my items will arrive tonight. Maybe the universe is cutting me some slack for once.

Then I order a takeaway.

Whatever is happening inside me demands food, and I'm not about to argue. If movies and books have taught me anything, it's that when you are dealing with a werewolf, vampire, or any other supernatural creature, you always feed the beast.

Chinese it is.

While I wait for both deliveries, I jump in the shower and scrub away the sweat from earlier. The exercise cleared my mind, but now I'm sticky and uncomfortable.

After towelling off, I grab a pair of scissors and tackle my hair.

Clumps of wet, unruly strands fall to the floor as I hack away. By the time I'm finished, it's still halfway down my back, but at least it's not as wild. It will do for now. I will go to a proper hairdresser eventually, but for now, I need to feel like I'm taking back control of my life.

I've got this.

Everything is going to be okay. I have to stay positive and keep moving forward.

When the deliveries arrive, I waste no time testing different fragrances.

The first few items are a bust—too strong, too weak, or just plain useless. But then I find a vanilla lip balm. I smear it across my lips and dab some under my nose. The scent is warm, sweet, and just strong enough to drown out the most overwhelming odours without stinging my nostrils.

The sunglasses help, too. They feel like a shield, even if

it's all in my head. The headphones are a godsend, silencing the constant drone of noise to a low, manageable hum.

Sure, I probably look completely ridiculous—a mismatched mess of sunglasses, headphones, and shiny vanilla-scented mouth and nose—but at least I'm no longer shoving cotton wool up my nose.

Small victories.

I settle down with the absurd amount of Chinese food I've ordered—enough for two—and eat every bite. By the time I'm finished, I feel stronger and steadier.

For the first time since all this started, I feel almost... okay.

If they don't kill me, I might just be all right.

CHAPTER SEVENTEEN

THE FOLLOWING DAY, my phone buzzes with instructions to be ready by 8 a.m. I'm outside, waiting, when a car pulls up. Merrick, apparently, couldn't be bothered to collect me himself.

Silly me for being disappointed.

I don't know where he stands in all this. Was he part of security that night, there to protect us? Or is he something else entirely?

I guess I will find out soon enough.

The blond shifter bodyguard is back, as smug as ever. His nostrils flare as he takes in my scent, and recognition flickers across his face almost instantly. Amusement dances in his green eyes as they land on my sunglasses and headphones, and his smirk widens like he has stumbled onto a private joke.

Under his breath, he mutters, "This will be good. He's gonna shit a brick."

Oh, great. Glad I can be entertaining.

He swings the back door open with a cocky smirk, and I slide inside, glaring at him. *Yeah, laugh it up, buddy. Laugh it up.* The urge to smack him in the back of the head is almost overwhelming, but I manage to refrain. *Be nice, Lark.*

Since I first woke up, my temper and hormones have been all over the place—like being thirteen again, but with added strength. I need to do something about it. Maybe hit the gym, punch a bag, or spar with someone. Right now, I feel like a live wire, crackling with uncontrollable energy, and the thing inside me keeps clawing to break free.

We don't stop at the Ministry's technological centre. Instead, the car drives past my usual stomping grounds, heading deeper into Zone Two's almost vehicle-free streets and unfamiliar territory. The road opens onto a broad square surrounded by historic buildings—tall, dark-stone structures with carved detailing from the early 1800s.

We pull up in front of one of these buildings, and a doorman in an immaculate uniform rushes forward to open my door.

"Good luck," Blondie says, grinning.

"Thanks for the lift," I reply, deliberately ignoring him as I step onto the pavement.

Polished stone steps lead to heavy wooden doors with intricate, weathered ironwork. The doorman darts ahead as I approach, pushing open the right door with a creak.

"This way, Mrs Emerson, this way," he says, gesturing grandly.

"Thank you."

I remove my sunglasses as I step inside. The dimly lit interior has polished stone floors and dark wood panelling on the walls. Through the layer of vanilla lip balm, I catch the faint smell of old books and leather.

A shifter woman waits nearby, her hair swept into a messy bun. She beckons me to follow, remaining silent as her heels click against the stone floor. At the far end of a long, shadowy corridor, we stop in front of an imposing oak door. She knocks once.

"Come in," a muffled voice calls.

She opens the door but does not step inside.

"Thank you," I say.

She nods, giving me a brief, almost apologetic smile before hurrying away. Her footsteps echo along the corridor like the hounds of hell are nipping at her heels.

I take a deep breath, gather my courage, and walk through the door.

It's a grand office with a high ceiling. To my left sits an old-fashioned fireplace, and the remaining walls are lined with shelves brimming with books and ancient magical artefacts that stretch from floor to ceiling.

At the centre of the room stands a huge desk carved from dark, glossy wood. Its edges are adorned with subtle claw-like designs. Papers lie in neat piles on its surface, and a fancy pen rests perfectly parallel to the edge.

I finally focus on the man behind the desk.

His fingers dig into the surface, as though he is forcing himself not to jump up and . . . grab me? Shake me? Hug me? The last one is probably wishful thinking, but I certainly wouldn't say no to a hug.

Merrick rises from his seat, looking effortlessly hand-some in a black suit and an icy blue tie that matches his piercing eyes. His expression is locked down tight—unreadable.

I wish I could master that kind of game face. Mine usually betrays every thought and flicker of emotion. It's gotten me into more trouble than I care to admit. Maybe this new face of mine will be different?

"Hi, Merrick, it's nice to see you," I say, flinging my hand in an awkward wave.

Merrick tilts his head, his gaze sweeping over me like a scanner. "Glad to see you are not a vampire," he says, his tone flat.

He must know about the vampire who prowled outside the wizard's house. His scent had to be everywhere.

I glance pointedly at the weak morning light spilling through the windows. "Yeah, not a vampire," I reply dryly. "If I were, I'd be either daytime dead or bursting into flames right now."

"Lark, what have you done to yourself?"

I let out a mortified laugh. "Oh yeah, this was totally my plan—the new 'get-bitten-by-a-shifter-and-fall-into-a-magic-house' diet. It's all the rage. Everyone's doing it."

I throw my hands up, yank the guest chair out, flop into it like a sulky teenager, and fold my arms. "Yes, I did it on purpose," I grumble.

Merrick makes an irritated sound in the back of his throat, as if biting back some harsh words. He smooths down his tie, then settles into his chair, resting his hands on the desk. His fingers are long, perfectly manicured, and annoyingly composed.

"The changes are... dramatic. Tell me what happened."

"Yes, they are," I mumble, tucking an uneven strand of hair behind my ear. My fingers brush its ragged edges—a reminder of my frantic attempt at control. I inhale deeply, forcing myself to meet his gaze.

I'm furious, frightened, and so bloody embarrassed. This entire situation is ridiculous.

I also don't understand why I'm here, spilling my guts to him of all people—except that he has saved me twice now. Once from being blasted by a mage at the hotel, and again on those stairs, pulling me from the jaws of that wolf.

He's the only person who seems to care.

They say things happen in threes, don't they?

Maybe he will save me one more time.

And the Ministry can't know about this—at least not yet. Not until I get some answers. I work for the shifter government, but that does not mean I trust them with whatever's happening to me.

My instincts say Merrick can help.

The thing inside me stirs, rolling restlessly under my skin. I stiffen and slap a hand over my chest as if I can smother it, but it refuses to calm.

"Tell me what happened," he repeats, his patience somehow more unsettling than outright anger.

I fidget with my headphones, adjusting them in a vain attempt to avoid his stare. Taking a shaky breath, I drop my hands, lean forward, and trace the smooth edge of the desk with my fingertips.

Then I talk.

I tell him everything. The bite, the vampire, passing out, waking in the wizard's house, the breakfast, seeing a stranger in the mirror, taking that nap, the explosion of senses. It all pours out in a jumbled rush. My throat aches from the effort of reliving the horror.

Merrick does not speak or interrupt. He watches me, his sharp eyes locked on mine. When my story ends, he stands without a word.

I follow him with my gaze as he crosses the room to a hidden sideboard and retrieves a crystal decanter. Even with noise-cancelling headphones, the sound of water pouring into a glass seems loud. He places the glass in front of me with the same measured calm, then returns to his seat, folding his hands together on the desk.

"Thank you," I mumble, my throat raw. I take a big gulp. "I'm sorry I was so rude. My temper and hormones are all over the place."

"It's understandable."

"It's still not fair. I'm asking for your help, yet I'm acting like a brat. I'm sorry." I gesture at myself. "Just warning you—it might be a while before I can rein this in." My voice rises, frustration cracking through my fake calm. "What is happening to me, Merrick? A bite doesn't just turn someone into a shifter. Isn't there supposed to be some super-secret ceremony? Bites don't change people. Right? This isn't how it's done." I despise the desperation in my tone, but I can't stop it.

He nods. "Before a human can become a shifter, there is magic and a ceremony," he says, his voice steady. "It's not something that happens from a simple bite and it's a complicated process. But it seems you are... a little different."

"What about the wizard's house? Do you think... you

said yourself there's magic involved. Could it have had a hand in this?"

"Possibly," he concedes with a slight nod. "At the very least, it kept you alive. An ordinary human would have died from those injuries, especially after wandering around the Enterprise Zone with a severely bitten arm."

I look down at the arm in question, hidden beneath my jumper. Merrick's gaze follows mine, and he nods at it.

"May I see it?" He holds out his hand, waiting.

I sigh, tug my sleeve, and place my hand in his palm. His hand is massive, completely enveloping mine, and so warm.

He inspects the damaged skin, rotating my arm gently, his thumb brushing over the scar tissue with clinical precision.

"You have healed remarkably well," he says, sounding thoughtful. "That, again, is unusual."

I bite my lip, ignoring the weird electric shock each time his thumb moves. *Married!* I remind myself sternly. *You are still married, and you're... whatever this is now.*

The reminder does not help.

Abruptly, I pull my arm away, tugging the sleeve down to hide the scars.

"I've been doing a little digging into your medical history." He taps the paper. "This is from your original human files."

Merrick slides the document towards me. My name leaps off the page. Beyond that, it's dense medical jargon that might as well be written in another language. The date is unmistakable—it's from my childhood.

"Okay, erm, thank you," I say, though I have no idea what he wants me to look at.

He sighs and gets up, moving around the desk to stand behind me. I freeze as he leans over my shoulder, his breath warm against my neck. He points to a highlighted section, and I force myself to focus on the bold words.

Human.
Shifter.
Mage.
Vampire.

I swallow hard and turn to look at him, wide-eyed. We're so close I can almost taste his breath. His expression remains unreadable.

"What does this mean?" I whisper.

"You have all four human derivatives in your blood," he says.

Oh.

So what? A little bit of shifter DNA shouldn't be enough to make me furry. Right? Maybe now's the time to consider telling him about my technomancy. Does he really need to know I've got mage powers?

Unless... I don't. I haven't tried them. Not once.

And with everything happening, there's a chance they have disappeared altogether. Or worse, what if they have... changed? What if I try to use them and end up frying someone's phone or blowing up a server?

My thoughts spiral, and I clamp my mouth shut. Years of keeping this secret have made silence second nature. It's not something I've ever felt comfortable talking about. And now, with all this DNA mutt business staring me in the face, I feel even less inclined to bring it up.

"Do you think the results would be different now?" I

ask, trying to sound casual. "Because, you know... I've changed."

Merrick shrugs noncommittally. "I don't know. We'd have to run tests."

"Tests?" I groan. "Great."

"We need to find out why you didn't need the ceremony. The wizard's house—or the bite—must have triggered something inside you. The shifter saliva likely caused an immune reaction, flipping a switch in your dormant DNA."

Oh.

I blink. "What does that mean?"

He smiles wryly. "It means, don't let a vampire bite you. We have no idea what you would turn into."

"Seriously? Now you are making jokes?"

He meets my gaze, all amusement gone. "I'm not joking, Lark. Don't let a vampire bite you."

I groan, frustration boiling over. "Okay, but seriously. Does this mean I'm... a shifter?"

"Yes," he replies. "It means you will be able to change shape."

"What? When?" My voice rises in panic. "Do I have to wait for the full moon?"

He exhales, shoulders tensing. I can almost see him dying a little inside at my flippant comment.

"The moon is irrelevant," he says, his voice clipped. "Your transformation will take time. You will have to adapt. And, frankly, no one's done this at your age."

Ouch.

"Wow, thanks," I grumble.

He continues, ignoring my sarcasm. "The transformation will wreak havoc on your physiology. You will get easily exhausted, or you might get angry."

Leaning forward, he presses his hand against the desk, his gaze fierce.

"On behalf of the Ministry, I extend our sincerest apologies. What happened to you is inexcusable, and you will be compensated and cared for." His voice resonates with quiet seriousness that makes my chest tighten.

Well, so much for the Shifter Ministry not knowing about my furry problems. I grind my teeth, wondering how much pressure it would take to crack one—and whether it would grow back. Shifters and their healing biology...

"But I don't think you fully understand your situation, Lark. Your contract with the sector has been revoked because you are no longer human. You are now under the jurisdiction of the Shifter Ministry, which means human laws no longer apply to you. The rules you lived by? They no longer exist."

I open my mouth to protest, but he silences me with a curt gesture.

"For everyone's safety," he says. His tone isn't cold; it brims with fierce compassion, clashing with my instinct to argue.

He places a glossy brochure on the desk and nudges it over.

"This explains everything. If it were me, I'd read it thoroughly. But you are an adult, and I'm not here to tell you what to do."

What? I can't believe shifters have a how-to brochure.

"You need to learn control," he continues, his tone

gentler. He opens a drawer and lifts out a sleek black band, placing it in front of me. "This will help."

I lean forward, pick it up, and rub my thumb over its smooth surface. Magic thrums quietly within.

"What does it do? Am I supposed to chant a spell or something?"

He shakes his head. "No spells needed. It activates automatically once you wear it."

I narrow my eyes. "And besides 'helping,' what does it actually do?"

Merrick drums his fingers on the desk, as though weighing how much to reveal. Eventually, he says, "It will track you—for medical reasons—and suppress your heightened senses and will stop most uncontrolled shifts. The first shift is risky. We don't want you hurting yourself or anyone else if you lose control. This ensures you won't shift alone, without medical oversight."

A tracker.

With everything I've been through—every smell, sound, and sensation tearing me apart—I will take whatever help I can get. I slide the band onto my wrist. It fits snugly.

"Take off your headphones," Merrick says.

My hands tremble as I remove them. Sound washes over me, yet I don't feel overwhelmed or bombarded. My vision seems softer too. I let out a shaky breath.

He hands me a tissue, and I roll my eyes but accept it anyway. "Thanks," I mutter, wiping away the protective vanilla lip balm from under my nose.

"With supervision, you can remove the band for short periods to build tolerance. Eventually, you will adjust, and you might not need it at all—or you might wear it only on special occasions, like a concert, so you can enjoy the music without hearing someone slurp their drink ten rows back."

"Good to know. Thank you." I tap the band. "Do newly turned shifters ever manage without magical help?"

"Some do," he replies. "It depends on the individual. Think of it as a spectrum. Some shifters wrestle with control, while others—like alphas—have near-flawless mastery. It's partly genetic. Call it 'uber-control.'"

That makes sense. Alphas are wired differently, exerting authority over their animals. I nod. "Okay. Thank you."

"I know you are an adult," Merrick says, "but every new shifter goes to the Facility until they have mastered their transformations. It's in Zone One, not deep in shifter territory. You will learn how to be a shifter, how to follow the rules, and what your strengths are. After that, we will find a place for you in a pack."

He says *pack* the way a human might say *family*.

"You have a place for me in a facility?" I snap, my temper sparking. "Hang on. I'm not going anywhere. I have a life and a job to do."

Now that I have this band, I can learn all this shifter stuff and figure the rest out on my own.

His eyes narrow, and his expression hardens into what I can only assume is his best alpha stare.

I stare back, no less indignant.

"You will do as you are told," he says, his voice low and commanding. "You are a shifter, Lark, and this isn't something—unlike your marriage—that you can run away from."

What?

Chapter Eighteen

"My what?" The words come out as a snarl. I'm on my feet before I realise I've moved, squaring up to him across the desk. My temper flares like a match struck against dry tinder, and the thing inside me responds with a feral hunger.

My fists twitch. I want to punch him in his smug, beautiful, infuriating face. I want to *bite* him, and it takes every ounce of willpower not to.

"What do you know about my marriage?" I growl, my voice shaking with rage.

Merrick's expression changes, watchful now, as though deciding whether I'm about to hit him or walk out. "You left your life in the Human Zone," he says evenly. "Left your husband for a job."

His words feel like a slap.

"I left my husband for a job?" I repeat incredulously, my voice rising with each syllable. "I. Left. My. Husband. For. A. Job? Is that what you think?"

I take a step closer, my voice razor-sharp enough to cut glass. "Let me tell you something, Mr High-and-Mighty Shifter. I left my husband because he screwed my sister. My *sister*. I caught them in bed together, so don't you dare stand there and judge me. I didn't throw away twenty-seven years of marriage for an effing job."

I'm shaking now, fury rolling off me in waves. "If you are going to have an opinion about my life, at least bloody well have the decency to ask me first!"

The words hang in the air, heavy with tension. Taking a deep, shuddering breath, I retreat until I bump into the chair behind me. Startled, I shuffle further back until my shoulders press against the shelves on the far wall.

I need to calm down.

Asking this man for help, then turning around and using my newfound strength to knock him senseless, would defeat the purpose.

Merrick rubs the back of his neck, wincing. "I apologise. I shouldn't have said that."

"Yeah, you shouldn't have." My voice remains tight.

Hurt.

I inhale deeply, trying to soothe the thing inside me. The fancy magical band isn't doing shit—she is prowling beneath the surface, feeding on my temper.

I close my eyes and wrestle with the magic within.

Before either of us can say more, a sharp bang and a hiss cut through the tense silence. The noise comes from one of

Merrick's desk drawers. He frowns, leaning down to investigate.

When he slides the drawer open, black, acrid smoke billows out.

"What on earth?" Merrick mutters, removing a smoking laptop. "It's switched off. How—?"

The device must be searingly hot; he juggles it from hand to hand, eyes flicking between confusion and annoyance.

Without hesitation, he stands, walks past me, and yanks open the office door. His voice booms down the corridor.

"Hannah! Can you bring me a new laptop, please?"

The rapid clicks of heels approach, followed by a quiet, hesitant reply. Merrick hands over the smouldering device without another word and shuts the door behind him.

The smell of burnt electronics lingers in the air, sharp and bitter.

I look away, biting my lip to stop myself grinning. My gaze drops to the floor, feigning innocence. I shouldn't have done it, but at least now I know my technomancy is still working.

Merrick sinks into his chair, dragging a hand over his face with a groan. "There's something else I need to tell you. I've arranged... I may have miscalculated."

That sounds ominous.

My smugness disappears. I keep my weight pressed against the shelves, the sharp edge digging into my back, bracing me against the panic rising in my chest. Merrick's usually stoic face is showing cracks.

What has he done?

"Merrick, what have you arranged?"

"You have an appointment today," he continues, voice low and steady. "Your solicitor will be here in half an hour, followed shortly after by your husband."

My knees buckle, and for a second, I think I might crumple to the floor. My fingers clamp around the shelf until my knuckles pale.

I have a creature clawing inside me, desperate to escape, and Merrick thinks adding Paul to this chaos is a good idea?

I'm hanging by a thread. Now this?

No.

"I can't. No. I can't." The words tumble out in a hoarse whisper before I repeat them, louder. "I can't, Merrick. I can't see him. Please, please don't make me see him. I will go to the Facility, learn how to be a shifter—then maybe, once I'm in control of myself—maybe then I can see him. But not now. Please. Not now." My voice breaks, betraying me. "Don't let him come here. Send him away. I don't want to see him."

Merrick's jaw tightens, though his expression remains resolute. "The paperwork's already done, and he is already in the Enterprise Zone. He's on his way. I'm sorry, Lark. There's nothing I can do."

Bullshit. This is Merrick's fault. "You interfered. You caused this to—to —what, to hurt me? To see me suffer?"

He flinches, guilt flashing in his blue eyes. "I don't want you suffering," he says quietly. "I don't want to see you hurt. But this is something you have to face."

"I know!" I snap, raking my hands over my face as if I could wipe away the despair. "Who are you to decide when? Look at me! I'm not the Lark he knew. My face, my hair— God, look at this mess. My clothes don't fit. I had a plan. I wanted to at least look... presentable before facing him. Not like some lunatic..."

I falter, glancing at Merrick in helpless frustration. "He will freak out. He is going to freak the eff out. He's anti-shifter. He hates shifters—he is an active member of Human First. The moment he sees me, he will lose it."

Or maybe, in the best-case scenario, Paul won't be able to look at me at all. Maybe he will sign the divorce papers without any more drama.

Merrick stands abruptly and strides to the door. He swings it open and shouts down the corridor. "Hannah! Bring me some scissors."

He shuts the door again and turns back to me, his gaze gentler. "We can at least fix your hair," he says softly. "Everything will be all right."

All right for him, maybe.

"Why did you do this?" My voice trembles. "If it's not out of cruelty or revenge, there must be—"

"Because it's something you have to deal with," Merrick interjects, firm but almost pleading. "And now it's more critical than ever, because it's not just about closure or dissolving your marriage. You are a shifter, and the change still isn't certain. You need to enter it with as few doubts as possible—no regrets, no ghosts in your past. If you don't, it could kill you. Do you understand? The transition still isn't guaranteed, Lark."

Do I understand? I nod, though the truth weighs heavily on me. I understand the logic—clear but crushing. Yes, I need to settle things with him, but am I strong enough to face Paul? Am I brave enough?

As much as he deserves my anger, I know he is not

dangerous. He isn't plotting against me. Honestly, I'm more worried about myself—about losing control, saying things I can't take back—or doing something I will regret, like going furry.

Merrick won't let that happen. Right?

"Is that why you brought up the state of my marriage—implying I left him for a job?" I eye him suspiciously. "Have you spoken to him?"

Merrick looks at me, his face unreadable. Maybe I see guilt again; I'm not sure. I don't know him well enough to interpret that stare.

"You are going to shove me in a room with the man who broke me, who tore my heart to shreds, and expect me to 'deal with it' so I can... what, turn into a monster?"

"Shifters aren't monsters, Lark."

"Most shifters aren't," I snap. "You are not a monster. But you said yourself—nobody my age has ever turned. You don't know what I will become."

My throat tightens as the enormity of everything presses down on me. The weight of it all seems to crush me. I'm teetering on the edge, about to splinter. This man standing across from me represents everything I don't understand, everything I can't control, the unknown, and now he is forcing me to face what I've been avoiding.

Paul.

"Couldn't you at least have given me a couple of days? A chance to get used to this face, this body, before making me confront my soon-to-be ex-husband?"

Fate has not just come knocking—it's kicked the door off its hinges. You can't run from your problems. I know that. But knowing it and being ready to face them is another matter entirely.

I want to be furious. I want to scream and shout.

Instead, I breathe, forcing down the fire in my chest.

Merrick is right—I need to face this. It's been gnawing at me for months. Maybe it's better with no warning—less time to spiral. Less time to overthink.

Still, I can't help but question him. *What is Merrick's job, exactly?* His role puzzles me. Is he Ministry security, a pack leader, or something else? The alpha aura is unmistakable, yet the thing inside me does not defer to him. It's... strange. What does that mean for me? Might I be an alpha? Or something else entirely?

I shove that thought away. One crisis at a time. One problem at a time. One bloody problem at a time. Let Paul sign the divorce papers, and then I will cope with the fallout later.

I take a deep breath and lift my chin.

"Okay, all right. I can do this. I need a computer with an internet connection."

"Why?" Suspicion edges his voice.

"If you are insisting I sit in a room with him, then I'm insisting on coming armed with evidence. I need proof—ammunition for my closure."

His brows lift slightly, but he does not speak.

"Paul's going to deny everything. He will twist the truth, act like the wronged party, make himself out to be the victim like he always does." *Like he did to you.* My hands form fists. "But this time, I will show him—every ugly, undeniable detail. I have a home video. Of him and—"

My throat constricts. I swallow hard.
The thing inside me rumbles, a low, approving purr.

Chapter Nineteen

Unwilling and dreading it, I follow Hannah to the conference room on the far side of Merrick's office building, the borrowed laptop tucked under my arm. She leaves me at the door, and my hand trembles as I press the handle.

Paul sits with his back to the door—who does that in a shifter building? Just seeing him makes me itch. Has he never heard of predators?

Even with the band's magic dulling my senses, I can smell his emotions: anxiety, anger, and something sour. It's strange—these scents are tied to his feelings, but I understand them instinctively, without conscious thought.

He is practically vibrating, a bundle of nervous energy barely contained. Whether he's angry at me, the situation, or the inconvenience of being kept waiting, I can't say.

To his left sits a broad, bald man whose face practically screams 'divorce solicitor.' To his right, leaning against him as though she needs support, is a woman who is all too familiar. Her dark, glossy hair is styled in perfect, voluminous curls. She seems thinner than when I last saw her—but then again, last time, she was naked and bouncing around.

Dove.

Of course he brought my sister.

My stomach twists into a painful knot, disbelief burning inside me. I realise my fingers are gripping the hem of my jumper. Today was already going to be hard enough, but this? This is a whole new level of insult.

They came together. To finalise our divorce.

I force myself over the threshold and hug the wall, keeping as much distance between us as possible. My movements are deliberate as I prowl around the conference table, each step heavier than the last, before finally settling in a seat opposite Paul.

Neither of them recognises me.

Paul glances up, his gaze skimming over my face. He dismisses me with a sneer—just another shifter, nothing more. Dove, on the other hand, gives me a once-over, her eyes narrowing as though I'm competition. She inches closer to Paul, resting a manicured hand on his arm in a possessive gesture.

I want to laugh. Really? This man isn't a prize. A husband who cheats on his wife with her sister isn't worth fighting over.

The laptop beside me feels like an anchor. If I could dream of the perfect scenario, this might make my top ten

—a chance to observe them without pretence or pity, without their emotions clouding my judgement.

Paul looks terrible. Dark circles under his eyes, unkempt hair, and the beginnings of a beard. For a brief moment, I almost pity him, but then I catch sight of Dove again, and that shred of compassion vanishes.

I only now notice the three guards stationed in the room, one of them the smirking blond who seems far too eager for a show. Blondie leans against the wall, arms folded, radiating amused anticipation. He wants me to lose control.

I roll my eyes and pour myself a glass of water. The crystal facets catch the light as I twist the glass, the whirlpool of liquid reflecting the storm brewing inside me. It also gives me eight little versions of an angry Paul.

"When am I going to see my wife?" Paul demands to the silent room, slamming his palm on the table. His voice is hoarse, like he's been shouting or recovering from a cold.

I set the glass down with deliberate care and lean forward, about to speak, when the door opens.

Merrick strides in with the effortless authority of someone who knows the room belongs to him. His presence changes the air, sharpens it. Paul stiffens; Dove straightens, flicking her hair and offering a nervous giggle.

The thing inside me stirs, and I fight the ridiculous urge to snarl. Dove can cling to Paul all she likes, but the moment her eyes flick towards Merrick, something primal in me flares to life.

Don't you dare look at him, you cow.

Barry, my shifter solicitor, follows Merrick in, his arms laden with files. "Apologies for the delay. I had to complete some additional revisions pertaining to this case," he says,

154

offering me a warm smile as he takes the seat beside me. "Good morning. Nasty business with the bite. How are you holding up?"

"I'm managing," I reply, glancing at the black sensory band on my wrist.

"Good to see you have got a band. That'll help immensely. Let's get this done quickly." He pats the stack of files, then leans back with a reassuring nod.

Merrick unbuttons his jacket and sits at the head of the table. He pours himself a glass of water, then regards Paul with cool detachment.

"Mr Emerson."

"Who the hell are you?" Paul snaps, his tone sharp enough to make the bodyguards twitch. Barry and the other solicitor wince.

Merrick does not bother answering. Instead, he flicks open the top folder and says, "What can I do for you, Mr Emerson?"

Paul slams his hand on the table again. "I'm here to get my wife!"

Merrick tilts his head, voice dangerously calm. "Are you now? Did you lose her?"

"Don't play games, you filthy beast," Paul snarls. "I told you on the phone—we had a disagreement, and now she's taken a job with the Ministry. I want to talk to her. I want her to come home. Whatever contract she has with you animals is null and void. She's human. She doesn't belong here."

"Mrs Emerson is an adult," Merrick replies smoothly, "and perfectly capable of making her own decisions. Can you tell me why she left?"

"That's none of your business," Paul growls, his expression darkening.

Merrick's gaze slides to me. "But I'd like to know."

Dove interjects, her voice syrupy sweet. "It was just a little misunderstanding. A tiny quarrel, nothing major."

Merrick arches a brow. "A small misunderstanding? She moved to an entirely different sector to get away from her husband. That's quite the disagreement. And you are?"

"I'm her sister, Dove," she replies with a simpering smile. "We have been so worried about her. She's not well, you see. It runs in the family—on *her* father's side."

Merrick's expression remains neutral. "That sounds serious."

"It is," Dove says, dropping her voice as though sharing a secret.

Paul leans forward, pleading. "Look, I love my wife. I'd never hurt her intentionally. This whole divorce thing is ridiculous. She can't just leave me!"

Merrick's eyes narrow, his next question slices through the room. "You both reek of each other. Do you and Mrs Emerson have an open relationship?"

Paul splutters, face reddening. Dove freezes, her smile faltering. I lean back, satisfied by the first crack in their united front.

"Mrs Emerson recorded a home video before she left you." Merrick continues, his voice calm, but the weight of his words and his poorly veiled anger presses down on the room. Dove and Paul exchange confused glances, not yet grasping the situation.

"If you would," Merrick says, nodding for me to

proceed. He is careful not to say my name. Which I appreciate.

Though my smile is strained, I slide the laptop to the centre of the table. The video is queued up, but I angle the screen away from myself—I don't need to relive it. The memory of that day is enough to twist my stomach into knots.

I press play, and the brief, damning fifteen seconds that changed everything. The sound is muted but unmistakable, the betrayal etched into every frame.

Paul's chair scrapes back violently, the crash as it hits the floor making me flinch. He is on his feet in an instant, lunging across the table to grab the laptop like a desperate man.

But Blondie is quicker. He sweeps the laptop out of reach and tucks it under his arm. "Now, now, no destroying Ministry property, Mr Emerson," he says with a toothy grin, his amusement barely concealed. "Did you have that temper with your wife?" He steps away as the other guards close in, their presence a silent warning.

Paul bristles, puffing out his chest like a cornered animal. "I would never lay a hand on her!" His voice cracks with indignation.

"No, you wouldn't," Merrick says smoothly, his tone razor-sharp. "But you would have awful sex with her sister."

"Awful?" Dove's face flushes red. "It wasn't awful!"

"It looked awful," Blondie mutters. "Like you were having some sort of episode."

A stunned silence hangs over the room. I clamp a hand over my mouth to stifle a laugh. I would have paid good money for him to say that. Is this really my life now?

Merrick does not miss a beat, his voice slicing through the quiet like a blade. "Let's try this again, shall we? With the truth this time. Your wife, Mrs Emerson, caught you in the act with her sister. She recorded it because she knew you would deny it—as you have done repeatedly."

Barry noisily jots something down in his file, shaking his head in disapproval.

Paul's face flushes an ugly shade of red, his fists clenched at his sides. Dove, ever the opportunist, jumps in. "We didn't think she'd be home!" she protests. "Paul said she'd be working late, that she had a big project. We didn't think it would hurt anyone."

"You didn't think it would hurt anyone?" Merrick's tone is incredulous. "Did it never occur to you, even for a second, how deeply it would shatter Lark to find out you were sneaking around with her husband? You didn't think she'd notice her sheets reeking of the two of you?"

Dove has the gall to look offended. "I'd have changed the sheets. Lark just needs to come home, and we can continue as we were. I mean, we need her salary to keep the house!"

Merrick blinks, his expression blank. "Charming."

Barry slides a document across the table to Paul's solicitor, who scans it before standing and gathering his things. "We're done here," he says briskly, avoiding Paul's attempts to grab his arm.

"Where the hell do you think you're going?" Paul snarls. "I paid you a fortune to be here!"

"There's not enough money in the world to fix this," the solicitor replies, straightening his tie. "Your wife is no longer your problem. The marriage has been annulled."

Paul's face twists with disbelief. "Annulled? That's bull-shit! You can't annul nearly thirty years of marriage!"

"The law says otherwise," Barry cuts in, pushing another set of documents towards Paul. "Here's your copy for reference."

Paul snatches the papers and reads them furiously. "It says here she was mauled by a shifter. What the hell does that mean? Is she dead?"

Dove lets out a theatrical gasp. "Lark's dead? Oh my God, my poor sister! A shifter killed her? Who's going to help me with—"

"WILL YOU SHUT UP!" Paul roars, silencing her. He turns back to Merrick, his face mottled with fury. "What does this mean?"

"It means your wife is no longer human," Merrick explains. "She is a ward of the Shifter Sector now. Her marriage to you is void, as she is legally considered deceased in the human world. All her property is being transferred to the Ministry."

"She's turned into a monster," Paul spits. "Did she agree to this? Was this part of her job?"

"No, it wasn't. Unfortunately, Lark was attacked while saving a colleague from being hurt. She is an incredibly brave woman." Merrick points to the document. "That's everything you will need for your records. If you can move out tonight, the Ministry will be selling the house and all joint assets. You will receive your share once the process is complete."

"They're selling the house?" Dove moans, clutching Paul's arm. He has gone a frightful shade of pale. "But how can you?"

"It's all legally binding," Barry says with a shrug, his voice almost cheerful.

Paul's hand shakes as he points at the document, his tone rising with confusion. "What's this name here?" He jabs a finger at the page. "This isn't her maiden name! Who is this Winters? Why has her surname changed?"

I blink, the words not making sense for a second. *Winters?* My surname has been changed? This is the first I've heard of it. I frown at Merrick, who meets my gaze with an exasperatingly calm expression.

"Lark, have you got anything else to add?" he asks, his voice like silk.

It takes me a moment to process his words. *Shit.* I manage a half-hearted wave, my throat suddenly tight. I want to puke. "Er... no, I'm fine. Thank you."

Paul's head snaps towards me at the sound of my voice. His eyes widen as he finally looks at me. *Really* looks. "Lark?" he croaks, disbelief in every syllable as his gaze drags over me, up and down. "Lark?"

Dove's squeal pierces the air like a boiling kettle. "But... you're *beautiful*! What on earth happened to you? You look like..." She narrows her eyes, studying me with a mix of jealousy and suspicion. "I thought you looked familiar. You look like our great-grandmother. Is that what happens when someone becomes a shifter?"

She is livid. *She's so, so livid,* she is seething with jealousy.

I fold my arms and lean back, biting my tongue to avoid saying something I might regret. If only she knew how little I care about her opinion now.

Merrick, utterly unbothered by the commotion, speaks

smoothly as if announcing the weather. "Well, your marriage is annulled, and this meeting is over. You can both leave now."

"Why Winters?" Paul snarls, glaring at me.

"Oh, isn't it obvious in the documents? Section four, paragraph seven. Lark Winters has taken her mate's name."

"Mate?' Paul and Dove say it in unison, the shock almost comical.

My own shock is no less severe. *Mate?* I mouth silently, my head spinning. I have a mate?

Merrick's grin turns predatory, his icy blue eyes locking onto mine before turning back to the unhappy couple. "Oh yes. Lark will soon be mated to the Alpha Prime."

"The Alpha Prime?" Dove wails, clutching Paul's arm tighter like he is her lifeline.

"Yes." Merrick's smile grows wider, more wolfish. "*Me.*"

Chapter Twenty

A KIND OF DARK, screaming panic wells up from behind my breastbone. My attention is fixed on Merrick—Merrick, the Alpha Prime. I'm still trying to process what just happened. He is the boss of all shifters, and yet he was the one who delivered my contract?

What the heck is going on?

"Lark, I forgive you for scaring me with the flowers! Lark! Tell them we can keep the house!" Dove's voice rises as Blondie physically removes her from the room. "I gave up my rental! I like your home, I like your street—tell them! Lark!" A satisfying 'oof' escapes her as Blondie deposits her outside.

Paul, meanwhile, stares at me as though I've sprouted a second head. "You left me for him? For *that guy*?" His tone drips with disbelief.

I sigh, pinching the bridge of my nose. *"You cheated on me,"* I want to shout, but what is the point? I'm numb. Too much has happened, one shock after another. I'm too emotionally drained to react to anything Paul says right now.

"He's practically a child!" Paul snaps.

Wrong again. He's Prime for a reason. Merrick's probably at least eighty, maybe older—shifters age differently. But explaining that to Paul would be like trying to teach calculus to a goldfish.

Another guard nudges him through the door, and it slams shut, thankfully cutting off his tirade.

Somewhere in the chaos, Barry must have slipped out— I didn't even notice him leave, and I never said thank you. My hands shake as I stare at them, willing them to stop. The room feels eerily quiet now.

The silence stretches. I should be angry—livid. Merrick has neglected to tell me far more than Paul ever did, yet all I feel is a weary sort of gratitude, a gratitude I don't want to examine too closely.

I sense Merrick's presence before I hear him.

"Are you all right?" His voice is softer than I expect.

I glance up. *No.* "Yeah, I'm just great. I'm legally dead, my name's been changed, and my ex-husband thinks I'm running off with a shifter." I wave my hands vaguely. "Alpha Prime? Seriously? You are the Alpha Prime. And you were the one dropping off my work contract? What was that about?"

Merrick settles on the edge of the table, looking far too calm for someone who just detonated my life. "I'm hands-on," he says with a shrug. "I get things done."

"Was this whole mate thing your way of 'getting things done'?"

"No."

"Did you make it up to speed along the paperwork?"

His lips twitch, amusement flickering in his eyes. "No."

"Then what, Merrick? How does any of this make sense?"

He leans forward, his voice steady and deliberate. "I knew the moment I saw you in the hotel lobby. You are my fated mate."

"Fated mate? I don't even know what that means."

"You will learn at the Facility," he says, daring to brush my forehead with a gentle kiss. "Don't worry about all this. Everything will be all right."

"All right?" My laugh comes out sharp. "I'm so confused."

"I know."

"I'm terrified."

"I'm sorry. I didn't mean to do this so publicly." His eyes lose their sharpness, regret shadowing his features. "But your ex pissed me off."

"Yeah, he has a knack for that."

"I should've talked to you first."

"Yeah, you should have. That was nuts, Merrick. This whole thing is nuts. Would you have told me about the mate thing if I hadn't been bitten?" I ask, my voice steady, although my heart pounds.

Merrick hesitates, the weight of the question settling over him. Finally, he sighs. "I don't know," he admits, his voice low, almost regretful. "I would have protected you, kept you safe from a distance. But... telling you? I don't know." He rubs the back of his neck, his gaze dropping to the floor. "It was hard enough to stay away as it was. I've had a security detail on you for months." His eyes lift to meet mine, and there's something raw in them. "My life is too dangerous for a human."

That's a no, then. A lump forms in my throat, sharp and painful. *Why does that hurt so much?* I knew we were different, that his world was nothing like mine. I knew he was out of my league. But hearing him say it—that he wouldn't have told me—hits me hard.

A small, insidious thought worms its way in, was the break-in really a terrorist attack?

Or was I set up? Could Merrick have decided it was better for me to be gone than to be his fated mate?

But no... He wouldn't have come for me if he'd wanted me dead. Right?

It's awfully convenient, though, isn't it? If I survive the change, I will go furry, and suddenly Merrick has a shifter partner who does not look like an old lady. My mind flickers back to Jo and Sandra—the way Sandra looked at Jo with such unshakable adoration. They make it work, but Sandra and Jo aren't us. Sandra isn't the Alpha Prime.

The bite, though... it does make things convenient for him.

I look twenty-five years younger now.

I rub my face, the motion doing little to ease the pressure building behind my eyes. This is all just too much. Everybody wants to be loved, to be adored for who they are —not for what some twist of fate decrees. Nobody wants to feel forced into a relationship because of some cosmic matchmaking.

First Paul. Now Merrick.

Neither of them really wants me.

Merrick catches a strand of my hair resting on my shoulder, twirling the end between his fingers. "Hannah did a good job," he says.

"She did," I admit.

Before the meeting, Hannah had evened out my hair, undoing the damage from my hasty, self-inflicted chop. It's not fancy, but at least I don't look like I lost a fight with a hedge trimmer.

"The things you will need have been packed and are in the car, ready to go. I know you don't want to leave, and you think you can handle this alone. But you can't. Trust me."

"Trust you?" I shoot back, my voice rising. "You set me up for your own amusement. Why should I trust you?"

"Because I'm your mate."

I throw my hands up. I'm his mate only when it suits him. "You didn't ask me. There's this crazy thing—it's called consent."

"I know." His voice is calm, unwavering. "But once you feel your animal, you will understand. You can't fight fate."

Oh, I can, and I will. I don't say it aloud, though. He is the Alpha Prime, after all.

Optimus Prime, I think, stifling a sigh under the weight of this ever-expanding disaster. I thought I'd skirt the Ministry and find help from an outsider. Instead, I walked straight into the jaws of the wolf himself.

"So, I'm leaving now?"

"Yes."

"To the Facility."

"Yes."

Okay, fine. I will go to the Facility. I will do the tests, endure the training, read the books—whatever they need me to do. I will prove myself, be the best bloody shifter they have ever seen. And then, hopefully, I can get back to work. I will keep my head down, focus on my job, and steer clear of Merrick.

I glare at him. "And what are you going to do? Go play Alpha Prime while I'm dealing with this mess?"

"You don't need me hovering. Riker will take you."

"Riker?"

"Your bodyguard."

"Blondie? The big blond guy?"

Merrick's laugh is warm and unexpected. "He will love that. Have you given me a nickname too?"

"Oh, yeah. You are Mr First Class."

"Mr First Class?" He smiles.

"Yeah. I thought you were a courier."

"Ah." His smile widens. "I will take it. I can be your Mr First Class anytime." He wiggles his eyebrows.

"No, you can't. I've got a new nickname for you."

"Oh? What is it?"

"Dickhead," I say, pushing myself up from the chair.

Merrick chuckles behind me. "Settle in, little mate. I will visit you soon. Be safe."

I wave over my shoulder without turning around. "Whatever, dickhead."

I yank open the door to find Blondie—Riker—leaning casually against the wall, his massive arms crossed.

"What's up, Alpha's mate?" His smirk is infuriating.

"Which way to the car?" I snap.

"This way, Alpha's mate."

"Stop calling me that."

"Why? Every time I say it, you look like you're gonna scream. It's hilarious. Mate, mate, mate, mate... Would you prefer Pup? Perhaps Blondie's ward might suit you better—"

I let out a frustrated scream, and he bursts into laughter, his deep chuckle echoing down the hall as he leads me to the car.

CHAPTER TWENTY-ONE

ZONE ONE IS ONLY forty minutes from Zone Two, but it feels like an entirely different world. While Zone Two is sleek and urbane, Zone One exudes military precision. It appears to be designed for training and discipline, a cross between a sprawling army camp and a reform school.

The Facility looms ahead, surrounded by a towering fence. I can only assume it's warded. The architecture is characteristic of shifters—equal parts imposing and practical. As we approach the gates, a guard waves us to a stop and checks our identification.

Riker hands over my new gold pass, replacing the blue one I'd barely grown accustomed to. The guard examines it then regards me with sharp, assessing eyes. After a moment, he offers me a shallow bow.

"It's a pleasure to meet you, Alpha's mate," he says.

I manage a tight smile. "Thank you." *Please don't let my eye twitch.*

Riker glances back at me, smirking. I dig my knee into the back of his seat and he laughs.

The guard hands the pass back, the gate opens, and we're waved through.

Although the familiar shifter greenery greets us as we drive in, the buildings here are starkly different. On the right is a squat structure that resembles an old gymnasium.

"That's the barracks," the driver announces in a tour guide tone. "That's where everyone stays. Each person has their own bedroom and bathroom, plus a communal area if you're feeling sociable."

We pass the barracks and pull up in front of a mansion-like building, which contrasts sharply with the utilitarian surroundings. It's the same building featured on the brochure—the one I've yet to open.

We step out of the car, and a man rushes down the steps to greet us. He beams as though I'm royalty.

"Miss Winters!" He clasps my hand in both of his, shaking it vigorously. "A pleasure to meet you! I'm Director Sullivan. I hope your stay with us will be both safe and pleasant. I heard about your attack—terribly unfortunate—and I want you to know we will take excellent care of you."

"Thank you," I say, resisting the urge to shake out my arm after his exuberant greeting. His enthusiasm is a little overwhelming, and his grip feels capable of detaching my arm altogether.

"We have scheduled some assessments for you later today," Mr Sullivan continues as we climb the steps. "Just a formality, of course, to ensure nothing will interfere with your progress. It's essential to be in the best possible frame of mind for this momentous occasion."

Momentous occasion. Right. Because being bitten and turned into a shifter is something to celebrate.

As he chatters on, I glance back at Riker. He coughs and mumbles something under his breath. Thanks to the sensory-dampening band, I can't catch it. I give him a questioning look and point at the band, but he only smirks again.

Mr Sullivan notices. "Ah, that band—an expensive model! Someone must care for you a great deal."

His smile makes me want to crawl out of my skin.

"You and your bodyguard will be staying in a suite in the main building. It's typically staff accommodation, but we—"

"Oh no, please don't do that," I interrupt, horrified. "I don't want any special privileges. I will stay in the barracks." I gesture back toward the squat building.

Mr Sullivan looks startled. "But you're the Alpha's—"

"It's fine," I say firmly. "I don't want to stand out."

The last thing I need is for everyone to assume I'm receiving preferential treatment. I've spent my whole life blending in, and I'm not about to start playing the privileged card now.

Mr Sullivan hesitates, clearly torn. "Well, if that's what you want, Miss Winters..."

I glance at Riker. "Is that all right with you?"

He shrugs. "Works for me."

"We have two available rooms," Mr Sullivan says, regaining his composure. "They are near each other, so your bodyguard will be close by."

I nod politely. "Thank you, Director. How long do you think I will need to stay here?" Please don't let it be months.

"Well," he says with a broad smile, "the full training course typically takes at least four months. Many of our trainees have been prepping for years. Most are born shifters going through their natural change, or turned candidates who've had extensive preparation. You, of course, are in a unique situation, so you will have additional classes to catch up."

My heart sinks. *Four months. Years of preparation.* And here I am, utterly clueless. It's as though I've been thrust into an advanced fighter jet programme with no idea how to fly a plane.

"A couple of weeks, perhaps. The Alpha Prime has requested that you remain here until you have learned to shift. After that, he will take you to the Capital for private tutoring."

The edge in his tone suggests he is less than thrilled about that arrangement. Evidently, my being whisked away by Merrick chafes his professional pride.

Fantastic. I'm already making friends.

CHAPTER TWENTY-TWO

I SIT through the psychologist's session, keeping my face blank and my mouth tightly reined. This isn't my chosen doctor. I didn't hire her. She is the Ministry's expert, and I'm fully aware her notes will end up in my file. So, I play along, answering her questions with upbeat, practised responses that sound perfectly adjusted and optimistic.

I lie through my teeth.

"Yes, large dogs make my heart race."

"Yes, I feel mildly anxious to be around shifters."

"Of course, I'm taking everything one day at a time."

She laps it up. By the end, I escape her office with a professional smile, a vague recommendation for 'a few more sessions,' and her assurance that I'm 'adjusting remarkably well.'"

Sure. Whatever gets me out of here.

On the way to my assigned room, pamphlets in hand, I spot a girl struggling with a large metal case. Sweat beads on her forehead, and her cheeks are flushed pink from the effort. She bites her lip, her palms bright red where they grip the handle.

"Hi," I say, stepping around her. "Need a hand?"

She blinks up at me with wide blue eyes, pale blonde curls framing her face. When our eyes meet, she dips her head, letting her hair fall like a protective curtain.

"Oh, I'm all right," she whispers.

"No, really, I can help. That looks heavy."

Her gaze flicks up again, uncertain. "Really?"

"Of course! Let me grab one side. Between the two of us, we can manage. Where are we headed to?"

"Just down the hall."

"No problem."

She moves to the front handle but hesitates before turning her back to me. "Thank you. It's a case from the shifter military—apparently, they used it for rockets, I think. But now..." She giggles nervously. "It's just packed with my stuff. Mostly books. I couldn't leave them behind. I'm a total bookaholic, and e-readers just don't smell the same, you know? I'm not bothered about clothes that much, so I stuffed the case full of—"

She keeps talking as we shuffle down the corridor, her end dipping precariously. I adjust to match her uneven grip, taking care not to lift too high as she struggles. *I'm much stronger than I should be.*

We finally reach her room, she opens the door, and I help manoeuvre the case inside. We set it down at the foot of her bed with a thud.

"Oh, look at my hands!" She rubs her red, sweaty palms on her jeans. "Thank you so much! That was so kind of you. I'm Alice."

"Lovely to meet you, Alice. I'm Lark."

"Lark," she says, smiling brightly. "That's such a pretty name. So, where are you from? I'm from a tiny coastal town. Our house is by the beach, and the view is so beautiful."

"Um, I'm from the Human Sector."

Alice doesn't skip a beat. Her smile widens. "Really? That's so interesting! I've never been, of course—protection and all that nonsense—but one day, when I'm older and fully shifted, I'd love to visit. Where would you recommend I go first?"

We chat about various places, and I mention sights I think she might enjoy. She even lights up at the idea of spying on vampires, though only from a safe distance.

"So, are you nervous about shifting?" she asks, bouncing on her toes. "I'm so excited! I've started meditating, but it's so difficult. How do people sit there and think about nothing? And the meditation instructor on the app keeps smacking his lips. It's so annoying!" She scrunches her nose in mock disgust, and I laugh.

"Yes, meditation isn't for everyone."

"What do you do for work?" she asks, tilting her head.

"I'm in IT."

"Oh, cool! So you, like, build computers?"

"Sort of. I do some building, but mostly programming."

"That's amazing. I run a cupcake business. I make weird and unusual cupcakes. If you want a Sunday dinner cupcake, I'm your girl. I can create the entire thing in fondant. Look." She takes out her phone and shows me pictures of intricately decorated cupcakes. They are amazing; some are shaped like flowers, others like miniature feasts, and more.

"Alice, these are incredible! You're really talented."

"Thanks!" She beams. "One thing shifters are great eaters, so it's a match made in heaven." She dashes to her metal case, flips it open, and pulls out a tin. Alice pops the lid to reveal a bouquet of cupcakes so lifelike they could be fresh flowers.

"Here, try one!" she offers.

"Thank you. I almost hate to ruin it—it's so pretty." Nonetheless, I take one and bite into it. The flavour is outstanding. "Alice, this is delicious."

Her face lights up. "I'm so glad you like it! Here, take another one for later." She presses a second cupcake into my hands, still smiling. "And thank you again for helping me."

"Well, I'd better get going."

"Oh, of course! I didn't mean to keep you. But... we'll chat later, right?"

"Yeah, definitely."

"Yay!" She claps her hands together, practically bouncing in place. "See you soon!"

Riker is waiting outside Alice's room, his expression turning melodramatic as I finish off the half-eaten cupcake.

"Seriously?" he says, feigning betrayal.

I grin, lick a stray crumb from my lip, and wave the second cupcake at him before stowing it in my room. "Not a chance."

His grumbling protest follows us all the way to my next

appointment, where an overly enthusiastic instructor hands me three massive tomes on shifter history and customs. Riker trails behind me as I trudge to the library.

The library is beautiful—towering shelves line the walls, and a fireplace is tucked into a cosy corner by the window. I settle into a chair and crack open the first book.

Fated mates. Fated mates... I dive into the index, flip to the page, and skim. According to shifter lore, fated mates are a rare gift from the gods, akin to human soulmates but with a deeper, primal bond. A fated mate can be anyone— human, shifter, vampire, or magic user. The connection is sacred, and shifters hold it in the highest esteem.

I pause at a section explaining that the animal within a shifter recognises its fated mate on sight, even if the mate does not have an animal. The text insists that with patience, work, and compassion, this bond can serve as the foundation for a loving, enduring partnership.

Sacred bonds, cosmic connections—sure. It all sounds like hokey pokey to me, but shifters swear by it. There's even a legal clause stating that discovering a fated mate can annul existing marriages.

Convenient. I suspect Merrick planned to invoke that rule if he'd pursued me when I was human. But I was bitten, and the rules—and my life—changed dramatically.

I flip through the other books. They echo the same sentiments. Fated mates are rare, sacred, powerful, and life-changing. Blah, blah, blah.

"Are you all right?" Riker asks, breaking my focus.

I glance up. He's bouncing on the balls of his feet, looking like he is itching to either run a marathon or punch someone.

"Do you need the toilet or something?" I ask with a cheeky grin.

He snorts. "No. I'm just bored. I was expecting more drama with your ex. It was... anticlimactic." He shifts his weight yet again, clearly yearning for action.

I shut the book with a thud. "Do you want to spar?"

His eyes sharpen as he arches a brow. "Spar? With you?"

"Yes, with me. I could use a proper fight."

He folds his arms, smirking. "Can you even fight?"

I gather the books, stack them neatly, and leave the library, heading for the barracks. "Thirty years of judo," I say lightly.

He stumbles mid-stride, then recovers. "You have done thirty years of judo? *You?*"

"I started in my teens," I explain, adjusting the books under my arm. "It's been the one constant in my life. I only stopped because... well, age. My joints didn't appreciate me throwing people around like I used to."

Riker gives me a long look, his expression turning into something close to admiration. "All right, Alpha's mate. Let's see what you've got."

I suppress a smile. "Careful what you wish for."

Chapter Twenty-Three

We get changed and head to the state-of-the-art training block. The place is impressive—there's an Olympic-sized pool, and I can hear the rhythmic slap of someone swimming laps. But it's the practice room that draws me in like a magnet.

It's built for combat. Thick blue mats cover every inch, providing a soft yet firm surface faintly textured for grip. The walls are lined with mirrors, giving the room a sense of space and allowing you to observe your every move. Along one side, storage racks hold training gear—pads, gloves, and a few practice weapons.

I warm up, stretching muscles that now feel almost new and strange with my enhanced body.

Riker mirrors me, talking about the thrilling subject of packs and shifter hierarchy while his sharp eyes track everything around us. He is constantly alert, watching the other trainees like a hawk searching for threats. It's obvious he's not just muscle—he is extremely good at his job.

The space is filled with activity. Some shifters fool around, while others spar with focus and precision. I ignore them. The looks and whispered comments have already started, mostly about who I am—the bitten human—rather than who I'm mated to.

I roll my eyes and tune them out. Let them talk.

"If someone's high-ranking in a pack," he continues his lesson, "they can't challenge someone lower than them. Challenges only go one way from lower to higher. Keeps it fair—stops higher ranks from picking off the weaker ones for sport." He shrugs, as though it's common sense. "Of course, it's different here. You're all considered unranked, so any trainee can be formally challenged."

I nod absently, more out of politeness than genuine interest. The concept of pack politics—challenges, ranks, hierarchies—feels like a distant world I've accidentally blundered into. I don't want any part of it. I have no burning desire to climb an imaginary ladder or prove my dominance. Being in charge of anyone, especially a group of shifters, sounds exhausting.

Poor Merrick.

Riker pauses, waiting for a question or comment, but when none comes, he grins. "Not a fan of the whole dominance thing, huh?"

"Nope," I say, shaking my head. "You can keep your ranks and challenges. All I want is peace—to be left alone and get through this absurd situation alive without more complications. I've had enough of people dictating my life, thank you very much."

Once we have finished warming up, we start with judo basics. Initially, Riker takes it easy, clearly testing the waters, but he soon realises I know what I'm doing. His grin widens as he switches gears, showing me shifter-specific moves—techniques meant for fighting in human form or half-shifted 'warrior form,' which sounds insane.

This is more like it. I'm enjoying myself for the first time in ages. Riker is skilled, and though he's careful, he does not hold back. That means I don't have to either. The sparring is invigorating—until it isn't.

A group of young men swagger into the space, their loud voices disrupting the room's focus. One of them, obnoxious and cocky, starts throwing out petty comments.

"Who let the girl in here? Isn't anywhere sacred from these bitches? Go make me a sandwich," he sneers, his tone dripping with disdain. His eyes flick to my arm. "Look at her—looks like she got chewed up and spat out."

His little pack of idiots laughs on cue.

This change in me isn't just affecting my movements and senses—it's making me more volatile. Where once I might have kept calm, now I've got a hair trigger. I need to watch myself.

I try to ignore them, I really do, but I see the muscle in Riker's jaw flexing as he grinds his teeth. He's annoyed, and I feel the tension shift. We keep working, trying to stay focused, but the guy won't shut up.

When we slow down to work on a more intricate move, it must look like I'm fumbling to the untrained eye. The loudmouth pounces on the opportunity to pipe up again.

"Who taught her to fight? Barbie's Ken?" he jeers. "Bet her arse is the only thing keeping her here."

I can tell instinctively he is an alpha—an overgrown, six-and-a-half-foot baby alpha, but still. The thing inside me is amused. I'm not. Alphas with unchecked egos don't last long, or so I've read. They are a liability in a society as aggressive as this.

He keeps up his commentary, getting cruder. I try to ignore him, but Riker's growing frustration distracts me, and eventually I snap.

"Oi, kid!" I snarl, turning to face him. "Shut the eff up. Nobody cares what you think."

He looks like he's never been challenged before. He freezes for a moment, hesitates, then his bravado kicks in.

"What's your problem, human?" he says, puffing his chest out and flexing his biceps. "You volunteering to teach me a lesson?"

I smile coldly, but I know better than to act without permission. "Can I take this one?" I ask Riker, keeping my voice casual. "Surely there are extra rules about beating up children."

Riker smirks. "You could, but you'd make him cry in front of his friends. Don't want to embarrass him, do you?"

The kid steps onto the mats, his face flushed with anger. "Come on, bitch," he spits.

The nauseating scent of an angry shifter ripples across the practice room.

"Is that a challenge, boy?" Riker asks evenly, his voice edged with warning.

"Yeah."

A challenge has been issued. I groan. My first shifter challenge, and it's with this idiot. Fantastic.

"Skin only, no permanent damage," Riker says, setting the terms.

Skin only. No fur. That means neither of us can shift. Great. It hadn't even occurred to me that he is a fully fledged shifter.

I'm about to fight a real shifter.

Shit.

Decades of sparring haven't truly prepared me for this. I've never fought for real—apart from choking out that guy at work—certainly not like this.

I step onto the mats, keeping my body loose, arms relaxed. Without warning, his massive fist slams into my face.

Hard.

Pain explodes behind my eyes like a firework, and my nose cracks. I hit the mats with a sickening *thud*, vision swimming as blood trickles down my face.

Sloppy, Lark. Real sloppy.

The room goes quiet.

I wipe my face, grimacing as I check my nose. It's broken. This new body might be incredible, but a broken nose is still a broken nose.

"Stay down!" the kid snarls.

Did that little shit just try to alpha-command me?

Something inside me coils, tight and furious. My body reacts instinctively, strength coursing through my veins. I kick up with both legs, my back arching as momentum jolts me upright onto my feet.

Pinching my nose between my fingers, I wrench it back

into place with a sickening crack, fresh blood gushes, streaming down my chin and soaking my shirt.

Around me, the trainees groan.

I glare at the kid through a haze of pain, tears, and rage. The thing inside me roars to life, furious and ready for vengeance. If I were still fully human, I'd be dead—and then he dared to order my animal side to stay down?

It's on.

Riker steps forward, looking ready to demolish the kid himself, but I hold up a bloodied hand. "I've got this, thanks." My voice is calm, underpinned with cold fury.

The kid freezes for a moment, then glances at his pack of idiots with a cocky grin. "Did you see how far she flew?"

Time to teach this toddler some manners, and I loosen the grip on my control.

I charge forward, a blur of motion. Before he can react, I pivot into him, driving my hip into his midsection. My hands grip his arm and collar, twisting sharply as I sweep his leg out from under him.

His massive frame flips over my hip, crashing to the mat with a satisfying *slap*.

I grin and mouth, "Who's the little bitch now?"

He is back on his feet in a heartbeat, growling as he throws a wild punch. I duck effortlessly, the rush of air brushing past my head. My old *sensei's* voice echoes in my mind. *Don't think. Move.*

Spinning on my heel, I drive my elbow into his jaw with bone-crushing force. The sharp crack reverberates up my arm, and blood sprays from his mouth as he stumbles.

"Wow, was that a tooth?"

He lunges, desperate and clumsy, trying to use his size

to overpower me. I feint backwards, baiting him. As he barrels forward, I plant my foot on his hip and pivot. My body arcs like a bow, using his momentum to flip him clean over. He lands hard, the impact driving the air from his lungs in a guttural gasp.

"Still think Ken trained me, Baby Alpha?"

He barely gets a chance to breathe before I'm on him again. Sliding one leg over his neck, I trap his arm with the other, locking him into a perfect reverse triangle choke. My legs squeeze like a steel vice, cutting off his airflow. He thrashes wildly, his face turning crimson as he claws at my thighs.

I release him just before he goes limp, shoving him off with a sneer of disgust. He collapses onto his hands and knees, coughing and gasping for air.

I don't let him recover.

Leaping forward, I bring my leg down in a precise axe kick. My heel connects with his shoulder, slamming him face-first into the mat with a roar of pain.

Chest heaving, I grab hold of his hair, tilt his head, and glare down at him, blood dripping from my nose. The thing inside me stirs, urging me to finish it, to rip his throat out with my teeth.

My hand curls into a fist as I fight the primal instinct clawing at my mind.

"We done?" I growl.

The kid nods, his face pale and sweaty.

I drop his head and walk away, leaving him crumpled and humiliated on the mat.

"That idiot asked her for a sandwich, and she turned him into a mop and cleaned the floor with his face!"

Riker steps forward, his voice a low, menacing snarl as he addresses the room. "Next time you so much as look at the Alpha Prime's mate, boy, I will kill you. That goes for the rest of you."

The room falls silent, tension crackling like static.

I don't look back as I walk out.

Let them whisper. Let them fear me.

Right now, I need a shower and a cup of coffee.

I don't belong here.

Chapter Twenty-Four

I shower and change, trying to shake off the lingering adrenaline. The rooms here are fine—basic, clean, and functional. They remind me of student accommodation. Not exactly cosy, but it will do. I hope Riker is comfortable in his space.

Anger churns inside me as I towel off my hair. How could I have let my guard down so easily? Never again. I need to remember that shifters don't abide by human rules.

In the mirror, I regard the alien face staring back at me. Even with a puffy nose, swelling, and bruises blossoming beneath her eyes, she still looks exquisite.

I hate her.

Lark, a mirror can't show your worth. It does not reflect your soul and the person you truly are inside.

She is still me. I am still me.

When I step out, Riker is leaning against the hallway wall, his damp hair curling slightly, his ever-watchful gaze sweeping the corridor.

"You all right, Rocky?" he teases.

"Yeah." I touch my nose gingerly, wincing at the tenderness. "At least a crooked nose will add character."

Riker's laugh echoes along the hallway, his good mood is annoyingly infectious.

"I'd stick to not getting punched in the face again. But don't be surprised if someone tries to rope you into another challenge. Some of these kids will be vying for dominance the moment they shift."

"Great," I mutter. "More idiots trying to prove themselves at my expense."

"I suspect they will be more worried about you after today. That throw was a thing of beauty."

I roll my eyes. "It was pure self-defence."

We head to the mess hall, the enticing aroma of food wafting down the corridor. I take a plate of spaghetti topped with cheese chunks and add some garlic bread, while Riker piles his tray high as though he has not eaten in weeks.

"You sure that's enough?" I tease.

"Barely," he replies with a grin, balancing a salad bowl precariously on the edge of his tray. "This is only round one."

We choose a table against the wall, instinctively securing a spot with a clear view of the mess. I take a tentative bite of garlic bread and glance around. Across the room, Alice's bright laughter catches my attention. She is seated at a nearby table, animatedly chatting with a small group of trainees.

I lift a hand to wave; she spots me immediately, her grin widening as she waves back enthusiastically, her curls bouncing with the motion.

"Making friends already," Riker says around a mouthful of food.

"She's nice," I reply, turning back to my plate.

"Sorry I outed you earlier."

I wave it off. "It does not matter. The whole Facility will know by morning anyway. Besides, the terrorists at the Ministry were after the Alpha Prime's mate—apparently me. It's no secret if the baddies already know."

His fork pauses mid-air. "You only just remembered this now?"

I nod. "I didn't piece it together until earlier. I suppose that punch to the face knocked something loose."

"You should've told us sooner."

His disapproving frown throws me off. "I know," I sigh. "It wasn't exactly at the top of my list of priorities. I only learned about my 'new status' this morning. I'm still trying to wrap my head around this 'fated mate' nonsense. Everything seems so up in the air I doubt I will ever catch up. Riker, why would they come after me?"

He leans back, the chair creaking under his weight. "Merrick has plenty of enemies," he begins, his tone calm but tinged with frustration. "The attack involved a motley crew—vampires, shifters, humans—a coalition of fools trying to make trouble. Don't worry; everyone involved has been dealt with."

I swallow, bracing myself. "The white wolf who bit me?"

"Dead," he replies bluntly. "You will never have to worry about that bastard again. Lark, Merrick should be telling you all this."

"I'm asking you."

Riker hesitates before nodding. "Some people dislike how Merrick rules. They resent the separation of sectors and want to blur the lines. They don't understand the necessity of our way of life. All they care about is power and profit. Money. They look at our land, our strength, the way Merrick runs things, and they want a piece of it. They want control." His gaze sharpens. "And they will destroy anyone who stands in their way—Merrick, you, anyone."

He pauses, his thoughts elsewhere. "What they don't realise is that, as shifters, we need structure. Without control, we become dangerous—not just to others but to ourselves. You know we're not cuddly animals. We're powerful. A shifter who can twist a steel bar with their bare hands needs boundaries; otherwise, it's chaos."

I nod slowly, nibbling my garlic bread.

"We have been on the brink of extinction before, and we learned the hard way. That's why everything is regulated now, to keep everyone—both strong and vulnerable—safe. Most of us appreciate that. We like the control, the sense of safety behind our walls. The security. But a small faction hates the restrictions. They hate needing visas to move in and out of the territory. They think Merrick's leadership is the problem, and if he were gone, the borders would open, and we'd live freely among humans and other sectors. What they don't get is that most of us want things to stay as they are."

His words weigh on me, and I pick at my food, my appetite fading.

"I don't belong," I murmur.

The tension in Riker's face softens. "That's where you're wrong. You have got more fight in you than most shifters I know. You belong here more than those clowns trying to tear it all down."

He offers a faint smile. "Besides, if anything happened to Merrick, nothing would really change. The system wouldn't implode. If someone dislikes it, they can leave. They can transfer out of the country. This is home, yes, but we're not trapped. Our sector works because it's been designed to."

I mull over his words for a moment, then ask, "So the people who attacked the Ministry... were they trying to abduct the Alpha Prime's mate to gain power?"

"Maybe," he concedes. "Or perhaps they just wanted to destabilise Merrick, to break him. He's never had a weakness before."

A weakness. He means *me*.

I wince. My poor nose aches, and I reach up to touch it gingerly.

Riker studies me. "We need to get you some ice for that nose. And no, you're not going to heal overnight. Shifters heal faster than humans, but it still takes time. Bruises might take a couple of days, a broken bone maybe a week. Shifting can speed things up, but there are risks. Sometimes bones heal improperly, and they have to be re-broken."

I grimace. "That sounds fun."

He shrugs, shovelling more spaghetti into his mouth. "It could be worse. Merrick's healing is so quick that if anything sets wrong, he endures twice the pain."

"Ouch. That must be horrible."

I think about the Alpha Prime, and since Riker is in a talking mood, I ask, "What about this mating thing? Everyone's acting like it's already decided."

Riker smirks. "You don't like him?"

I stab at my spaghetti. "I can't stand him. He is bossy and overbearing. He put me through hell this morning. But..." My inner voice finishes the thought. *He is also infuriatingly handsome, surprisingly kind, and makes my heart race. No one's ever fought for me like that before.*

"But?" Riker prompts. When I don't answer, he continues. "He's also the one who risked his life to save you. When he realised you were in danger the night you were bitten, he came for you without waiting for backup."

I sigh, dropping my fork. My fingers trace the scars twisting around my arm. "I didn't know that. He saved my life, and I'm grateful—so grateful—but it doesn't erase what happened. He lied to me."

He also shielded me from both Dove and Paul.

Riker leans back, a knowing smile playing on his lips. "So, what are you going to do about it?"

"I've no idea." The truth is heavier than any glib reply. "It's only been three months since my marriage fell apart." How can I trust anyone again—let alone a man like Merrick? It's madness. I wouldn't survive the fallout.

Riker says nothing, watching me wrestle with my thoughts.

I twist the spaghetti around my fork, my gaze drifting

across the mess hall at my fellow trainees—many look to be in their early twenties—young and brimming with potential yet dealing with the same life-altering event. Some were born shifters, predestined from their first breath—while others were chosen or volunteered to be turned.

I'd expect more nerves, more hesitation. Their faces betray no fear; there's no sign of the enormity of their situation—just grim determination and, for some, a competitive spark. Whether born or bitten, they all share the same resolve. The same confidence.

They come from different ethnic backgrounds, different upbringings, yet they are bound by that odd strand of junk DNA setting them apart from the rest of humanity. It's unsettling. Overwhelming. They have accepted their place here long before they arrived. I haven't. *Will I ever?*

I can't quiet the little voice in my head insisting I don't belong.

A loud crash yanks my attention to another table. Alice's tray hits the floor, food scattering everywhere. She stares blankly ahead, her big blue eyes wide with shock, her face pale. Then, without a sound, she crumples, collapsing off her chair and hitting the ground with a sickening *thud*.

Her body convulses violently.

Oh my God, no.

Riker gently grips my arm, holding me back as I instinctively move to help. Shouts ripple through the room as staff rush forward. Trainees scatter—some stepping back, others frozen. A staff member clears the food debris while another carefully lays Alice flat. Someone murmurs, "She is not breathing," and panic seizes the entire room.

"Medic!"

There is nothing I can do.

Within seconds, a medical team dashes in. One medic begins chest compressions while another readies a defibrillator. Alice's jumper is torn open, her pale chest exposed as they attach electrodes.

"Clear!" the medic shouts, and Alice's body jerks under the electric shock.

I clasp my hands, silently pleading for her to come back. "Don't they have a med mage?" I whisper, unable to tear my gaze away from the frantic scene. "Please, please, Alice, breathe."

The medics work tirelessly, shocking her repeatedly, but her small frame remains unresponsive. At last, the lead medic shakes his head and says quietly, "She is gone."

Alice's arm flops to the side, revealing a patch of fur on her wrist. Her hand is half-shifted, the beginnings of claws visible.

This is exactly what Merrick was afraid of. He worried this might happen.

CHAPTER TWENTY-FIVE

AFTER WATCHING Alice die in the mess hall, I abandoned my food. Hunger felt like a distant concept. Back in my room, I freak out and then spent hours poring over the books describing the changes ahead—but so much of it does not apply to me, because I'm different.

Alice's cupcake sits innocently on the side, mocking me.

Sad, edgy, and restless, I knock on Riker's door, but there's no answer. Guilt prickles at me. After what happened today, should I really be wandering about without my bodyguard? Still, this is a secure base, not some unpredictable city street.

Besides, the idea of running into that kid and his cronies does not bother me anymore. I'm too numb to care.

Knowing these trainees could die is entirely different from seeing it happen right in front of me.

Oh God, I'm so sorry, Alice.

In the small kitchen, I find an instant coffee stash. I make myself a cup and take it outside, the mug warm in my hands. Night has fallen.

It feels strange to be out here after dark when I've spent most of my life locking myself in at night. The base's high perimeter fence, floodlights, and vigilant guards give me a sense of security, but a hum of awareness thrums beneath my skin. I'm not human anymore, and the night does not feel the same.

It's sharper, more alive with sounds and scents I never noticed before, even with the band—leaves rustling, the faint tang of metal on the air, the whisper of distant footsteps.

I sip my coffee and set the mug on a post near the barracks, planning to grab it when I'm done. A nearby running track catches my eye, and the urge to move surges. This is exactly why I live in jogging bottoms—for spontaneous decisions like this.

I run.

The steady rhythm of my feet on the track and the cool night air calm the restlessness inside me. I hit a loping pace, fast but sustainable.

My thoughts wander, tracing everything that's happened over the past few days. It's almost incomprehensible. The psychologist was wrong. I haven't truly acclimatised—I've just buried my feelings beneath sheer willpower. If I stop, it might all collapse. So I keep running.

I run farther than I have in years—perhaps even farther

than I did in my twenties. Next time, I will bring a weighted backpack to challenge myself more.

The track loops near the fence, its imposing presence strangely comforting. Checking it satisfies an odd, itching need I didn't realise I had.

Maybe I'm part guard dog?

The books say shifters thrive in packs, stronger together than alone. But I've never been a team player. I step up when necessary, yet I've always been content working independently. That has not changed; if anything, I feel more withdrawn—more wary.

Out of the corner of my eye, I see movement. At first, I assume it's a guard. Then I hear my name, sung in a mocking tone.

"Laaaarrrrk."

I falter, slowing to a stop. The fence's floodlights wash everything in stark brightness, ruining my night vision. Stepping off the track, I scan the darkness, trainers crunching on the grass. My instincts scream caution.

"Hello, Lark," a voice purrs.

A figure materialises from the shadows.

The vampire. The one from the wizard's house.

How does he know my name?

His red eyes glow like embers, locked onto me. My breath catches, and I almost stumble, but my sharpened reflexes keep me steady. I avoid meeting his gaze, fearful he will try to trap me with it. My heart pounds, more from shock than fear.

How did he know I was here?

He inclines his head. "I would have loved to turn you, Lark. Shame the shifters got to you first. Once human, no longer human—look at you." His slow, glacial gaze sweeps over me, lingering with deranged intensity. "What a makeover, if we ignore the black eyes and puffy nose. Still making friends, I see."

Every hair on my body stands on end. The night is too quiet. It's just him, me, and a thin fence humming with magic between us.

"I've been looking for you," he continues, his grin stretching unnervingly wide, fangs catching the light. "Hunting you. Craving a proper taste."

I resist the urge to step back. "Sorry," I say, forcing my voice steady. "I'm off the menu."

He chuckles, a low, sinister sound that makes my skin crawl. "Ah, an exclusive delicacy, then." His tongue darts over his teeth as he steps closer to the fence.

Slowly, he raises one hand, black claws glinting in the harsh lights. As they scrape the metal, sparks erupt where the protective ward flares. Energy crackles over his pale skin, but he doesn't so much as flinch. "The shifters do love their little protective borders, don't they? Does it not feel like a cage, Lark? My pretty little birdie, trapped with nothing but mangy animals for company."

The grating sound of his claws against the ward sets my teeth on edge. A distant shout slices through the silence—a triggered alarm, no doubt.

He bares his fangs in a gleaming smile. "I will be seeing you soon, little birdie."

In an instant, he vanishes into the darkness, leaving me cold and shaken.

I barely have time to process what has happened before a pounding of feet announces the arrival of two guards and

Riker. He takes one look at me, frustration and concern in his eyes.

"What are you doing out here? Did you touch the fence?" he barks.

"No." I peer into the shadows, my heart still racing. "It was the vampire."

He growls low in his throat. "Vampire?"

"Yeah—the one that tracked me to the wizard's house."

"What was he doing here?"

"Hunting," I reply grimly. "Hunting me."

Riker issues a sharp command. "Turn off the fence!"

Without waiting, he yanks off his clothes, tossing them carelessly onto the ground. I blink in surprise, but then something even more startling happens—he starts to shift.

I'd imagined the transformation to be subtle or quick. It's neither. It's loud and visceral. Bones crack, reshaping with gut-wrenching precision. Riker groans as his body swells, white fur erupting across his skin.

I stagger back, my stomach lurching at the sight. When it finishes, he is no longer Riker but a colossal polar bear. Round ears twitch, black eyes glittering in the half-light, and thick white fur covers his hulking frame. He radiates raw, primal power.

One guard nods. "Fence is down!"

Riker does not hesitate. The ground trembles under his massive paws as they dig into the dirt, and with a mighty leap, he clears the ten-foot fence. Barbs snare wisps of his fur, but he keeps moving. Nose low to the ground, he sniffs once, twice, then bolts into the night—a white blur swallowed by darkness.

I stand there for a moment, clutching his discarded

clothes. "Is he going to be all right?" I whisper to the nearest guard.

The guard does not respond, his expression hard.

Another guard sneers. "Go back to your room, trainee. You will be called soon enough."

I square my shoulders, annoyance flaring at his tone. Who the heck does he think he is talking to? But I know better than to pick a fight right now. Instead, so Riker can find them when he returns, I fold his clothes neatly on top of his boots, turn on my heel, and jog back toward the barracks.

The steady thud of my feet soothes my jangled nerves somewhat, but my mind is still in turmoil. Can one shifter —even a massive polar bear—take on a vampire? I don't know.

Once inside, I retrieve my now-cold coffee from where I left it and rinse the cup in the kitchen sink. The mundane act grounds me, yet the worry gnaws at the edges of my thoughts.

I hope Riker will be all right.

I can't lose another friend today.

CHAPTER TWENTY-SIX

THE MESS HALL buzzes with morning chatter and the clatter of trays as I work through my breakfast sandwich with exaggerated gusto. Across from me, Riker scowls, displeasure radiating off him. He is clearly still annoyed about my late-night run.

I swallow and sigh. "Why are you still glowering at me? You do realise I'm an adult, right? The base—the one you have kept insisting is secure—seemed safe enough. I needed to move, Riker. You understand that, right? Alice's death was a shock."

"Oh, I understand," he growls, his tone heavy with disapproval. "Doesn't mean I agree with you. What the hell were you thinking, Lark?"

"I thought I was safe, and it wouldn't be a problem," I say with a shrug.

"It's not just about external threats. It's about these little shits inside too. Any one of them could have hurt you."

"I wasn't—" I start, but he cuts me off.

"No, you were not thinking, and that's the issue. Naturally, you then bump into a psychotic vampire who stopped by for a Lark snack." He throws up his hands, muttering something about suicidal women.

I shrug again and focus on my breakfast. I'm starving. After last night's events, I was too edgy to eat, and now my body feels jittery. As I chew, I run a hand over my hip bones, frowning. I've been losing weight too quickly, as though my body is burning through itself to deal with all these changes.

"How many calories do I need to eat a day, roughly?"

Riker doesn't miss a beat. "About six thousand, given your weight and height."

"Six thousand?" I stare. "That's three times my normal intake."

"Welcome to being a shifter. You can talk to the doctor later about blood tests and all that. They will explain."

"Ah, tests," I say, pushing the sandwich aside and reaching for my coffee. It's dark and bitter—not great, but better than last night's instant swill. At least it gives me the caffeine jolt I need.

A sudden hush falls over the hall like a wave receding, and the surrounding chatter dies. I glance up, puzzled. Riker snorts, stifling a laugh.

"What?" I whisper.

He doesn't reply; instead, his gaze shifts to something—or someone—behind me.

I turn and see Merrick.

The Alpha Prime prowls through the mess, his icy blue eyes fixed on me. Under his coat, he's wearing a dark blue T-shirt and designer jeans. The shirt clings to his defined muscles, rippling as he walks.

My heart hitches. Where's his suit? I glance at his feet—high-end trainers. Now I've seen it all.

The Prime looks *good*.

"Lark." Merrick leans against the table, his eyes roving over me like I'm the only person here.

I lift my coffee, meeting his intense gaze with forced calm. "Dickhead," I reply, deadpan.

Riker nearly topples from his chair, howling with laughter. Merrick's lips twitch, his icy façade cracking just enough to reveal a hint of warmth. The rest of the mess hall is deathly silent, disbelief hanging in the air.

A chair scrapes, followed by a muffled whisper, "Did the human just call the Alpha Prime a dickhead?"

"Shush, she's his fated mate."

Merrick shakes his head and leans in, pressing a gentle kiss to my forehead. Ever since announcing his intentions, the man has become insufferably touchy-feely.

"Hello, little mate," he says, his tone laced with affection. "I've missed you."

"It's only been a day," I point out.

"A day is plenty of time to see you are not safe here. After your medical exam today, we're leaving."

"Leaving?" I echo, thrown off-guard. A vampire on the prowl has not exactly helped my nerves—or Riker's—but a surge of relief washes over me. I've never felt comfortable here.

He nods, his expression gentle. "You will be safer with me."

Safer with him. I sip my coffee, rolling the idea around in my head. At least it won't be dull.

"He's been here all night, ever since you ran into that vampire," Riker says, sounding smug.

My chest tightens at the thought. "That's... nice. Sorry if I caused you any trouble. I didn't mean for anyone to be dragged out in the middle of the night."

"You will never be a problem, Lark," Merrick says, his voice unwavering. "Now, come on—you have got a medical appointment. I will walk you."

I down the last sip of coffee, grab what is left of my sandwich, wave goodbye to Riker and follow him.

He slows his pace, closing the distance between us as if he can't resist being near me, nudging my shoulder lightly with his. I huff and sidestep; he smiles that infuriatingly soft smile.

Outside, the morning air is crisp. Merrick gestures towards the main building. "The clinic's around the back."

"Thank you."

I finish the sandwich just as he opens the door. We enter, met by a receptionist whose fluttering lashes and saccharine smile are aimed right at Merrick.

"Alpha Prime," she coos. "We have been expecting you."

Merrick's voice hardens. "You are expecting Lark Winters, not me." He does not acknowledge her attempts at charm, nor does he even look at her.

I grin childishly.

She blinks, nodding. "Of course. Lark Winters. Right

this way." She barely glances at me. I might as well be invisible so much for equal footing.

She leads us to an examination room, where a doctor waits behind a desk, a bright, eager smile plastered on her face. She nods politely at Merrick but focuses on me with a vaguely predatory gleam in her eyes—the same one the receptionist gave Merrick. It's like the look you would give a decadent dessert.

"Hello, I'm Doctor Sheridan. Please, Miss Winters, take a seat."

"Thank you," I say, sitting down where she indicates.

"We have several tests planned," she says, scrolling through data on her tablet. "I'm particularly interested in your case. We'd like cerebrospinal fluid, bone marrow—"

Merrick's low growl silences her. "That's not why Miss Winters is here. She is here for basic tests to confirm she is fit to leave—nothing else. She is not your lab rat."

Doctor Sheridan's expression falls. "Of course not, Alpha Prime. I would never—"

His eyes narrow. "We discussed this. Just the basics, Doctor."

She lowers her gaze. "Yes, Alpha."

I exhale, relieved she won't be poking and prodding beyond reason. Once Merrick leaves, she continues with the standard tests, clearly disappointed.

Twenty minutes later, I'm finished. Everything looks normal. I'm unlikely to shift for a few more days, and I'm otherwise healthy.

Doctor Sheridan can't resist telling me I'm developing faster than expected, implying more tests would be ideal. I ignore her.

When I step outside, Merrick is waiting—silent, seething with anger that radiates off him.

"Are you all right?" I ask quietly.

"I'm fine," he says, though he does not look fine at all. "That was absurd. I'm sorry. No one should subject you to extra procedures without explanation. I'm glad I was there." He pauses, gaze distant. "Doctor Sheridan is good at her job, which is the only reason she is here. She got... carried away. I will have someone keep an eye on her."

He types furiously on his phone. I begin heading for the barracks, but without looking up, Merrick gently takes my elbow and steers me towards the car park instead. A sleek black car waits.

"Fancy. The Alpha Prime must come with some great perks."

"It was a gift from the Vampire Court."

"Oh?" I raise an eyebrow. "Do they often give you presents, or is this a special gift?" My inner voice adds sarcastically, *Like, for when one of theirs is stalking your mate?*

"They send things occasionally, but I don't always accept them."

"And this one?" I ask, gesturing at the gleaming bonnet.

He shrugs. "I needed a new car. So this one's mine."

Of course it is.

"Riker will bring your belongings."

I'm grateful I left my room tidy.

Merrick turns to me. "Before we go, I have something for you."

He produces a delicate necklace, the chain gleaming—

white gold or platinum—with a tiny vial of swirling blue liquid suspended at its centre.

"It's a spell," he explains. "Protection. If you are in danger, crack the vial and let the liquid absorb into your skin—or fur. It creates a powerful ward around you, shielding one person only. Two, and it fails. Once activated, no one—shifter, vampire, whatever—can detect you, not even if you are injured. It will keep you safe until I find you."

The vial looks priceless. Accepting something so valuable feels strange, but with a vampire sniffing around, I'd be foolish to refuse.

"Thank you," I say, taking it.

Merrick steps closer, lifting my hair as he helps slip the chain over my head. His fingers brush my neck, and I shiver.

"Always," he murmurs, voice warm.

Awkwardly, I slide into the car. "So, um," I say, desperate to fill the silence, "what is your favourite colour?"

He chuckles—a sound that sends a tiny thrill through me. "Silver. Though it used to be warm brown."

I tilt my head. "Oh, that's interesting." Then, feigning a huff, I add, "Silver like my eyes, eh? You old flirt."

His mouth curves. "You caught me."

I roll my eyes, my cheeks warming. "My favourite colour is pink."

"Pink? But you don't wear anything pink."

"I know, but it's still my favourite. It's so bright and cheerful."

Merrick hums under his breath.

I smirk. "What do you do for fun, Alpha Prime? Besides bossing people about?"

"Martial arts and fitness training," he replies with a lazy grin. Then his gaze hardens. "Speaking of martial arts, I heard about your fight—and your broken nose." He glances at me briefly before returning his focus to the road. "You have healed impressively fast."

"I have, haven't I?" I play it off, though I'm as surprised as he is. Overnight, the swelling vanished, the bruises faded. "I'm officially done looking like a panda. But whatever you do, don't tell Doctor Sheridan."

He growls softly. "Your secret's safe with me."

We drive out through the gates, the guards dipping their heads in respectful bows. I glance at Merrick. "Doesn't that get old? Everyone kissing your arse?"

"All the time," he admits, amused. "But not everyone does. You and Riker are especially bad at it. Perhaps I should give you lessons."

I snort. "No thanks. You're not my alpha."

"No, I'm your mate. And I'm glad no one else will ever be your alpha."

We lapse into a companionable silence, the road winding through dense woodland as the militarised land-scape of Zone One falls behind. That's when it happens.

A lorry comes out of nowhere.

It smashes into the driver's side with a thunderous crash, and the car flips, spinning like a leaf in a storm. The world is a blur—up, down, sideways—until it finally slams to a stop, upside down.

Hair falls over my face, and my seat belt digs painfully into my neck and chest. Blood trickles from a cut on my forehead, and my ankle aches, but I'm alive.

"Merrick?" My voice trembles. "Merrick, are you okay?"

His side of the car is crushed, blood smearing his face. He's unconscious, but his chest still rises and falls. Relief floods me—he is alive.

I fumble with my seat belt, stopping myself before I land headfirst on the roof. Through the shattered windscreen, I see movement. The lorry must have hit us full pelt —it's halfway down the road—and two... no, four men leap out with alarming purpose.

Shit. They are not lorry drivers. This is an ambush.

The door groans and pops as I force it open, kicking it wide. At least we have an exit.

"Merrick, wake up!" I shake him. "There are guys with guns. Merrick!"

His belt is jammed. I pull and twist until it finally gives. He falls, and I lower his head gently, easing him from the wreck. My new shifter strength helps me drag him—just about. Shifters weigh a tonne, all dense bone and muscle.

We roll down a shallow, dry ditch at the roadside. I lay him on his side, slip off my hoodie, and cushion his head. *Clear his airway, Lark.* My hands shake as I wipe blood from his nose and mouth.

I've never felt so helpless—or so terrified.

I pat his pockets and find his phone, unlocking it with his thumb. My fingers quiver as I dial Riker.

"Ello—"

"Riker, we have been run off the road—a lorry—" I blurt the plate number. "Four men. Merrick's unconscious."

"Run," Riker demands. "Leave him and run."

"No, I'm not leaving him." I position Merrick carefully, heart hammering. "Can you track his phone?"

"Lark, he'd want you to be safe."

"Well, I'm not doing it. Can you track his phone?"

"Yes. Now get out of there!"

I have no time to argue. Another car and a van screech to a halt, disgorging more men who fan out, advancing on us.

I place the phone by Merrick's head, tug the necklace from my throat, and crack the vial. As the magic liquid seeps into his limp hand, I step back, and the ward springs to life, shimmering faintly before becoming invisible.

He should be hidden now, safe from detection.

Shit. They are closing in, their figures silhouetted against the wreckage. I inch toward the trees, but one of them spots me.

I expected that.

"Mrs Emerson," he calls, mocking. "Where's your guard dog?"

"He ran," I lie, willing my voice to stay calm.

He laughs, motioning for the others. They are human —and armed. "Let's not make this harder than it needs to be."

He points his gun at me, and I hold my trembling hands up.

He seizes my wrists and yanks them behind my back, cinching them with a zip tie. His fingers brush my scars, and his face tightens.

"Damn. That's ugly. Can't believe you survived."

"I can't believe you are kidnapping me," I shoot back.

He tuts. "Ah, that's Human First for you. You call it

kidnapping; we call it justice. Your husband put out the word. The shifters had no right to turn you. By our laws, you're still human—and breaking them. So we're taking you in."

"You are taking me back to the Human Sector for a trial?"

"Humans who break our laws," he says, smiling coldly, "don't get trials."

I glare, refusing to show fear. "So what are you going to do, kill me?"

"Oh, we will make it quick," he answers, voice dripping with mock sympathy.

"Dignified, even. Think of it as a service—we're happy to put you out of your misery."

CHAPTER TWENTY-SEVEN

MY HEART POUNDS and adrenaline surges as they shove me into the back of the van. The interior is caged like a police transport, its metal bench cold and unyielding beneath me. Two armed men climb in, one on each side. The chatty one sits opposite me, grinning like a loon as though this is some grand victory.

Paul. Bloody Paul. It all comes back to him. He couldn't just let me go—couldn't accept that our marriage was finished. How do you promise to love someone forever, then hand them over to Human First like a sacrificial lamb?

Twenty-eight years. *Twenty-eight years!* And I meant nothing to him. The instant I stopped being human, he decided he'd rather see me dead.

My heart aches, raw and jagged. The pain slices so deep it feels like it might tear me apart. Was I so blind? Was he always this selfish, or was I simply that... amenable—easy to overlook, easy to take for granted, easy to bend?

What a mug I am.

And now here I am, trapped in this strange, fated bond with Merrick—destiny, not choice. Yet like a fool, I sacrificed myself for him.

The worst part is I'd do it again, because it felt right. The world needs more men like him. I'm not the kind of person who can stand by and watch someone die in my place. It's not in me to look the other way, to pretend it's not my problem.

Maybe that makes me foolish. Maybe I have some hero complex, or I'm just missing the critical component that screams naïve or lacking self-preservation. It does not matter.

The van lurches, and my body sways with the movement. My stiff arms, bound behind my back, protest with every jolt. Pain radiates through my chest and shoulders, a cruel reminder of the crash.

Please, Merrick, be okay.

Each bump ignites a new wave of agony. I can already feel the bloom of seat belt bruises forming along my torso, dark marks to match the turmoil within.

I can't decide if I'm frightened or furious. My emotions collide, fragmenting in every direction. Fear threatens to take hold, dragging me into helplessness, into being a victim. But anger—anger is something I understand. It hones my thoughts and sharpens my focus. I inhale deeply, fuelling that fury and clinging to it like a lifeline. Fear clouds the mind, but anger? Anger keeps me alive.

Part of me wonders why they haven't killed me yet. They could have done it on the roadside without any fuss.

"What are you waiting for?" I blurt out, my voice steady despite the roiling emotions underneath. "You want to kill me—why not do it now?"

Chatty smirks, evidently pleased with himself. "Oh, we will get there. But a dignified ending requires planning. You know how it goes—sometimes, you have to make a spectacle for the message to really sink in. Killing you isn't only about you—it's about sending a message. Human First needs the world to see what happens when humans betray their own. It will put us on the map."

"I haven't betrayed anyone."

"You turned," he spits, his grin slipping briefly. "That's enough."

He pulls out a roll of duct tape, rips off a strip with his teeth, and slaps it across my mouth. The adhesive stings. "I'm sick of your talking," he mutters.

One of his companions laughs. "What is it with you people? Always wanting to defend yourselves. Always with the 'why me?' questions."

They share a hearty laugh like it's the best joke they have ever heard.

Inside, I'm coiled tight, but I keep my expression calm and cast my gaze to the floor. There's no point in arguing. Arguing with zealots is pointless. Let them think they have won for now. I will wait for the right moment to save myself. There will be a moment, and they won't see it coming.

Human First. I mentally snarl. I always knew they were dangerous, but I never thought they would stoop to outright murder. Then again, why wouldn't they? Organisations fuelled by hate. Hate groups are tinderboxes—just a single spark away from an inferno. Hatred breeds violence. It's only a matter of time before rhetoric becomes weaponry and protest becomes bloodshed.

Chatty lounges back, arms crossed. "You should've died with dignity when they mauled you. Now look at you —all mangled up and... one of them." Disgust twists his features, though his gaze flicks towards my chest, lingering.

Disgust and fury churn within me, but I focus on my breathing.

The thing inside me stirs. She hates this. Her anger is raw and feral, and even with the band, I sense her scratching to get out. My mind flicks to Alice. *Not yet. Please, not now.*

I bow my head, pain flaring in my lower back as the van rattles on.

I might actually die here.

My thoughts flit to Paul. Was there ever a scenario where this didn't end like this? Then Merrick crosses my mind—his fierce protection, his unwavering strength. It's not only his impossible beauty; it's his presence, his certainty. I should be furious with him for barging into my life, yet I'm so grateful he did.

I recall Paul's shocked face when Merrick claimed me, Dove's jealousy souring the air. It wasn't the closure I'd imagined, but it was a measure of justice—a hilariously perfect mic-drop moment. And Merrick, Riker—they have both stood by me. In mere days, I've found more loyalty than I ever had in nearly three decades of marriage.

Life is short—too short to stay loyal to the wrong

people, too short to stay silent or let fear rule. More than anything, I don't want to die here. Not like this.

They have underestimated me.

I inhale and sink into the spiky warmth of my magic, feeling out the tech around me. One of the men has a phone in his pocket. I tug at its software, sending a quick message to Riker with the van's number plate and granting him access to the phone's GPS.

There will be repercussions if I survive, questions I can't answer without revealing my technomancy, but secrecy doesn't matter much if I'm dead.

An hour passes. We have crossed two zones, and from their conversation, it's clear we're heading for Zone Four—the coast. They discuss bribed patrols, smugglers, and ways to slip past Shifter Ministry sea defences.

When we arrive, they haul me from the van into a cavernous warehouse that reeks of damp, rust, and abandonment. Water puddles across the uneven floor, reflecting stray beams of light. A pigeon flutters through a hole in the roof, its wings a frantic blur in the dingy space.

"This is redevelopment territory," Chatty says. "Shifters have been knocking these old buildings down to build new ones. But this relic is still here—pre-sector." He sighs, almost wistful. "The good old days, before everything went to pot."

The good old days. He can't be more than thirty, so what does he know? Nostalgia is a funny thing—selective and warped; people remember what they choose.

I focus on the men, the shadows, and possible exits. They swap the zip ties for metal cuffs that bite into my wrists. This time my hands are secured in front. They drag me to the centre of the warehouse, where a wobbly chair is being hastily set up. Forced onto it, I feel the floor's uneven ground beneath me as they chain me in place.

In front of me stands a complete camera rig, its lights glaring and hot.

"This has to be perfect," barks one of the men, sounding like a second-rate, overzealous film director. Nearby, another man in a balaclava sharpens a long, gleaming knife.

Great. Just great.

'Camera Guy' crouches to adjust the lens. "Quiet, everyone!" he orders, then begins recording.

Using a voice distorter, Chatty steps forward and delivers a pompous spiel. They are not editing; it's being broadcast live. I stare into the camera, my breath rasping against the duct tape. I don't need to fake the tears. I sniff. If my nose clogs completely with snot, I will suffocate.

"We're here today..." Chatty decrees an absurd list of fabricated charges against me. Apparently, I'm guilty of betraying humanity by using 'magical means' to survive the bite and turn shifter. He rails about quotas and how Human First is here to 'correct the injustice' and destroy the 'traitor.'

As his tirade drags on, the man in the balaclava creeps forward, knife glinting. I reach for my magic, sinking into the circuits of their equipment. Smoke curls from the camera, and the feed dies with a sizzle.

"What the hell?" Camera Guy exclaims, smacking the device. "Damn thing just died, and it's only six months old!"

"At least it's under warranty," someone mutters.

Camera Guy scowls and stomps off. Balaclava gives me a meaningful look before backing away. A technical glitch has spared me—temporarily.

The delay gives me time to trace and dismantle the live feed, tearing it apart. By the time I'm done, there's no trace left.

Fifteen tense minutes later, Camera Guy returns with an older backup camera. He meticulously sets up the replacement, adjusting the angle and muttering under his breath.

"It's not going to be as high quality," he complains.

"Just get on with it!" Chatty snaps, pacing.

"Fine, fine. Silence, please," Camera Guy says, fiddling with the backup camera before finally hitting record.

I bide my time, and as soon as Balaclava steps forward again, I trace its signals, destroy the feed, and fry the circuits in the backup camera.

Another puff of smoke. Another severed connection. Another round of curses.

"Why does this keep happening?" Chatty fumes, spinning towards me.

"Maybe there's anti-tech interference?" Camera Guy suggests lamely.

They all turn to me.

"You're something else, aren't you?" Chatty growls, moving closer. "What are you doing?"

Behind the duct tape, I smile.

"Someone find the Magic Hunter!" Chatty yells.

Magic Hunter? My heart falters. That can't be good.

"Isn't he on watch duty?" one man mumbles.

"Get him! We just need five minutes before this place is

swarming with shifters—long enough to slit this bitch's throat."

The Magic Hunter strides in, kitted out in combat gear. White-blond hair stark against his sharp features. Pale eyes sweep the room, landing on me. "What now? You're paying me to watch for shifters, not play babysitter," he snaps.

"She's messing with the camera equipment. Do something, Hunter!" Chatty retorts, nearly shoving him but stopping short at the last second.

The Hunter's lips twist into a mocking smirk. "You're filming this? Amateurs." He snorts, then narrows his gaze at me.

"You're being paid, so earn your keep and fix it," Chatty snaps, waving a hand at the smoking camera. "Fix it. We need to execute her and send a message."

The Hunter's eyes narrow. "You think she's a magic user?" He steps closer, his thigh brushing the chair.

I tense as he leans in, surveying me with cool interest. "A half-changed shifter and an untrained, baby techno-mancer, eh? I can taste the magic. Nicely done, love." His fingers clamp my chin, tilting my face into the light. Then he raises his voice for the others, "I've seen the file. She's far too young to be forty-seven. Turning shifter doesn't change your face, so are you sure you have got the right woman?"

Chatty shrugs and hands over his phone. "Paul Emerson swore this was her."

The Hunter holds the screen next to my face as though comparing antiques. "She looks nothing like that photo. I'm no expert on shifters, but they don't alter eye colour, hair—none of that changes." His voice sharpens. "So I will ask again, are you certain this is Mrs Emerson?"

Chatty squirms. "Paul said her appearance changed."

"Sure he did," the Hunter scoffs. "You're taking a part-time nobody's word for it?"

"She said her bodyguard ran off," Chatty mutters.

"Did you see him run?" The Hunter folds his arms. "No? Then how do you know the guard didn't stay behind?"

"She told us," Chatty says weakly.

The Hunter's expression hardens. "For all you know, this is some random shifter covering for Mrs Emerson. You kill her, film it, and she's done nothing wrong..." His voice drops into a venomous hiss. "That's murder. And guess what happens next? Every faction in the land will want our heads. Is that your goal?"

Nervous silence settles over the men.

The Hunter rips the tape from my mouth, making me wince. I flinch as it tears at my skin. "What's your name, love?"

My heart hammers. To hell with it. "Lark Winters."

"She's lying," Chatty snaps.

"Emerson or Winters?" The Hunter studies me with a mix of curiosity and mild irritation. "Who's your mate?"

I hesitate, then say quietly, "The Alpha Prime."

The Hunter groans and drags a hand down his face. "You idiots kidnapped the Alpha Prime's mate and tried to broadcast her murder? Are you insane?"

"Well, technically—" one of them starts.

"Shut it!" The Hunter swings around to glare at Chatty. "Do you have any clue what you have done? You fuckwits have signed our death warrants. Harm her, and the Prime won't just kill you—he will wipe out your entire bloodline. Granny, aunties, cousins—anyone with your DNA is toast, every last one. And guess what? He will be justified."

Chatty bristles, his hands twitching near his weapon. "Paul Emerson said she—"

"I don't care what Paul Emerson said!" The Hunter snaps. He faces me, bowing his head. "Mrs Winters, accept my apologies for this... misunderstanding. Let her go."

My pulse pounds as I look between them, every nerve screaming.

"We don't need your help," Chatty snarls.

The Hunter stands between me and Chatty, menace radiating from his stance. "You will release her now."

There's a click as Chatty raises his rifle. "No one tells me what to do. I can kill you more easily than I can kill her."

The Hunter does not flinch. His tone drips with dark amusement. "Try me. Go on. But I promise you will regret it."

Chapter Twenty-Eight

Chatty's grip on the rifle shifts. He twists it as if wielding a club, and the stock slams into the Magic Hunter's face with brutal efficiency—once, then twice. Horrified, I watch as blood sprays, and the Hunter crumples to the ground, unconscious, crimson streaming from his nose.

He didn't see that coming. I hope he will be all right.

Chatty barks a harsh laugh. "What a fool. Finish the girl, and let's get out of here."

Silence. No one moves.

His confidence falters as Balaclava shifts uneasily, his knife hanging slack at his side. Shaking his head, he steps back. "No way, buddy. I'm out. I love my mum."

"You can't be out!" Chatty snaps, frustration spilling over. "Get back here and do your damn job!"

But Balaclava does not look back. He keeps walking, footsteps echoing in the cavernous warehouse. One by one, the others exchange uneasy glances and follow. Their loyalty —or perhaps their courage—vanishes as quickly as the Hunter hit the floor.

Two of them pause long enough to drag the groaning, bleeding man away.

Left alone, Chatty groans, exasperated. "If you want something done right..." He pulls a red Swiss Army Knife from his pocket, a small, almost harmless-looking tool that suddenly appears menacing in his hands.

He flicks open the blade, the sharp sound loud in the oppressive stillness, and strides towards me.

Before I can react, his boot connects with the chair, sending it skidding. The chains strain, and it topples over.

I fall backwards, slamming onto the cold, unforgiving concrete. Pain explodes across my spine and the back of my head. My vision blurs with starbursts, and part of me almost wishes I could lose consciousness.

But I can't.

Chatty leans in, his breath hot and foul against my cheek as the knife's cold edge presses to my throat. "I'm not going to kill you," he whispers, voice low and venomous.

The blade skims along my skin, scraping the delicate flesh of my cheek. "If I had a few more minutes, I'd peel the nose right off your face. You wouldn't be so pretty then."

The knife lingers, threatening, before sliding lower.

"But I'll do the next best thing." The blade snags my clothes, plucking at the fabric as it traces a deliberate line down my chest, between my breasts, and halts at my stomach.

His eyes gleam with cruel anticipation.

If he had the time, I'm certain he'd do worse.

The blade pivots and he shifts his focus to my forearm, the tip of the blade gliding over soft skin. For a second, I brace for him to slash my wrist. Instead, with a swift, practised flick, he severs something far worse—the black sensory band circling my arm.

The moment it drops, the floodgates burst open. A groan escapes before I can stop it as every suppressed shifter sense crashes into me like a tidal wave. The world rushes in —overwhelming, unrelenting and deafening. Scents, sounds and vision, all sharpen and stab. My skull feels ready to split in two.

Instinctively, I try to lift my cuffed hands to shield my ears, desperate for relief.

His hand slams them back down onto the concrete with brutal force. "No," he snarls, his voice booming in my shattered world, the single word reverberating like a megaphone in my ears.

From his pocket, he takes out a small, innocuous-looking pouch. He rustles it, the faint crackle of dried leaves setting my teeth on edge. "Wolfsbane," he says with a cruel smile. "Poison to shifters."

He grips my face, his fingers crushing my jaw, and slips the blade between my lips, cold steel clinking against my teeth, prying them apart. Pain blooms as it nicks my tongue and cheek, flooding my mouth with the metallic tang of blood.

I groan, defying him, as he pours the gritty, pungent contents into my mouth.

The blade is gone, but before I can spit the wolfsbane

out, he clamps his hand over my mouth and I can't breathe as he pinches my nose shut. "Swallow, bitch," he hisses.

I jerk my head violently, refusing to give in, but my lungs scream for air. The world tilts, darkness creeping in at the edges. Panic bubbles up as my body's need for oxygen takes over. I gasp, desperate for relief, and wolfsbane scorches its way down my throat.

Its toxic burn seeps through me, setting my insides ablaze.

I choke and splutter, agony gripping my throat.

Chatty steps back with a triumphant sneer. "Yeah, that's it. You're done for. Nature's fixing the mistake." His laughter echoes in the warehouse as he turns to leave, footsteps fading.

Pain rips through me in waves.

The thing inside me is no longer quiet.

She is awake—angry, raw, fighting back. I feel her clawing, tearing at my insides, determined to protect us both.

My ribs crack. The sharp snap of bone is drowned by my ragged breathing. A broken whine rises from my throat, raw and agonised. Control slips through my fingers. My senses overflow, my body convulsing in a brutal, unstoppable rhythm.

Whenever I imagined my first shift, I assumed Merrick or Riker would guide me. I thought I'd be safe. Instead, I'm chained, alone, in agony.

My body spasms. Each snapped bone reforms, reshaping beneath my skin. It's excruciating, torture, but the thing's voice murmurs in my mind. *We've got this. I've got you. Let go.* She is calm, reassuring, and I trust her.

So I surrender, letting her—another side of me, not some murderous alien thing—take over. She is me.

Fur erupts along my skin, twisting and stretching me into something new. Something wild.

The cuffs strain and groan. Broken bones in my wrists narrow just enough for my paw to slip through. The other follows, the handcuffs and chains clattering to the floor.

I slump forward, trembling. My breath is ragged, and my chest heaves. This new form feels alien yet familiar, powerful yet fragile. My paws—brown fur streaked with white—quiver as I try, and fail, to stand.

A deep, feral roar cuts through the pounding of my heart.

My ears swivel toward the sound, and I lift my head weakly.

The warehouse door is torn from its hinges, crashing to the floor. A towering figure in half-shifted warrior form charges in, snarling, his glowing eyes focusing on me.

Merrick.

He came for me.

His gaze meets mine, and his snarl eases into a soft whine. The beast shrinks away as his fur recedes and human skin returns. He falls to his knees beside me.

"Lark." His hands find me straightaway, stroking my damp fur, his touch steady and comforting. "You are a beautiful wolf," he whispers, his voice thick with emotion.

A wolf. Wow. Fantastic. I was secretly hoping for a dragon—or a unicorn.

"Why—why, Lark," he says, voice unsteady, "didn't you use the ward on yourself? Why protect me?"

Tears prick my eyes, hot and unexpected, as I grasp the

reality of what I am—what we are. My tongue lolls out, and I weakly lick his wrist to reassure him I'm still here.

Still his mate.

"Fuck, they gave her wolfsbane," Riker growls from behind him.

"I'm so sorry, little mate. I will find whoever did this to you and rip them apart," Merrick murmurs, his hands trembling as he cradles my head. He lowers his forehead to mine. "The one person who is truly mine, and I failed you. I should have protected you better. Forgive me."

My tongue sneaks out, and I lick him again, more gently.

At last, I feel safe. Even as the wolfsbane's poison threatens to drown me, I know I'm not alone.

If I live, I will never be alone again.

I see it now.

The sound of boots rushing into the warehouse fades, growing distant as the world dims. Merrick's heartbeat echoes in my ears, the final sound I notice before darkness takes me.

Chapter Twenty-Nine

THE WORLD SWIMS into focus slowly, like a camera lens clicking frame by frame.

Click.

Merrick's alpha command reverberates in my mind, desperate yet futile. The shock in his voice, disbelief tangible as the Alpha Prime himself fails to compel me to shift.

"She's a sigma," someone whispers. The words hang in the air, heavy with meaning I don't quite understand.

Click.

"Please, Lark, shift for me," Merrick pleads, the authority gone from his tone, replaced by raw intensity. My body stirs at the fated connection between us, even though commands don't work. I shift.

Click.

Overhead, helicopter blades whirr, sending a gust of air that carries shouts I can't decipher.

Click.

Merrick's tone turns icy. "If she dies, I will kill you all."

CHAPTER THIRTY

THE NEXT THING I KNOW, my eyes flutter open. The sterile white of a medical room greets me. I'm alive, and I'm human again.

Merrick slumps in a chair beside me, his large hand holding mine. His head tilts at an awkward angle, exhaustion etched into every line of his face. Even in sleep, he looks like a storm barely contained.

I shift slightly, wincing as soreness ripples through my body.

"Here." A gruff voice draws my attention. Riker stands at the door, a silent sentinel. He crosses the room, pours water from a jug, and offers me a glass.

I sip carefully, rinsing the foul taste from my mouth before swallowing. Who knew water could taste so divine?

"Hi," I croak, managing a weak smile.

Riker scowls, arms folded, his imposing frame blocking half the doorway.

"Sorry I didn't listen," I rasp. "The Alpha Prime is worth twenty of me. I didn't realise it at the time, but my wolf knew. She knew we had to protect our mate."

"We?" He arches a blond eyebrow, scepticism plain on his face.

"When I say 'we,' I mean me," I explain. "There's no separate entity, no scary monster—just me. But now I have a... wilder side. A furry inner voice."

He narrows his eyes. "That's strange. Most shifters describe their animal as a separate being, even alphas. But you... you're one and the same, aren't you?"

I shrug and glance at Merrick. "I suppose so. I was only a wolf for about five minutes."

Of course, I'm not normal; I never was, and I will embrace it.

Riker follows my gaze. "He only just fell asleep. Four days straight, he's been up, watching over you. It took complete exhaustion to knock him out."

Guilt knots my stomach. "I'm sorry I frightened him," I whisper. "I'm sorry I frightened you."

Riker tilts his head back, staring at the ceiling. "You're the bravest person I've ever met," he says quietly. "You have got more heart than anyone. I've seen people break under less."

I let out a shaky laugh. "I felt like a mouse. Maybe a very scared caterpillar."

"No." He straightens, his tone firm. "You're a wolf shifter with the heart of a lion. I'm glad you are all right."

"Thank you." My voice cracks, and I blink away threatening tears.

"Thank you for saving my best friend's life." Riker presses a button above the bed, summoning the medical staff. "The nurses will want to check you over, and the doctor will probably want to run some tests."

I groan. "Tests. Great."

"You deserve them." He smirks. "I hope they poke you with all the needles."

Despite everything, I laugh. "Thanks, Riker."

A warm hand squeezes mine gently. Merrick is awake. His piercing blue eyes soften as they meet mine.

"You're awake," I whisper.

He nods, smiling tiredly. "You are back," he says, voice gravelly. "Never scare me like that again."

"I'm sorry," I reply, shaking my head. "But if you are in danger and I can keep you safe..." I shrug. "I will always take that chance. I will always pick you."

His jaw tightens, and his eyes flash with emotion. "It's not like I can stop you. My alpha command does not work on you." He exhales. "You are a sigma, Lark. Do you realise how rare that is?"

"I don't even know what that means," I admit.

"We will talk about it later," he says, brushing a strand of hair from my face. "For now, you need to focus on getting better."

"For now, we need to focus on Human First."

At the mention of the group, his face hardens. "Human First? It was them?"

I nod.

Fury blazes in his eyes. "They will pay for what they have done."

I reach up and brush his cheek, smoothing the harshness. "Paul tipped them off," I murmur.

Merrick's gaze snaps to Riker, who nods and leaves the room without a word.

"What will you do to him?" I ask hesitantly. I spent most of my life with Paul, and despite everything, I don't want him physically hurt.

"Paul?" Merrick's voice is low and lethal. "What I want is to take him apart piece by piece—open his abdomen, pull out his intestines, and wrap them round his throat. But there are laws, and I will follow them—for now." He sighs. "Justice will be served. I will make sure of it. He will never be in a position to harm you again."

"Good. Let's whack him with the law like a piñata and see what falls out."

Merrick gives a soft chuckle, though his gaze stays intense. "You rest. We will deal with revenge later."

"I will rest because I need my strength to hunt them down."

"Not from a hospital bed," he counters. "I will find them, little mate."

Not if I find them first.

A mischievous smile curves my lips as I test my magic. I've woven a delicate web around their gadgets—smartwatches, phones—beacons ripe for tracking. I can trace them all, follow their every movement, unravel their plans.

Especially Chatty.

He thinks he is safe, that I'm just another victim, but I know exactly where he is. Where they all are.

The thought sends a surge of energy through me. My shifter and technomancer powers hum under my skin—eager, coiled, ready.

They tried to erase me. Instead, they have handed me the map to their downfall.

I lean back against the pillows, a predator feigning rest. They set this game in motion; they just don't realise I'm the one holding the pieces now.

I smirk. "We'll see, big mate. We will see."

CHAPTER THIRTY-ONE

AFTER SEVERAL DAYS OF OBSERVATION, I'm finally discharged from the medical centre and—for vampire security reasons—end up at Merrick's Zone Two residence, in his office building. But it's more than an office. He has a whole apartment here, and Riker lives here too.

Human First denies any involvement, claiming the attackers were part of a rogue chapter, not an official affiliate. It's absurd, of course, but what can you do? It won't stop Merrick from pursuing those responsible.

Although I wasn't exactly invited, I don't let that keep me from crashing today's meeting.

I'm in a high-tech war room, waiting. Along the walls, antique bookcases have been modified with hidden panels, revealing rows of high-resolution screens showing live feeds, maps, and encrypted data. In the centre sits a polished oak table, its surface dotted with sleek touchscreens and holographic projectors. Shifters, apparently, appreciate style.

My magic thrums with anticipation. The things I could do in this room...

The door opens, and Merrick and Riker stride in. Merrick wears black combat trousers, bunched slightly at the tops of his tactical boots, and a black long-sleeved T-shirt. He isn't just dressed for war—he *is* war.

Wow.

My mate is ridiculously beautiful.

They both spot me at once. Merrick's reaction is immediate. He shakes his head, voice resolute. "No. You are not going. This isn't your concern."

"Not my concern. Huh. Right."

Tension radiates off him. "Must you be such a nightmare? Lark, they poisoned you with wolfsbane. If you hadn't shifted—if you were not this strong—you would be dead. It should have killed you. I'm not letting you near them. It's my job to deal with it. I will deal with them."

I squirm in the chair, irritation prickling beneath my skin. "You're really not used to being defied, are you?"

He shoots me a look, and I fold my arms, huffing. No one's ever protected me like this before—Paul never cared enough—but Merrick cares a little too much. I know he's worried, but I'm forty-seven, not a child.

Besides, I have the information they need and the skills to help.

"You can't protect me from everything, Merrick."

"I can try. Since I met you, I've aged a hundred years." He tries to sound light, but there's sincerity in his words.

"I will have nightmares about that day," I say softly, the admission slipping out. "Leaving you bleeding, unconscious. I need some control back. I'm not saying I want to kill them, but I need to see them caught. Punished. And I can help."

He regards me for a moment, and I catch that flicker of sadness again—fear lurking under the surface of his gaze.

"If you come, you will see a side of me I don't want you to. A side—"

"A side that what?" I cut him off. "Merrick, I know you are the Alpha Prime. I've heard the rumours. Nothing you do will make me afraid or drive me away. But if you insist on controlling me, then we have got a problem." His jaw clenches, so I press on. "We're mates. I feel it, deep down. That does not mean I will roll over and accept your decisions. You have to help me do this. I have to see this through. I need closure."

He groans, running a hand over his face. "You can barely shift. You have been sick—"

"I know."

"You have lost weight—"

"I know."

He glowers, and I hold his gaze.

"God, you will be the death of me," he says, louder now. "No, Lark. No. It's not safe and you are not trained. I swear I will punish them for you."

"You are going to do this without me?" I demand.

"Yes."

"Oh? So you have found them?"

Don't grin, Lark. Don't grin.

He scowls, a flash of frustration in his eyes. He has not.

237

"It's been a week. The trail must have gone awfully cold," I continue, adding my final blow. "If I can't help, I'm not telling you where they are." I meet his glare with one of my own.

"Just give me the info. I will go myself. Riker, the team—"

"So," Riker drawls, leaning against the door, "you're going to do your 'magic' thing?" He flicks a hand in my direction and wiggles his fingers.

I freeze. "Magic?" I echo, my heart hammering.

"Yes, magic," Riker repeats, his smirk widening. "I noticed you glossed over how you got that GPS data during the debrief. You didn't fool me."

"Riker," Merrick growls. We both ignore him.

My stomach drops. "What makes you think it's magic?" I try for indignation, but my voice betrays me with a slight squeak. "Maybe I'm just a super-talented hacker."

Riker shrugs, his grin turning sly. "A hacker? You, Little Miss Goody Two Shoes? Or maybe you are someone who blends tech and magic together." He leans in slightly. "Lark, drop the act. You're a technomancer."

I wince, then school my face into a glare, fists clenching. "Now what? You going to tell everyone?"

"Calm down," Riker says. "Your secret's safe with us— and with the Ministry of Magic."

"The Ministry of Magic?" My chest tightens. "What about them?"

Merrick pulls a sealed envelope from a hidden drawer. The paper almost crackles with contained magic.

"I *was* going to broach this subject with you delicately,"

he scowls at Riker. "You must have had a good reason to keep your magic secret. While you were unconscious, they sent a summons," he says quietly, his eyes fixed on my face.

"A summons?" That does *not* sound good.

My hands tremble as I stare at the envelope.

CHAPTER THIRTY-TWO

"It's all right," Merrick says, his tone gentle. "You are safe, and we have checked the document. There's no nefarious magic. They just want to talk—to you, to us."

I wiggle in my chair, trying to put some distance between myself and the glowing envelope. The fear rising inside me must be obvious, because Merrick moves faster than I can react, sweeping me up as though I weigh nothing. He sits, pulling me into his lap.

"What the heck?" My surprise momentarily pushes the fear away.

Riker bursts out laughing at my expression. "Priceless."

"Merrick," I protest.

"I know." His arms tighten around me. "But please humour me. I need to hold you. I don't like seeing you frightened."

Heat rushes to my cheeks as I groan in embarrassment. "I'm not frightened." Despite myself, I relax against him, my head resting on his solid chest. "Fine. What is going to happen?"

"It's not us who are in a conundrum," Merrick says, his voice low and steady. "The human government, however, is going to have a problem." He cuddles me closer, but there's a flicker of sadness in his eyes.

My stomach twists. "What is wrong?"

He hesitates, his jaw tightening. "I read your medical file. At fifteen, the human government sterilised you," he says, his tone sharp with disbelief and grief.

I shrug, brushing it off. "Yeah, it happens. They do it to everyone with faulty DNA. They sterilised a lot of us. They didn't know I was a magic user."

"You kept your magic hidden."

"Yeah." I pause, choosing my words carefully. "It didn't show up until later, until after I was sterilised. I always thought it was stress-induced. I never told anyone. I kept it a secret for over thirty years, so this"—I gesture towards the summons—"didn't happen. That Magic Hunter at the warehouse, the one who tried to help me, knew what I could do. He said he could taste my magic."

I glare at Riker. "And now you guys know. Oh, and the entire Ministry of Magic, apparently. What do they want?" I ask, eyeing the envelope as though it might explode. "I'm not touching that."

"It's safe. My magic staff checked it thoroughly," Merrick assures me.

Reluctantly, I pull the spiky-feeling envelope towards

me. The magic pricks at my skin, but I break the seal and extract the heavy parchment.

"Dear Mrs Winters," I read aloud, then glance at Merrick. "Look at that. I've been upgraded."

He kisses the top of my head. "Yeah, you have been upgraded, little mate."

"Without my consent."

"Hospital thing," he says with a shrug.

"Uh-huh. Hospital thing." I shake my head and skim the letter. "This feels like I'm getting an invitation to Hogwarts."

"Not quite as exciting," Merrick replies dryly.

"They want to speak to me. In person." I look up at him. "Are we going?" I'm certainly not going by myself.

"As soon as we deal with Human First, we will."

I fiddle with the edge of the parchment. "And... the Ministry of Magic—will they make me stay with them?" The thought sends a shiver down my spine.

"They can't. You are no longer human. You're a shifter —part of our society. Your magic changes nothing. You are my mate, and they wouldn't dare harm a single hair on your head." Merrick plucks the letter from my hands and sets it aside.

Riker gestures to the wall of screens. "All right, techno-mancer. Do your thing."

I arch an eyebrow. "I'm not some performing puppy, Riker. And I've already stated my terms—I will help, but only if I come too."

I lock eyes with Merrick, neither of us backing down.

"Fine." Merrick's voice cuts through the tension, gruff.

"You can come, but only under my direct supervision." His eyes narrow, the weight of his alpha authority pressing down. "You stay by my side. No arguments."

Riker leans back in his chair, smirking. "Under the thumb already, Alpha Prime? Impressive." His gaze flicks to me. "You are such a troublemaker. We will need to double the strike teams to keep you out of trouble."

I shrug, unrepentant. "Maybe. But I'm still going, aren't I? Can I please have a laptop?"

"Yes, of course. Riker, grab the laptop, please," Merrick asks.

Riker rolls his eyes but obliges, muttering something about 'high-maintenance technomancers' under his breath.

I sigh. I don't want to leave Merrick's warmth and the shelter of his arms. He lets out a low, gruff sound—half growl, half protest—as I reluctantly slide off his lap and settle back into my chair. The loss of his touch is immediate and unsettling.

Riker places the computer in front of me. "Thanks," I mutter.

Merrick's gaze never leaves me, a subtle intensity in his eyes, as if willing me to stay close. I swallow the lump in my throat, forcing myself to focus. There's work to be done. I blink. "It's my laptop."

Of course it is.

"Yep, all your stuff's here," Riker says with a grin.

All my stuff? I glance at Merrick, suspicion narrowing my eyes. "So, we're living together now?"

He smiles that soft, disarming smile and bumps his shoulder against mine—bloody touchy-feely shifter. Little touches on my neck. Sneaky kisses on my temple. Always there. Making my heart skip. Making my skin hum with electricity and my resolve dangerously pliable.

"I want my own space. My own bed," I add quickly, even as goosebumps race up my arms. "This does not mean you get to skip out on dating me first. Fate might have spoken, but we still need to get to know each other. All the hanky-panky stuff can wait."

"Of course," he murmurs, a mischievous gleam in his eye. "I will court you properly."

Court me? I bite my lip to stop the smile. Damn it, I like him. Not just because of fate, his stupid beauty, or the way he makes me feel alive. I like *him*.

I focus on the laptop, logging in and pulling up a mapping programme. My magic hums at the ready. "Here." I tap a key and send the data to the wall of monitors. The screens flicker and then display a detailed map, street views, and nearby security surveillance.

"They are in this building here," I say, pointing. I use my magic to zoom in. "All of them, except the Magic Hunter—I can't track him properly; it might be because he's too far away. But the rest? They are clustered together in the Human Sector. Waiting for something."

Merrick leans forward, his jaw tight. "Planning another attack?"

"More than likely," Riker says.

"And before you ask, no, it's not a decoy. They are using their devices—actively. It's real."

Merrick growls low under his breath, the sound reverberating through the room. "This building is in the Human

Sector. I will need to deal with the human police before we plan anything." His tone turns deadly. "It will take a little... persuasion."

Watching Merrick work is fascinating. Once I pull up all the data, he calls in the troops. The war room transforms into a hive of activity—men and women, all impeccably trained, moving with purpose and deferring to Merrick's authority. He spends most of his time on the phone, negotiating with his contacts in the Human Sector.

The sticking point? The humans want their people present during the operation. Merrick isn't having it. Eventually, they settle on one human observer—a compromise, but a win for him.

By the time late afternoon rolls around, the plan is set, the team ready. We grab a quick meal—which feels more like a feast, given how shifters eat—and everyone leaves to prepare. We will head out just before dark. The drive to the target—an old office building closed for renovations—will take a couple of hours.

I keep a light, magical connection on the 'bad guys' while Merrick's human police contacts monitor the area.

The building has an old, active security system, but it's a closed circuit—no internet connection. I will need to access it manually when we arrive. Merrick does not want to risk tipping them off. After how quickly they left the Shifter Sector following my abduction and attack, it's clear they are jumpy and far smarter than we'd assumed.

Meanwhile, Paul is missing. They have been hunting him since I named him as the one who tipped off Human First, but he has vanished. The annulment wrecked his finances, and with the forced sale of the house, he's been reduced to crashing at a friend's place.

Dove, unsurprisingly, left him. She told the police it was all my fault. According to her, if I'd 'kept hold of my husband,' none of this would have happened.

Chapter Thirty-Three

THE GUEST ROOM is at the back of Merrick's building, next door to his apartment—close enough to feel connected yet still private. It's breathtaking, vast and luxurious. The space must span at least twenty feet, dominated by a massive sleigh bed piled high with pillows and cushions in various shades of pink.

"He remembered my favourite colour!" I grin and hug one of the pillows.

An outfit waits neatly on the duvet, with sturdy boots on the floor beneath. I run my fingers over the fabric—black, strong, magical. I'm not sure what spells are woven into it, but there's power here—protection, perhaps—to stop a knife or slow down a magic blast like the ones at the hotel. Now that I think about it, it feels similar to Merrick's suits. No wonder he always looks so pristine; the magic probably self-cleans.

At least it's not some awkward jumpsuit, either—thank God.

I have my very own fancy, badarse military outfit: combat trousers with enough pockets to stash half the war room, a form-fitting top, a lightweight jacket, thick socks, and handmade military boots. Everything is comfortable, practical, and ready for anything—even fingerless gloves are included.

I finish getting dressed, and there's a knock at the door. It's Hannah. "How are you settling in? Need anything?" she asks, already eyeing the mess I've made of my hair.

"Honestly, I need a miracle," I admit.

"Here, let me." She sits me down and begins French-plaiting the strands, weaving them close to the scalp into two neat plaits—sleek, practical, and impossible to grab. Fancy combat-ready pigtails.

"You are a hero," I tell her when she's done. "Thank you."

"You're welcome. I'd better get going."

"I'm so sorry for keeping you so late."

"Don't worry about it. I don't usually work these hours. The Alpha Prime's rarely here—he spends most of his time in the Capital. I manage things in the Enterprise Zone, so having him here for three months has been... unusual."

"I bet it's been a long three months."

She shakes her head, a soft smile playing on her lips. "No. It's been good. I'm glad he met you. You have softened him—and made him stronger."

Her words catch me off guard, but I smile and give her a quick side hug.

After slapping on some moisturiser, I leave the apartment and follow the distant hum of voices and movement. It leads me to a door that's slightly ajar—beyond it lies a weapons storage room. An armoury.

The men and women joining us are gearing up. The air hums with preparation—boots thudding, weapons clicking, quiet orders exchanged. Riker, ever casual in the chaos, slings a spare jacket over his arm.

"Ah, there you are," he says with a grin. "Look at you, all military chic."

I roll my eyes. "Yeah, a real shifter fashionista. Shifter Lara Croft is the look of the season."

He wiggles the jacket at me. "Unfortunately, you will hate this addition. It's going to be hot as hell, so don't put it on just yet. When it's go-time—busting down doors, kicking arse—you will need this."

I take the jacket from him and nearly drop it. "Bloody hell, what's this made of? Concrete?"

"Bulletproof. Spellproof. Top-tier shifter military tech," Riker says smugly. "Merrick would wrap you head-to-toe in this stuff for the rest of your life if he thought he could get away with it. I'd check your wardrobe after this—bet it's already been replaced with magic-proof everything."

I dig my elbow into his ribs, and he laughs, unfazed.

Merrick strides in, prowling toward us with that lethal mix of authority and warmth. His eyes flick between me and Riker, and without a word, he bumps his shoulder against mine.

I frown and try to step away, only to be spun back into

his hold, his arm snug around my waist. Bloody touchy-feely shifter.

"Let's get you outfitted," he says, guiding me toward the walls of weapons. "Can you fire a gun?"

"No. But I discovered I'm pretty good with a dart gun."

Merrick arches a brow, amused, and hands me a solid dart gun—sleek, familiar. "This one's loaded with tranquilliser darts strong enough to drop any derivatives."

He starts filling my pockets like I'm a walking arsenal—knives, extra darts, torches, little gadgets I don't even question. I take it all because, honestly, it makes me feel better to have something—anything—on me.

Then Merrick pulls something delicate from his pocket: a new necklace, its blue vial shimmering faintly in the light. It's identical to the one I used a few days ago. He steps behind me and fastens it around my neck with careful hands, taking extra care not to disturb my newly-plaited hair.

His touch lingers. "There," he murmurs.

"Thank you," I whisper, tucking the vial safely under my top.

He cups the back of my neck gently, his thumb brushing my jaw as he leans closer. "Promise me you will use that for yourself this time. Not anyone else."

"I can't promise that," I reply, honesty winning out.

Merrick sighs, his frustration visible as he closes his eyes for a moment. When he opens them, his gaze grows gentle. "I know. It's not in you. And that's why I love you—not just because we're fated mates, but because of who you are. I've never met anyone so selfless."

The air evaporates from my lungs. "Selfless? I wouldn't

say that," I stammer, my heart thundering as his confession sinks in. "You... love me?"

"Yes," he says simply, as though it's the most obvious thing in the world. "Of course I love you. You are very easy to love. Don't worry—you don't have to say it back. I just didn't want us to walk into danger without you knowing."

"Oh," I say faintly, my mouth opening and closing like a fish. My mind is a blank slate. Merrick loves me. *Me.* How is that even possible?

He kisses my forehead—soft, reassuring—and pulls away. "Come on. While everyone finishes prepping, we need to talk about who you are. Your place in the pack."

"What I am, you mean? A sigma?" The word feels heavy on my tongue, and I swallow nervously.

"Yes." He leads me from the armoury, down the corridor, and into his private office. The quiet is a stark contrast to the hum of preparation outside. My nerves jitter in my stomach. I don't know what being a sigma really means, but I pray it isn't something bad.

Before I can slump into one of his visitor's chairs, Merrick scoops me up effortlessly and sits me on his desk. He nudges my thighs open and steps between them, his presence a mix of warmth and dominance that steals my breath.

"Sigmas are very rare," he says, his voice low and measured, as if sharing a secret. "They exist outside the traditional pack hierarchy. Not alphas, not betas, but something entirely their own. Successful, respected, but rebellious. Lone wolves who are untouchable. They bring balance, Lark, and because of that, we protect them. We cherish them."

I stare up at him, my pulse quickening. "So... what does this mean for us?"

His gaze softens, though his expression remains intense. "It means," he says, brushing a kiss on my nose, "I'm the luckiest man alive. The last known sigma died over two hundred years ago. You are something my kind has only whispered about. You can't be commanded by an alpha. Your healing, your shifting—it will all be faster, stronger. And your gifts..." His lips quirk into a small smile. "We will discover them together. I will be with you every step of the way."

"Thank you," I whisper, my voice catching on the sudden emotion rising in my chest.

"You don't have to thank me. It's an honour to help my mate." His thumb brushes my cheek, lingering near my lips. "Can I kiss you?"

The question steals the air from my lungs. I swallow hard, my eyes wide as they meet his.

"Courage, mate," he murmurs, his breath feathering over my lips, warm and teasing. I nod, unable to form words, and then he leans in.

The moment his mouth meets mine, it's like a bolt of lightning hits me—fire and electricity racing through my veins. His scent surrounds me, intoxicating. My entire body shudders, and I lose all sense of reason. My hands reach up instinctively, threading through his hair and pulling him closer as my body arches into him.

He tips me back over the desk, and I don't care when he follows me down. I don't think. Thought is obliterated, replaced by sensation—his lips firm and sure, the sweep of his tongue making me tremble, burning heat surging through every inch of me.

I'm gone.

Nothing exists except this kiss, this man, and the fire he has lit inside me. I've never known a kiss like this. It's... *everything*.

A loud fist pounds on the door, rattling the frame. "Come on, you two! We're loading up!" Riker's voice booms, equal parts exasperated and amused.

Reluctantly, Merrick and I pull apart. My lips tingle, still buzzing with sensation. I can't help but touch them, breathless.

"He has impeccable timing," I rasp, trying to collect myself.

"The absolute worst." Merrick's voice is low, rough, and edged with frustration. "If he were not so damn useful, I'd kill him—just so I could keep kissing you."

He helps me down from the desk with infuriating care, his touch lingering. Then he takes my hand, weaving his fingers through mine as though he refuses to let go, and together, we head outside to join the others.

CHAPTER THIRTY-FOUR

HE KISSED ME. I almost choke on the thought. And wow —that kiss. Let's just say I didn't know people could kiss like that. The connection, the fire, the everything. It's both exhilarating and terrifying. How can a kiss make me feel so unmoored yet so grounded at the same time?

When I get outside, I still feel dazed and have to shake myself awake.

There are seventeen of us—three groups of four, then our group of five. I've made the numbers wonky. *Great start, Lark.*

Each team has its own transport, sturdy vans with heavily tinted windows and bench seating in the back. It's a very different experience from the time I was stuffed into one of these.

Our vehicle is the last to pull away from the kerb. As we drive, familiar streets roll past my window. My old workplace disappears behind us, and further down, I spot the massive oak tree and... I squint, pressing my palm to the window and leaning in so far, my cheek smushes against the glass.

I stare back at the empty plot where the house used to stand. "The wizard's house is gone," I say, disbelieving.

"Yes," Merrick says. "With everything that happened, I forgot to tell you. It disappeared the day you were abducted."

A small, distressed noise escapes me before I can stop it. "Gone? Just like that?"

"It can go anywhere in the world," he says. "Anywhere it wants to be. Some say they move where they are needed. But I will admit, I'm glad it's the last wizard's house in my territory. You think it helped you, but houses like that can hinder just as easily."

"I know," I mumble, swallowing the lump in my throat. "But it *did* help me. It saved me from the vampire and gave me somewhere safe to heal."

A strange ache settles in my chest. It's ridiculous, really, to mourn a house. But it wasn't just brick and mortar—it felt alive, like it had been waiting for me for decades, holding space for someone who needed it most. Silly thoughts, I know, and ones I'm not brave enough to share. Still, I close my eyes and whisper a silent thank you to the house and the wizard's soul within it. *Wherever you have gone, I hope you are safe too.*

Forty minutes later, the van rolls through the border checkpoint and the tunnel of doom. I brace myself instinctively, waiting for the familiar gut-wrenching slap of the border's magic.

But... nothing happens.

I blink in surprise. Riker catches my expression and bursts into laughter, smugness radiating off him.

"The magic won't bother you now you're a shifter," he says, grinning.

"What?" I gape at him. "All that time, I thought you and the driver were total badarses. Turns out you were just... unaffected?"

He leans back, still smirking.

I narrow my eyes at him. "Do we need a hankie to mop up all the smugness dripping off your face?"

His laughter booms, echoing through the van.

It takes another hour and twenty minutes to reach the location. The human representative greets Merrick with a curt nod and firm handshake before stepping aside to observe, his presence stiff and silent.

At Merrick's signal, I send out a pulse of magic, severing all communications in the office building. "Communications are down," I report, pulling on the heavy jacket as the teams split off.

Merrick's lips curl into a sharp, predatory smile as his eyes flick my way. The look is brief, but I catch it—a silent reassurance, tinged with pride. I nod back, though my stomach twists into knots. His soft words cut through the tension. "Hold on to my belt and do exactly as I do."

Meeting his steady gaze, I step closer, my fingers brushing the thick fabric of his jacket before gripping his sturdy leather belt. I hold it tight, careful not to restrict his movements.

For a brief moment, the air hangs heavy and still. Then, with a subtle motion of Merrick's hand, we move. I mirror his crouched steps, heart pounding, as Riker stays close behind me.

We reach the front entrance. The other teams are already in position, silently preparing to converge or intercept anyone trying to flee. The lead shifter kicks in the glass doors with a thunderous crash that reverberates through the empty hallway. Weapons are drawn as we step inside.

My stomach lurches at the metallic tang of blood. I step over a thick, dark pool, the scent cutting through even my sensory band. It's worse than I imagined, blood, meat, and the acrid stench of bowels emptied. I clench my jaw, fighting the gag rising in my throat.

The air is thick with human fear. I can taste it—feel it clawing at my senses like an invisible predator.

Something terrible happened here.

We follow a grisly trail of blood into the central office. The furniture has been shoved to the edges of the room, creating an open space dominated by a massive TV screen and a single, misplaced sofa. The screen flickers red, displaying grim words in jagged, looping text: GAME OVER. YOU'RE DEAD. GAME OVER. YOU'RE DEAD.

"They were playing some kind of shooter game," I say, my words catching in my throat.

"Are you okay?" Merrick asks, bumping his shoulder gently against mine.

"I'm fine," I say, though my voice cracks. I let go of Merrick's belt and cough, trying to clear the lump in my throat. My legs itch to bolt from the suffocating horror of this place, but I can't. I won't. Instead, I pretend it's all fake —just a set, just makeup.

But no amount of pretending can erase the reality.

The Camera Guy is missing his head.

They are all dead.

Something—or someone—has ripped them apart.

"This wasn't a shifter," says the big guy who breached the doors. He sniffs the air, grimacing at the sight.

Once the building is cleared, the human observer is brought in. He surveys the scene, jaw tight. "Try not to touch anything," he warns, composure fraying despite his professional façade.

"Can I turn off the screen? I don't have to touch it," I ask—the flashing GAME OVER message is drilling into my skull.

"That's fine," he says, waving a distracted hand.

I wave mine, and the screen goes black. The sudden darkness makes the room feel even more oppressive. Nausea claws at my throat, and I force myself to breathe steadily. The floor is a minefield of blood, gore, and... bits. My knees threaten to buckle.

"Riker, take Lark back to the van," Merrick says. His voice is calm but edged with worry.

"Sure thing. Come on, Rocky, you're looking a little pale."

"Wait." My voice wavers, but I force myself to continue. "Do you... want to see what happened to them?"

Merrick's intense gaze softens. He sets his hands on my shoulders. "Are you still willing to access the security system?"

I nod. "Yeah, and I can replay it on the TV."

He hesitates. "Are you sure you want to see that?"

I swallow hard, ignoring the bile rising in my throat. "We have to know what happened."

"Okay, little mate."

"If it helps," a woman from one of the rear-entry teams chimes in, "they came through the front. The back doors were chained shut, and the chains hadn't been touched in years."

"That is helpful, thank you," I reply, turning my attention to the tech. I draw on my magic to sift through the building's digital history, starting with the cameras and scrubbing through the footage.

The interior cameras show nothing unusual—the group is alive, absorbed in their game. "Their device activity slowed just before dark," I mutter, mostly to myself. I fast-forward, isolate the footage, and bring up a split screen on the TV. Four feeds fill the display, each focused on a different part of the building.

As night falls, a pizza delivery guy appears on the street cameras, his cap obscuring his face. He pounds on the glass door, and one of the Human First members gets up, wallet in hand, and heads to the main entrance.

What happens next makes my blood run cold.

The Pizza Guy drops the box and lunges, his hands morphing into claws as he rips out the man's throat in one brutal motion. No one else reacts—they are too absorbed in the game. On the feed, the Pizza Guy killer drags the lifeless body by the hair, leaving a dark, glistening trail of blood. He dumps the corpse behind the sofa, and still—no one notices.

The room fills with the wet sounds of carnage as he

moves impossibly fast, faster than the cameras can track. I let out a shaky breath and make the main room feed full screen. We watch as he tears through the remaining Human First members, each kill as vicious as the last. It's a massacre.

He spends extra time on Chatty, the sound of ripping and snarling filling the room. When he uses the red Swiss Army Knife to pluck out Chatty's eyeballs, I clamp my eyes shut, unable to watch until the noises stop.

When I open them again, the blood-soaked killer is staring directly into the camera. His red eyes glint, and his pale face tilts in amusement. His voice comes through the speakers, unnervingly melodic.

"They dared to mess with my hunt," he says, lips pulling back in a sharp grin that exposes his fangs. "I will be seeing you soon, little birdie Lark."

Oh, shit.

CHAPTER THIRTY-FIVE

EVERYONE in the room turns to look at me. Weapons are drawn, and the shifters instinctively form a protective barrier around Merrick and me. It's almost comical—the notion of guarding against a vampire that fast. He is long gone, but their instincts won't let them relax.

I keep my eyes on the screen, watching until the vampire leaves. He places something on the arm of the sofa, then blurs through the hallway and out the main doors. In a flash, he's gone. I stop the recording and turn off the TV.

"I've sent the footage to the war room server," I say, my voice tight.

"Is this the vampire who came to the Facility? The one hunting you?" Merrick asks.

"Yeah, that's him."

"I have his scent," Riker says from behind me, his voice low and grim.

The shifters exchange uneasy glances. Even they look rattled, and I don't blame them. The Alpha Prime's mate is being stalked by a psychopathic vampire. Human First decided to toy with me, and he responded by wiping them out in a gruesome bloodbath.

It's a message. A warning.

I feel hollow and cold, as though all the blood in my body has drained away. My mouth is dry, and my heart pounds so hard it feels as though it might crack my ribs. Exhaustion drags at me, but it's the smell that pushes me over the edge.

The scent of raw, mutilated human flesh is suffocating. My head spins. The shifters might be able to tolerate it, but I'm not built for this. It's too much.

It's way too much.

"What did he leave?" someone asks, breaking the tension.

Riker steps carefully through the carnage, his boots squelching on the blood-slick floor. He tilts his head, examining the object on the sofa's arm. When his green eyes flick back to me, his expression is troubled.

"What is it?" I ask, my voice barely above a whisper.

Riker glances at Merrick. Without a word, they have an entire silent conversation—raised eyebrows, subtle nods.

Whatever it is, it's bad.

"Two squads, take Lark back to the van," Merrick growls.

It feels like I'm being dismissed, a child sent to bed

while the adults deal with something unspeakable. Frustration flares in my chest.

"What is going on? What did he leave?" My gut churns with the certainty that this 'gift' is meant for me—and I'm not going to like it.

"You don't need to see this, Lark," Merrick says. "You are swaying on your feet. We will talk about it later."

I frown, shaking my head, unwilling to leave.

"Trust me," he says, locking his gaze onto mine.

Trust him. I force myself to nod. I don't want to undermine him in front of his people. "Okay. Later," I say, my voice hollow.

With a final glance at Merrick, I follow the four shifters assigned to escort me out, another four trailing close behind. Riker catches up quickly, falling into step beside me as we head back to the van. Human authorities arrive just as we round the corner, their vehicles flooding the street. I'm relieved to be leaving the chaos behind.

Inside the van, my thoughts spiral as I shrug off the heavy jacket and place it across my lap like a weighted blanket.

"What did you see, Riker?" I ask quietly.

He does not answer immediately, his jaw tight as he stares out the window.

"Riker, please. What did you see?"

He glances at me, lips pressing into a thin line. "We will talk about it later," he says, tone evasive.

"Tell me now," I insist, my voice trembling. "Please."

He sighs, running a hand through his hair. "There was a driving licence."

"A driving licence?" My brow furrows. "Whose?"

He hesitates, shoulders stiffening. When he finally looks at me, his expression is resigned. "Lark," he says softly, "it was Paul's."

"Oh." The word escapes me in a whisper. "Do you think the vampire got him?"

Riker shrugs. "Probably."

The vampire wouldn't have Paul's driving licence if he hadn't taken him. "So that's where he went. He didn't just run off. He was taken, or he is already dead." Bloody Paul.

I stare at the van's ceiling, my mind spinning. The vampire went after Human First because they abducted me, messed with his hunt, and ruined his fun. He went after Paul because he gave them my name. Is this vampire clearing my slate of enemies, or is he simply enjoying the carnage?

I don't know, and I don't want to try to understand the mind of a serial killer.

"Do we know who he is? The vampire?" I ask, trying to keep my voice steady despite my frayed nerves.

Riker looks at me carefully, jaw tightening. "Not yet. But we will. We have got pictures, and I've got his scent. He won't stay hidden for long."

I nod, locking away the chaos swirling inside me. I'm not sure how to feel. Paul is no longer my responsibility; he gave up that right when he betrayed me with Dove and sold me out to Human First.

What he has done is unforgivable. Is he even worth saving?

No, he's not.

Yet guilt cuts through me like a blade. I don't know if I can live with myself if I let him suffer and die. Unlike Paul, I can't lie, cheat, or switch off my emotions at will. Even though I hate him for what he did, a tiny, broken, and battered part of me will always care.

"What will Merrick do?"

Riker exhales through his nose, shoulders lowering slightly. "This is tied to you, so Merrick will go after the vampire. Not to save your ex," he adds, meeting my gaze. "Merrick couldn't care less about him. But he will do it for you—to keep you safe. He knows that if anything happens to Paul, it will hurt you. And hurting you? That's not something Merrick will allow."

He knows Merrick so well.

I pull the heavy coat tighter around me, trying to quell the trembling in my hands. "Why is this so hard?" I whisper.

Riker's demeanour shifts, sympathy crossing his face. "Because you're a good person, Lark. You care, even when you don't want to."

I bite my bottom lip, holding back a surge of emotion.

"We will figure this out," he continues. "We will find out who this vampire is, where he's hiding. And then we will sort it—if you give us the chance."

I nod, my throat too tight for words. "Thank you," I manage after a moment, my voice hoarse.

Leaning my head against the cool window, I close my eyes and let myself shut down, piece by piece, until there's nothing left but the muted thrum of my heartbeat.

Chapter Thirty-Six

I BURROW DEEPER under the covers, my nose barely peeking out from beneath the pillow. A stretch pulls through my limbs, and my nails clack against the sheets.

Wait—nails?

My heart skips a beat. I stare at my hand.

It's not a hand.

It's a paw.

A *freaking* paw.

I yelp, jerking upright, only to tumble off the bed in a flurry of fur and limbs. The floor greets me in an undignified heap.

I'm furry.

I'm furry!

What the actual heck is going on? Why am I furry?

This must be a nightmare. I squeeze my eyes shut, willing myself to wake up, but when I open them, the fur is still there. I bang my head lightly against the bed frame. Nope—definitely not a dream. Shouldn't the sensory band have stopped this? The damn thing is still on my furry wrist. Wasn't it supposed to control my shifts?

I slump back onto the floor and bury my face behind my paws.

My paws.

Taking a deep breath, I force myself to think rationally. *Okay, think human thoughts. Skin. Fingers. Toenails. Earwax.* (Why earwax? I have no idea, but I'm grasping at straws here.)

I imagine my normal body.

Nothing happens.

Maybe I need to burn off some energy. Yeah, maybe that's it.

Thank goodness the bedroom is big enough to accommodate a restless wolf. I push myself up on all fours, wobbling slightly. The sensation is bizarre but not unmanageable. The pads of my paws press into the carpet as I take a cautious step, letting my body move naturally.

Surprisingly, it feels... good.

I widen my stride, rolling my shoulders and dipping my head, testing my range of movement. A little stretch here, a little bounce there. I try a downward stretch, only to yelp when my tail smacks me between my back legs.

That is so weird.

Undeterred, I pace the length of the room, turning at the wall to head back towards the window. Each lap is faster than the last. Soon, I'm jogging lightly, then bounding in springy strides. I push off with my hind legs and leap onto the bed, bouncing once before landing on the floor.

This is amazing.

I can't help myself—I do it again. And again. Sometimes I clear the bed entirely; other times, I bounce like an overexcited puppy. My tail wags embarrassingly, my tongue lolling out, but I don't care.

It's fun.

I'm so caught up in the joy of my impromptu acrobatics that I don't notice the figure standing in the doorway until I screech to a halt, misjudge the timing, and skid chin-first across the carpet.

Oof.

Wide-eyed, I glance up to see Merrick, arms crossed, one eyebrow arched high.

"What are you doing?" he asks, his voice laced with amused confusion.

I try to answer, but it comes out as a jumble of yaps and whines.

"Yeah, uh... I don't speak wolf, little mate. Are you all right?"

I nod.

"You shifted. Was that on purpose?"

I shake my head vehemently. No, I absolutely did not plan to wake up as my furry self.

"Ah, so it happened while you were asleep?"

I nod again, a soft whine slipping out.

"Have you tried shifting back?"

Another nod, this one more frustrated.

"You are fine," Merrick says, his tone gentle. "May I come in?"

I nod, clumsily rising from the floor. After a full-body shake, I prance to the bed and leap onto the rumpled covers. The once-pristine bedding is now a disaster zone—pink pillows and cushions scattered everywhere. I flop onto my side with a long huff.

Merrick steps in and sits on the edge of the mattress. His fingers move through my fur, stroking in a slow, soothing rhythm. It feels incredible. When he scratches behind my left ear, my back leg betrays me, thumping uncontrollably.

He chuckles, low and rich. "You are adorable as a wolf, you know."

I growl and turn my head to glare at him.

He tugs gently at the fur on my neck and gives me a mock shake. "Don't be mean. That was a compliment."

I feel a twinge of guilt and lick his wrist in apology. His lips quirk into a smile.

"Sometimes this happens when you are stressed," he says, still stroking my fur. "It's nothing to worry about. It's normal. You will get a handle on it. After the first couple of years, it will stop. For now, it's completely routine."

I close my eyes, leaning into the steady motion of his hand.

"Everything's going to be all right. Do you want help transforming back?"

I sniff, uncertain. I'd like to try on my own, but what if I can't?

"It's an alpha's job to help the pack," Merrick continues gently. "And I'm your mate, so I'm here for whatever you need. If you would rather stay in wolf form for a while, that's fine too."

A soft whine escapes as I tilt my head toward him.

"Okay," he says, understanding. "Do you want my help?"

I nod, ears flicking forward.

"All right then. Close your eyes."

I do as he says, and a strange warmth floods my body— like liquid magic, soothing and coaxing. Alpha magic, maybe. Pack magic. I'm not sure, but it works.

Slowly, my body begins to shift. Ouch—it hurts. Bones crack, and ligaments stretch and twist as my muscles rearrange. It feels like an eternity, though it must only take a few minutes to transform back. I can't believe I slept through this earlier.

"You are okay," Merrick murmurs, brushing my hair back from my face. His voice is a steady anchor, pulling me back to reality.

Then the cool air hits my skin. My eyes snap open, and I let out an undignified squeak as I realise—I'm naked.

For a forty-seven-year-old woman, freaking out like this is mortifying. Scrambling, I dive under the covers, wrapping myself in the sheets like a human burrito. My fingers fumble desperately until I find my discarded pyjamas, which must have been kicked off during the shift. Some-how, I manage to wriggle back into them beneath the covers.

When I finally poke my head out, Merrick is laughing, his eyes crinkling at the corners. "You might be the funniest person I know," he says affectionately.

"I forgot I'd be naked," I mumble, cheeks burning. I

find a wrinkle on the duvet particularly interesting. I smooth it with my fingertips, avoiding his gaze. "It was just... a bit of a shock."

He grins. "Shifters are okay with being in the buff, you know. It's pretty normal."

"Yeah, well," I reply, glaring half-heartedly, "I was human for a very long time. It will take me a while to get used to this whole nudity thing."

Probably never.

"I will leave you to get some sleep."

"I don't think I will be able to," I say, then immediately betray myself with a yawn. The running around in wolf form clearly took it out of me. "How did you know I'd shifted and needed help?"

"Because it sounded like a herd of elephants stampeding in your room," he says with a quiet laugh. "I wanted to check you were not fighting a vampire."

"Oh." My cheeks heat. "Right. Sorry about that."

"It's no problem," he says gently. "I will take you somewhere proper next time—somewhere you can run free and feel the grass under your paws, wind in your fur. Your first proper shift, and you had to do it in your bedroom." He shakes his head, regret clouding his face. His voice drops, rough with exhaustion. "I'm sorry, Lark. I should've been here. I'm a pretty poor excuse for a mate, letting you go through that alone."

"I'm okay," I say softly. "You are here now. I'm sorry for waking you."

"Don't be. I wasn't sleeping—I couldn't. I was in the gym, taking it out on the punching bag." He leans back, rubbing a hand over his face. "I have all this rage and nowhere to direct it because everyone's either abducted, hiding, or already dead."

Gently, I reach over and squeeze his hand. He curls his fingers around mine, and for a moment, his gaze lingers on me. Then he leans in, pressing a light kiss to my forehead.

"So," I say, quieter now, "do you have any updates on the vampire? Or about Paul? Is he... alive?"

I feel bad asking—it's only been a few hours.

"We don't know yet. But it's odd for the vampire to leave Paul's driving licence without leaving..." He pauses, watching for my reaction.

"His body," I rasp.

"We might find him in a couple of days—or not at all."

A chill settles over me. I don't want him to be dead. Miserable? Yes. Dead? No.

Maybe the vampire is using Paul as bait—how sporting.

"Do we know who he is?" I ask, my throat tight.

"Yes."

"We do?" My mouth falls open.

"His name is Leonidas," Merrick says grimly. "He is an old vampire. He used to serve on the Vampire Council about two hundred years ago—long before my time as the Alpha Prime. They have been keeping tabs on him. I've got a full dossier."

"Can I see it?"

He hesitates. "Are you sure? It's not light reading."

"Yes, please."

"All right," he relents. "Why don't you get changed, and I will meet you in my apartment?"

"Okay. Thank you. Oh, and Merrick? I *love* the pink cushions—thank you so much." I beam a smile at him.

His icy blue gaze drops to my lips for just a second, and he visibly restrains himself, chuckling under his breath as he steps back. "You are going to be the death of me," he murmurs, voice low. Then he prowls to the door.

He pauses, looking back at me with a soft, lingering expression, before gently closing it behind him.

Chapter Thirty-Seven

Whatever he is imagining, he can forget it. Yes, he's seen a glimpse of my bare skin by accident, and sure, we have kissed—once. It was the kiss to end all kisses, an epic kiss, but I've got bigger things on my plate.

I know life is fleeting, and part of me thinks I should be climbing Merrick like a tree—but I won't. Not yet. I have so many things I'm dealing with, and adding intimacy to the mix isn't wise, especially when my wolfish hormones are all over the place.

The least he can do is take me on a proper date.

I slip out of my pyjamas and into something comfortable: leggings and a jumper. After a quick check in the mirror, I pad down the hall and knock on his door.

"Come in," Merrick calls.

Stepping inside, his scent hits me like a tidal wave. It's

everywhere, saturating the room, wrapping around me. The man smells ridiculously good—cedarwood and leather, with a warm hint of amber. My wolf stirs, and a wild part of me wants to roll around on the carpet to soak it in. Must be a wolf thing, because that's just plain weird.

The thick grey carpet muffles my steps as I cross to his sofa and sink into it. Merrick's apartment blends the building's gorgeous architecture with a sleek, modern twist. It feels effortlessly elegant yet lived in—a reflection of its owner. If this is just his temporary accommodation, I'd love to see his permanent home.

"Do you want a drink?" he asks.

After running through a few suggestions, I opt for coffee. As he wanders off to make it, I can't help checking him out. Bare feet, grey, low-slung jogging bottoms, and a white T-shirt clinging to every sculpted muscle. The man is a walking dream.

"The laptop's on the side," Merrick calls from the kitchen. "No password. You will find the information on the desktop."

"Okay, thanks."

I pick up the sleek device and open it. There's a detailed report on Leonidas. No recorded last name—maybe a string of them over the centuries, lost to time. Who knows? What is clear is that this vampire is ancient, around two thousand years old, and one of the last of the oldest vampires.

And he is hunting me.

Of course he is. Why not throw an ancient, psychotic vampire into the mix? If life's going to pile on, it might as well be over-the-top. Give me a magic nobody recognises, turn me into a super-rare shifter, and pair me with the head of the entire shifter world. I'm over it. Somebody else can be the centre of the universe for a change.

I don't want to be greedy.

Why is it that people who want to stay in the shadows always get dragged into the spotlight?

I shake off my internal moaning and refocus on the report. Leonidas is described as brilliant and unhinged. It seems some vampires, after living so long, lose themselves. Many find hobbies or passions to stay sane; Leonidas appears to have chosen hunting people. And he has been busy.

I deliberately skip the photos and detailed case notes—enough death for one lifetime. Next time Merrick suggests I sit something out, I might actually listen.

Leonidas does not seem to have a specific type for his victims. Perhaps something in the blood calls to him. I look up from the laptop, letting my thoughts drift. How hard must it be to live for centuries, watching everyone around you fade away while you endure? Our DNA may have evolved, but we're still human and deeply flawed—capable of kindness but also great cruelty. Nature went all out when it made the derivatives.

Now I'm a shifter, and my lifespan has increased immensely. I might live three to four hundred years. It's mind-blowing and scary.

The sharp clink of cups on the coffee table jolts me out of my thoughts, and I flinch.

"Are you all right, Lark? You have gone a bit pale," Merrick asks, concern colouring his tone.

"I'm just overtired, and this document is... horrible."

"Yes, it is," he agrees, studying me with narrowed eyes. "What else is wrong?"

"Nothing." The lie comes easily, but guilt churns in my gut. Years of burying things with Paul have left their mark. Old habits die hard.

Merrick tilts his head, unconvinced. I huff. Hiding won't work—not with him. Not when he can scent my emotions. Not when he is my mate. I can either shut him out or trust him to help carry it.

My chest tightens at the thought, but I take the leap.

"This is my fault," I finally say, the guilt dragging the words out. "If I'd just stayed in the stairway, if I hadn't run and bled all over Zone Two... I'm so sorry."

His expression softens, but I can't stop.

"And now this vampire—Leonidas—he's going to hurt you, or Riker, or someone else I care about. I can't figure out his endgame, other than... my death." I shake my head, my eyes stinging with tears. "I know this is my mess, but how do I fix it? My wolf is barely competent. I've shifted twice, both times by accident. Fight with teeth and claws? I can't even walk across carpet without tripping over my nails."

A brittle laugh escapes me. "This is a nightmare."

Merrick does not answer right away. Instead, he leans forward and cups the side of my face, his thumb brushing away my frustrated tears.

"Lark," he says softly, "you are forgetting a few things."

I meet his gaze. The warmth there is almost overwhelming.

"If you hadn't run," he continues, "you might never

have fallen into the wizard's house garden, and you might not be here now."

He is right. That house saved my life. Running wasn't all bad.

"You are not alone anymore. You are a shifter, with a fated mate who adores you and an entire country of shifters at your back. Whatever happens, we will face it together."

"I don't know how to deal with all that," I whisper. This feels like yanking out a festering splinter lodged deep beneath my skin.

"I know." His lips twitch in a faint smile. "It will take time."

Sensing my need for a change of subject, "We got your test results back. Would you like to hear about them?"

I nod, snapping the laptop shut. He leans back, expression gentling.

"They compared all your results—from the hospital, the Facility, and the older ones from your youth. Your DNA profile has changed drastically."

I sit straighter, bracing myself.

"The good news is the shifter DNA has locked in. Your shifter and technomancer traits have merged and stabilised, so you are a magical shifter."

"So... no vampire fangs if I get bitten?"

"Correct," he says, smirking slightly.

"Good to know."

"The Ministry of Magic will definitely want you to do some training," he adds.

I shrug. "Do they know what part the wizard's house played in my change?"

"No. They are baffled. There's no record of a wizard's

house ever being linked to a shifter. The Ministry suspects distant magical lineage might connect you to it, but that's only speculation. There's no precedent for a magic user being turned into a shifter."

"So, it's all guesswork," I murmur.

"For now. We will know more tomorrow."

"Tomorrow?" I ask, taken aback. "So soon?"

"Yes," Merrick says. "We're going to the Magic Sector. You have recovered from wolfsbane poisoning, we have dealt with the rogue Human First chapter, and the Ministry has already given us as much time as they are willing. They need to ensure you are not a threat. We can't risk a war."

"And Leonidas? The vampire?"

"We will travel during the day, so there's less risk. By night, we will keep you behind a strong ward. I'm taking a small, highly trained team. If I arrived with half the Shifter Sector, it would look both aggressive and insecure. I won't let them think I don't trust the Ministry of Magic to protect you. That said, I'm not leaving your side."

I force a smile, but unease coils in my stomach.

This does not feel right.

CHAPTER THIRTY-EIGHT

FOR OBVIOUS REASONS, I've never visited the Magic Sector before. Determined not to embarrass Merrick, I accept several business-style outfits made from spell-and-bite-proof material. Riker wasn't joking about my mate's obsession with wrapping me in magical bubble wrap.

In this case, I'm all for 'power dressing.' If I end up meeting that vampire again, I will take whatever protection I can get before he tries to drain me dry.

I hadn't thought about how we'd actually travel there—my mind's been busy ignoring the visit altogether. When we climb into a car and drive to the nearest airport, it finally hits me: we're flying.

For some reason, I'd assumed we'd be on the road for hours.

Our country isn't huge, and the jet is barely in the air

for an hour and a half before we begin our descent into the Magic Sector.

Riker clears his throat, his tone sharp. "Listen up, boys and girls. Once we hit the ground, it's full lockdown on all communication. Keep conversations to a minimum. Assume everything is monitored and recorded. Code words only. Understood?"

A murmur of agreement ripples through the group, but I turn to Merrick, leaning in to keep my voice low. "Do I need a code word?"

"No."

I narrow my eyes and drop my voice further. "If I tell you I'd love a cup of tea, just know the shit has officially hit the fan."

His lips twitch, a hint of a smile crossing his usual stoicism. "All right. Tea means trouble. Got it."

I grin.

From above, the Magic Sector looks deceptively like any Human Sector city. Only as we get closer do the layers of magic and illusion reveal themselves. The security team— eight highly trained shifters—arrange themselves into a precise formation I don't pretend to understand. My nerves are on edge, and I'm glad they are with us as we step off the plane.

The moment my feet touch the tarmac, the ley lines slam into me like a bolt of magic. My knees wobble, and it feels as though every hair on my body is standing on end. Even the sensory band on my wrist goes haywire, blasting me with waves of sound that fade as quickly as they appear. The world tilts. *Shit.*

"Lark?" Merrick steadies me, his arm firm around my

waist as he shoots a dark look at the magic users who've come to meet us. They clearly chose this runway on purpose. I try to pull myself together, determined not to make a scene.

"I'm okay."

"Alpha Prime, Mrs Winters," one of them says, bowing slightly, their tone polished and diplomatic. "Thank you for gracing us with your presence. We have your transport waiting. This way, please."

The official-looking cars, decorated with diplomatic flags, hum with arcane energy. I slide in between Riker and Merrick, my heart pounding, my technomancer magic pressing against the edges of my control. The enchanted vehicles glide silently, so I distract myself by looking out the window.

We head into the city's heart, a vibrant sprawl of modern technology fused with ancient magic. Sleek skyscrapers gleam in the sunlight, their glass and steel façades adorned with faintly glowing runes powered by invisible currents of magic that flow through the city like electricity. Ivy-covered cottages nestle beside futuristic towers, their chimneys emitting enchanted smoke. The sheer saturation of power is overwhelming. I struggle to breathe, as though trying to draw air through a straw.

For the hundredth time today, I wonder if sneaking back home would really be so bad.

There's no mistaking the Ministry of Magic's main building. All roads converge at its base. It's clad in a strange black stone that seems to devour light, creating a void against the city's magical glow. Silver runes coil across its surface, shifting like serpents whispering secrets I'm too human—or too untrained—to comprehend.

Our car glides into an underground entrance, plunging us into the fortress-like bowels of the structure. The atmosphere is dense and oppressive. I stare at the walls as Merrick helps me out of the car, thinking how dramatic his border crossing had seemed—until now.

As planned, we remain silent as we're led inside, guards from both sides taking up a brisk, echoing formation. The interior is a cavernous space that seems to stretch on forever, with ceilings so high they vanish into darkness. The same light-absorbing black stone lines the walls, shot through with glowing silver veins that pulse with magic, casting an eerie light on the chequered floor. Enchanted sconces flare along the corridors, which twist and turn in a disorienting labyrinth.

Eventually, we're shown into the council chambers—a grand room dominated by a massive circular stone table, black and alive with the same shifting silver runes. As more people file in, the table expands seamlessly, creating extra chairs in perfect symmetry. Sleek black seats match the eerie elegance of the space.

Unease prickles at my skin. Before Merrick can sit, I rest my fingertips on his seat, scanning for malicious magic. Nothing. I sense only layered spells, none of which seem harmful. I nod, and we both take our places.

My eyes widen as the chair shifts beneath me—an odd sensation, as though I'm suspended in mid-air. It's as if I'm floating, cradled by an invisible magical current. The feeling is creepy. Is all this classed as normal in the Magic Sector?

Riker stands behind me, flanked by the rest of our security team.

My hands rest in my lap, fingers nervously twitching against the spell-resistant fabric of my clothing. Merrick notices. Without a word, he places his hand over mine, warmth radiating through me. He gently squeezes, anchoring me, and bumps his thigh against mine, a silent reminder: *I've got you*.

I've spent a lifetime avoiding magic users, hiding the secret of my technomancy. After meeting Merrick and being bitten, my entire world has flipped upside down.

Now, here I am, in their most powerful stronghold, surrounded by the people I once feared. My pulse pounds, but I hold my head high. I can do this. With Merrick and Riker by my side, I can be brave enough to take on any challenge—one small step at a time.

The door swings open, and another group begins to file in.

"The Ministry of Magic's Council," Merrick says, leaning towards me. Some of them acknowledge him with polite nods; others sweep past in lively conversation. As they take their seats, their voices mingle with the faint scrape of chairs.

The room grows crowded quickly, and I focus on breathing evenly, trying not to fidget under their scrutiny.

Then I see her.

My breath hitches, and I have to force my gaze back to the table to stop myself from staring. It's the redhead from the hotel—the one who found her husband cheating. Dayna. Or was it Dana? She looks almost unrecognisable:

thinner, more severe, as though she's been through hell. My chest tightens. I hope she and her three children are all right.

Another face draws my attention—a man with white-blond hair. He laughs loudly, scanning the room, and a jolt of recognition shoots through me. I murmur out of the side of my mouth, "Blond hair, third chair on the left—that's the Magic Hunter."

Merrick's chin dips, his gaze following the man. His silent intensity is both comforting and terrifying. The man notices and offers a sly smile as he sits.

"Good afternoon," he says, his voice warm yet under-pinned by something sharper. The table's magic reacts, creating an illusion of intimacy—shrinking the distance between us as though we're mere inches apart, even though neither of us has moved.

It's as though the Magic Hunter is right beside me.

His pale eyes settle on me. "Mrs Winters, it's a pleasure to see you again. I'm glad you're recovering after your ordeal."

My throat tightens, but I manage to keep my voice level. "What is going on?" I demand quietly. "Why are you here?"

His smile widens. "Ah, how rude of me. You know me as the Magic Hunter. After our little encounter, my cover with Human First was compromised. So here I am, back on official council duties. Allow me to introduce myself prop-erly—I'm Lander Kane."

He leans back, utterly at ease, as though revealing his dual identity is no big deal.

Lander Kane. A council member who spent who-knows-how-long infiltrating terrorist groups. My mind reels, struggling to reconcile his roles.

"When I returned," he continues smoothly, "I informed the council of certain developments—like a rogue techno-mancer wandering about. And, of course," his eyes gleam, "the baby shifter she's become."

I swallow, my fingers tightening around Merrick's hand. What does one even say to that? *Thank you?* The man was deeply embedded in Human First and now sits here like it's all perfectly normal.

Sure, he helped save me, but he also sold me out to the Ministry of Magic.

"Ah, the classic game of tit for tat," I say, my tone edged with sarcasm. "You exposed my secret; I exposed yours. Well played, Councillor Kane."

His eyes flash with amusement, but before he can respond, Merrick's voice cuts cleanly through the chatter.

"The shifters appreciate your intervention during my mate's rescue," he says, measured but with an undercurrent of warning. Instantly, the room quiets.

"I'm glad you were there, Councillor Kane, to help contain the Human First threat. For that, we are in your debt." He squeezes my hand, then lifts it to his lips, his gaze sweeping the chamber with a dangerous glint.

"Lark is more precious to me than anything in this world," he says, his voice punctuated with a low growl. "The Sectors would burn before I let harm come to her."

The weight of his declaration presses down on us, silence stretching taut.

Kane's smug grin never falters. "That's funny," he says

lightly, "because I've seen and heard a lot about this 'precious mate' of yours. Wolfsbane shoved down her throat, her first shift in some filthy warehouse, terrified out of her mind—some protector you were then, huh, Alpha Prime. Did I miss the epic fire?"

CHAPTER THIRTY-NINE

MY JAW nearly hits the floor at this man's sheer audacity. Merrick is practically vibrating with barely contained rage. The hand that isn't holding mine is clenched so tightly that his knuckles have turned white.

Lander, oblivious or simply reckless, opens his mouth to continue without a care, utterly unaware of how close he is to having his head ripped off his shoulders.

Dayna cuts in, her sharp tone slicing through the tension. "No. None of that. We all know the Human First chapter responsible for the abduction ended up in little pieces in the Human Sector."

"Sure," Lander interjects, his smirk widening. "But it wasn't the Alpha Prime doing the ripping apart, was it? That honour goes to a vampire." His eyes gleam with thinly veiled malice as he ticks points off on his fingers. "Let's summarise, shall we? First, the Shifter Ministry's technological centre gets attacked, which leads to your technomancer and fated mate being bitten and turned. Then there's a wizard's house—how convenient. Follow that with her abduction by Human First, and, to top it off, an ancient vampire decides to 'clean up' under the guise of a hunt. It looks like you have got more than a few problems on your plate, pal."

Merrick's muscles bunch like coiled springs, tension radiating from every inch of him.

"Lander!" Dayna snaps, her voice ringing with authority. "Enough. We do not pick fights with allies."

"I'm merely stating facts, sister dear," Lander drawls, though the glint in his eyes is anything but innocent. "Nobody's fighting here."

For a moment, I'm certain Merrick will lunge across the table and tear Lander's throat out. Then he exhales slowly. His entire body relaxes as he sinks back in his chair, his thumb brushing gentle circles against my wrist—a silent reassurance that he's in control. For now.

At least Lander Kane does not know about the mage battle at the hotel with his sister, where I almost got fried. If he did, he'd probably twist that into Merrick's fault too. My gaze drifts to Dayna, her face a portrait of exasperation. I can almost hear the internal sigh as she watches Lander with the kind of patience usually reserved for unruly children.

"The wizard's house," Merrick says, his voice low and measured, his mask of civility firmly in place. "Can you explain why my mate—a forty-seven-year-old human—entered it bleeding and emerged a shifter, looking decades younger? Do you know anything about that?"

"We don't," Dayna replies, her expression firm. Despite her youthful appearance, there's a weight to her presence suggesting she is high-ranking in the council—and not by accident.

"We're investigating it," she continues. "The house seems to have disappeared—relocated to another sector or possibly another country. We will track it down and analyse it. Councillor Kane," she adds pointedly, "will be involved in that investigation."

Lander scowls, crossing his arms. "Will I now?"

"Yes, you will," Dayna says through gritted teeth. "And pack it in."

I glance around the room, fighting the urge to bolt. The other council members watch quietly, and this place feels more suffocating by the second.

"We have a human government representative arriving shortly," Dayna announces, checking a sleek, enchanted watch on her wrist. "Twenty minutes, to be exact. They will explain why we were not notified of a technomancer in their midst." Her voice sharpens. "We will also discuss compensation on behalf of the Alpha Prime, Mrs Winters and the Magic Sector. The sterilisation of a rare mage is a gross overstep, and from now on, all non-consensual magical sterilisations are suspended until Parliament reviews the matter. I also move to ban the practice entirely. It's barbaric."

A chorus of agreement ripples around the table.

I find myself nodding.

"Does anyone have any questions?" Dayna asks, scanning the table. When no one speaks, she adds, "No? Excellent. Let's take a short break for refreshments."

I'm exhausted and uncomfortably sweaty, the magic and atmosphere in here are taking their toll. Just as I'm about to sag with relief, Merrick speaks.

"We will be leaving now. There's nothing further we need to discuss."

"We haven't covered Mrs Winters's magic," a man pipes up.

"We have covered enough," Merrick says firmly, though there's no mistaking the growl beneath his words.

"She will need to be assessed and trained," a woman interjects, her lined face stern. "We can't have someone untrained wandering the country and blowing things up. Laws exist for a reason. You are not above the law, Alpha Prime."

"And I can't believe you work in IT," Lander Kane says with an infuriating grin. "That means your control must be impressive, but we need to ensure it's sufficient. You have already passed small tests without knowing it. If this is your first time in the Magic Sector, the ambient power alone can drive an unprepared magic user mad—most cope only because they grew up here."

Well, it would've been nice to know that *before* stepping off the plane. Still, I keep my face blank.

"My assessment," the same woman continues, her gaze boring into me, "is that Mrs Winters has good control. From what Councillor Kane told us, she is well-grounded —no doubt self-taught. But she is powerful." Her eyes are sharp and probing, as though dissecting me.

I shrug, refusing to give her anything more.

"In our history," a man chimes in, adjusting his glasses, "we have never had a magic shifter. Surviving being bitten, turning, and retaining powers is unprecedented. Theoretically, magic would be the first thing to go—along with their humanity."

"Shifters are human," I say, my voice tight with anger, the words snapping out before I can stop them.

"Of course they are. Of course," he backpedals, waving a dismissive hand that makes me want to shove his chair over.

"So we agree Mrs Winters will stay for a few days to be assessed and trained," the woman declares, as if it's already decided and they don't need my consent.

"I didn't agree to anything," Merrick snarls, every inch of him taut with fury.

"I'd prefer a couple of months," the woman adds, ignoring him.

Tea! my mind screams as everything begins to spiral out of control. I want to shout, *"You promised me! You promised they wouldn't make me stay!"* But I clamp my frustrated words behind my teeth. This isn't Merrick's fault. Having a tantrum won't help; it will only make things worse.

Sometimes, you can't fight the current—you have to go with it.

It's only two days.

I inhale, steadying the turbulence inside. It would be foolish to refuse the chance to learn more about my magic. Even a day or two with a real tutor could help me refine my control.

Merrick looks torn, guilt and devastation warring on his face. He promised me, but he can't fix this. We're not above the law, and both of us know it. It must be horrible to wield so much power yet have a mate who keeps landing in trouble—though, to be fair, it's never intentional.

"I've managed my magic for over thirty years without anyone knowing what I am," I say. "I think I can handle two days of training." I rest a hand on his arm. "It's okay. You said yourself, we don't want to start a war."

"Absolutely not," Merrick growls, fury roughening his voice. He glares at the Council. "This is not what we discussed."

Behind me, Riker rolls his shoulders and cracks his knuckles.

The tension in the room tightens like a noose. The other shifters bristle, poised for a fight.

Chapter Forty

MY PULSE RACES. Oh no. This is bad. They don't understand what they are up against. These magic users aren't merely bureaucrats; they are powerful and will defend their authority with lethal force. If a fight breaks out, someone on our side will die—maybe everyone.

I can't let that happen. Two days isn't worth anyone's life.

Merrick moves as though he is about to stand, but before he can, I clamp my hand around his forearm. My grip is steady and firm, even though I'm trembling inside. "It's okay," I say again, forcing calm into my tone. "I can do two days."

His jaw clenches, muscles flexing beneath my hand. "No."

"Can you stay with me?" I ask, hoping for a compromise.

"No," the stern woman cuts in before Merrick can respond. Her smile is thin, her tone dismissive. "It's only two days. You will be perfectly safe here, Mrs Winters. Nothing will happen to you."

Merrick's nostrils flare, his anger barely contained. He tucks a stray strand of hair behind my ear, his touch almost painfully gentle. "We will all wait for you," he says quietly, his voice hoarse. "We will find accommodation close by. We can be here within minutes if you need us."

"Excellent." The woman's smile broadens, as if she's just scored a victory and won a prize. "I look forward to working with you."

Not if I've got anything to say about it. "I'm not working with you," I tell her flatly. Her expression darkens. "I don't trust you. I don't like you, and frankly, you have been nothing but rude."

Colour flushes her cheeks. "Well, you need to work with someone," she snaps.

"I will work with the lady in the blue cardigan, if she is willing." I glance towards the elderly woman I've been watching.

Her grey hair is neatly pinned into a bun, and her kind brown eyes are quietly observant. Throughout the meeting, she's remained calm, her reactions more genuine than performative—like when she winced when the man with the glasses declared that shifters were not human. The subtle anger that flickered in her gaze felt like a defence of us —not just politeness.

Real empathy.

She is the only one here I feel I can trust. If I'm going to learn, I want someone who values what I am, not someone who barely tolerates my existence.

"Me?" she asks, pressing a hand to her chest in surprise. Her voice holds warmth and uncertainty. I nod, meeting her gaze.

"Well, Mary," Dayna says with a hint of a smile, "do you have time? Will you help?"

"Of course, I would love to."

"The Professor is long retired," the sharp-tongued woman interjects, her voice almost frantic. "She does not—"

"It would be an honour to help guide the Alpha's mate," Mary interrupts smoothly, her gaze never leaving mine. "I have time," she adds, her smile deepening. Her measured tone leaves no room for argument. The other woman snaps her mouth shut, frustration etched across her features.

"Thank you," I say.

Mary dips her head in acknowledgement.

The chamber door creaks open, and the human official in a sharply tailored suit strides in, adjusting his collar. A sheen of sweat glistens under the magical lighting, and his gaze settles on me with undisguised contempt.

"Ah, Minister, thank you so much for coming," Dayna greets him. "The Alpha and his mate were just leaving. Mary will escort Mrs Winters to the training room."

Mary stands, her steps slow as she beckons me forward. "This way, dear."

Reluctantly, I follow the two women into the corridor, Merrick following close behind. His fingers brush mine.

"You can say your goodbyes now," the sharp-tongued woman announces, looking between Merrick and me, then at Mary. "Mary, can I have a word, please?"

Mary offers a serene smile, her endless patience evident as she allows herself to be led down the corridor. The woman's voice drifts back, sharp and clipped, "Mrs Winters needs to learn..."

I tune her out. My full attention settles on Merrick. "What about the vampire problem?"

"You will be perfectly safe," he reassures me. "This place is a fortress. No one is going to get near you here."

Including you? The thought coils in my stomach. What if I'm trapped here? My breath catches, and I force myself to exhale slowly. The Council can't hold me indefinitely unless they decide I'm a threat. Then I might never get out at all.

Merrick's voice pierces my spiralling thoughts. "While you are continuing your education," he says carefully, "I will organise the search for Paul. My best team is already on it. If he is findable, they will find him, Lark."

The knot in my chest pulls tighter. "I don't want to see him if you do. I just want him safe and far away from me."

"We can arrange that," Merrick promises.

"Thank you."

His expression softens. "Are you sure you will be all right? You don't have to do this if you are not ready."

I bump him lightly with my shoulder, forcing a small smile. "I will be fine. I'm nervous—maybe even a little scared. Perhaps a little excited. I guess it's better to get this over with now."

"If you need me, call." His lips tilt in a faint smile. "Remember your code word?"

"Yeah, yeah, funny guy," I say with an exaggerated eye-roll, failing to hide a grin.

He leans in and presses a soft kiss to my cheek, leaving me with a pang of longing. "Stay safe. I will have your things sent over."

Riker gives me a sheepish, almost guilty smile as he walks past. "Have fun with the magic stuff," he teases, though his eyes betray his worry.

"I will," I promise.

With one last reassuring squeeze of my hand, Merrick and the other shifters disappear down one corridor, while Mary and I head down another.

Her steps are short and shuffling—her pace slow. I adjust mine to match hers and glance back just once before the corridor curves, blocking Merrick, who gives me a final wave, from view.

"It's a pleasure to meet you, my dear," Mary says kindly. "You must have been terribly frightened. May I ask why you never told anyone you were a technomancer? We are not as bad as you think—if you would have come to us, you would have had nothing to fear. You could have avoided all this unpleasantness."

"I didn't even know about my magic until I was fifteen," I admit. "By then, I'd already been sterilised. I was terrified the human government would find out, and they would kill me to prevent an international incident."

Mary's brown eyes widen, her brows knitting in concern. "My goodness, you are quite perceptive. I daresay you were probably right. The human government can be...

shortsighted." She shakes her head, her voice gentler now. "And you have kept this secret all these years? Taught yourself? You were just a little girl."

"I did what I could," I say, the words heavier than I intend. "I didn't have a choice. The magic seemed... quite willing, almost eager, once I realised it was tied to my emotions. If I kept myself under control, the magic followed."

A sparkle lights Mary's eyes, deepening the lines at the corners. "Remarkable. Truly remarkable. And your magic —it came quite naturally, didn't it? Quite willing, as you put it."

I nod, unsure how to elaborate.

She pats my arm gently. "I noticed you scan the chair and the Council's table. That isn't something just anyone can do. Your instincts are good, your basic skills are excellent, and you have a deep well of untapped potential. Not many can taste magic."

"Taste magic?" I echo, surprised. My mind flicks to Lander's words in the warehouse. I'd been too scared then to consider what he meant.

"Oh yes, dear," she replies, laughing lightly. "Very rare, very exciting. I haven't met a technomancer in years. My grandmother was one. Of course, back in her day, technology wasn't nearly as advanced as it is now. She only had radio waves to work with, and she made them do all sorts of interesting things. But you—oh, with modern technology, I can only imagine your potential."

She tilts her head, her eyes gleaming with curiosity. "So, tell me—what can you do?"

Hesitantly, I explain my knack for working with computers and networks, tracing and manipulating data.

Mary's smile grows with every word. "Oh, that's excellent! Absolutely marvellous! Your human education must have been a great help, giving you a solid understanding of how these systems work. A grasp of technology, blended with magic? You are quite formidable. You are a clever girl."

"I'm forty-seven," I say gently, hardly a 'girl.'

Mary chuckles, the sound soft and chiming. "Eighty-three," she counters, "and to me, you are a spring chicken. I remember being your age—so young and full of promise. Now look at you, on the cusp of something extraordinary." She gives my arm a reassuring squeeze. "I'm not sure who'll learn more, me or you. But I promise, when you leave, you will take away some valuable knowledge, techniques, and, I hope, new friends. And remember this: you are not alone anymore. You have a magical family now."

I swallow hard, the lump in my throat is making it difficult for me to speak. "Thank you," I manage, my voice barely above a whisper.

"And you are a shifter too," she adds, her tone brightening. "You have the shifters, your mate, and I hear you are a sigma. You really are remarkable, Lark. Truly remarkable. May I call you Lark?"

"Yes," I whisper, my throat still tight. "Of course."

"Splendid!" Mary exclaims, clapping her hands lightly. "Now, you are probably exhausted after your journey, but I thought we'd work through lunch. There's so much to do, and I'm eager to begin."

"That's fine with me."

"Excellent! So, what do you like to eat? Do you find

yourself leaning more towards a carnivorous diet these days, or do you still enjoy—"

"Pasta," I cut in, relieved by such a simple question. "I love pasta."

Mary's entire face lights up, as though I've just shared a marvellous secret. "Ah, pasta! Do you know, I believe they are making lasagne today!"

Her excitement is infectious. For the first time since arriving in this sector, I feel a spark of warmth and a quiet reassurance that somehow, everything might be okay.

CHAPTER FORTY-ONE

AFTER WE HAVE EATEN, Mary takes me to her study, a cosy room where floor-to-ceiling bookshelves bulge with volumes that hum with latent magic. A soft, bright rug covers the floor, lending the space an inviting warmth.

We sit at her desk, which is buried under a chaotic sprawl of paperwork and trinkets. With practised ease, Mary shuffles the clutter aside, carving out a clear workspace.

"That little sensory band on your wrist is dreadful," she says, wrinkling her nose. "Whoever made that deserves a good slap on the chops. May I?" She gestures towards the band, her expression brimming with morbid curiosity.

I hesitate. I'd noticed how her gaze lingered on the band throughout lunch.

Before I can reply, she mumbles, "What am I thinking? You will need some extra help."

She picks up a wand from the desk and gives it an elegant flick. Words, lyrical and fluid, spill from her lips in a Latin chant, and the room is suddenly enveloped in a shimmering bubble of silence. Everything takes on a soothing blue tint, softening the light's harsh edges.

"There—that boundary spell should hold while I poke around with this thing," she says, wiggling her fingers with a mischievous grin.

Reluctantly, I slip the band off my wrist and place it in her palm. I'm relieved to find the boundary spell does its job. Everything is fine.

Mary closes her eyes, murmuring under her breath as her fingers glide over the band. "Tell me, what do you feel when you use this?"

I think for a moment. "It tingles a bit, and then everything quiets down. My senses retreat—sound, smell, touch, all of it."

She hums in acknowledgement. "That's your shifter side. Now, what does the magical side say? Push away the shifter magic for a moment and focus on the technomancer side."

I blink at her, baffled.

"What does your shifter magic feel like?" she prompts gently.

"It's wild," I reply slowly, "raw, emotional—like a storm rolling through me."

"And your technomancer magic?"

"It's... a kind of cool, calm blackness."

"What did it feel like when you first noticed this magic?"

"Pure chaos," I admit, memories of my earlier struggles drifting to the surface.

Her lips curl into a triumphant smile. "Exactly. If your technomancer magic was once chaotic and you managed to mould it into calm blackness, why can't you do the same with your shifter magic? You are a sigma, Lark—control is your gift. That wildness does not have to define you; it's still part of you, but you can decide how it flows. Imagine it not as a raging storm but as a smooth, glassy surface, or a gently lapping stream."

Her words resonate, and I nod.

"Good. Now, try this: take that wild shifter energy, and instead of letting it rule, box it up. Tame it as you did with your technomancer magic. Then, with the chaos out of the way, use your magical senses and tell me what you feel about this band."

I take a deep breath, closing my eyes to focus inward. I tackle the storm inside me, approaching it with the same logic I used when I first learned to stop blowing up gadgets. Slowly, I visualise the wildness as a puddle of muddy water on the side of a road. The image makes me smile—why a pothole, of all things?—but it works. The turbulence settles, and I gently push it to the side, boxing it away.

The difference is immediate. My mind feels clearer, lighter, as though a dull ache I hadn't noticed has suddenly gone. For the first time, I feel balanced.

I open my eyes and smile. "It worked."

Mary beams. "I knew it would. Look at you, my dear— you are stronger than you think. Right, now tell me about this band." She places it back in my hand, her expression twisting in mild disgust.

"Oh," I say, wrinkling my nose. "That's... bad."

"Yes, isn't it just," Mary agrees wryly.

"The band is *bitey*. It's like someone stuffed mismatched magic into it. They have tried to fix scent, sight, sound—everything—in one messy bundle. Then they slapped a tracking spell on top, but instead of smoothing it out, they knotted it all together. It's like someone tipped out a bag of knitting yarn, mixed it up, and tied impossible knots. It's horrible."

I drop it onto the desk, poking it away from me.

"Precisely. You must not have that horrid thing near you; it will do more harm than good," Mary exclaims, her voice edged with indignation. "So we will do better—no, *you will* do better. Your magic isn't limited to technology. You are powerful enough to fix these things yourself. Honestly, I hate to put someone out of a job, but if they are making rubbish like this, they deserve it. It's shameful. Our educational system should be producing better mages."

She pauses, her gaze sharpening thoughtfully. "Unless, of course, the Council *wants* the shifters to have subpar magical tools. If that's the case, Landon will have a very stern conversation with them."

Her words strike a chord. My thoughts wander to Alice and her sensory band—the one that failed her when she needed it most. It never stopped her from shifting; it didn't protect her. Maybe it even hindered her.

A wave of sadness tightens my chest, making me lower my head. How many young shifters like Alice might have lived if these bands had been better? If the enchantments had been stronger?

Mary's earlier comment resonates in my mind: "*You are powerful enough to fix them.*"

If that's not worth doing, an important calling, I don't know what is. Alice may be gone, but maybe I can stop others from suffering the same fate.

Chapter Forty-Two

"Mary," I say, lifting my gaze to meet hers. Determination sparks in my chest as I hold up the band. "Will you really show me how to make these? Something that actually works?"

Her features soften, understanding flickering in her kind eyes, and she nods. "Absolutely, my dear. It will be my pleasure to teach you. Together, we will create something far better than this mess."

"Thank you."

Mary smiles warmly and nods towards the necklace Merrick gave me. "Now, that's a beautiful piece of work."

I shift my focus to the necklace; Mary is right. It's nothing like the band. The warding magic is intricate, layered with a precision that radiates protection and care. I can feel its strength through my fingertips.

"It's beautiful," I say, awe filling my voice. "Merrick gave it to me."

"The Alpha Prime must truly love you," Mary says with a knowing smile. "With your magic balanced and that awful band gone, let's concentrate on your shifter magic and fix your sensory issues. You can't craft effective magic bands if you are not fully in control of yourself. Close your eyes."

I obey, letting my eyelids fall shut as I focus inward.

"Good. Now, tell me—how does your shifter magic feel now?"

"It's not so wild anymore," I reply, my voice distant. I sense the still-boxed energy inside me. "It's calmer."

"Excellent. You are already maintaining control. Remember, shifter magic can be powerful and unpredictable, but it does not have to be chaotic. I'd like you to pull a thread of that magic and direct it towards your ears."

My ears?

Though hesitant, I concentrate, imagining a strand of magic moving to them. Suddenly, my hearing sharpens, overriding Mary's boundary spell. "I can hear faint conversations far away," I say in amazement.

"Perfect. Now pull it back."

I focus once more, and the enhanced hearing fades, returning to normal.

"Well done. Now let's try your sight." Mary gestures at a bookshelf on the other side of the room. "Can you read the spines from here?"

I squint, but the letters remain blurred. "No."

"All right. Push the magic to your eyes."

I draw on that magic again, directing it to my vision. Instantly, the book spines come into sharp focus. I can even make out the smallest lettering, and beyond that, the wood's grain, the texture of the stone walls, and faint silver filaments—tiny inscriptions carved into the stone.

"I can see them," I say, wonder thick in my voice.

"Brilliant. Pull it back now."

I let the magic recede, my sight returning to its usual range.

"You can do this with all your senses—smell, taste, touch. It's about directing the magic where it's needed, the same way you use your technomancer abilities. You already have discipline, and that's a big advantage. Soon, it will become second nature, responding before you even think about it."

"Thank you," I murmur, gratitude flooding me.

"Do you think you will be all right if I drop the boundary spell?" Mary asks.

I pause, checking my shifter magic. The wild energy remains firmly in its box. Feeling stable, I smile and nod. "I will be fine."

"Excellent." With a swift flick of her wand, the soft blue glow around us dissolves. I brace myself, expecting a sudden onslaught of sound, but the world remains calm. Everything hums at a normal level.

Mary's smile is warm, her pride unmistakable. "Well done, Lark. You have taken to this more quickly than I anticipated. Feeling better?"

"Much better, thank you." The tension in my shoulders finally eases.

She picks up the sensory band, holding it gingerly between her fingers as though it might bite. "You don't need this anymore. May I dispose of it?"

"Please," I say, eager to be rid of it.

Mary crosses to a sealed bin marked MAGIC WASTE and drops the band in without ceremony. As it lands, the faint hum of its magic sputters and fades, winking out of my senses.

"Good riddance," she mutters, brushing her hands together as if shaking off its lingering essence.

"Now, let's talk about shifting. How many times have you shifted?"

"Twice," I reply. "Once when I completed my transformation at the warehouse, and once in my sleep."

She hums thoughtfully. "A resting brain—your shifter magic decided to be sneaky. It shouldn't happen again. Did it hurt?"

"Not when I shifted in my sleep," I admit, "but the first time was incredibly painful."

Mary leans forward, eyes gleaming with interest. "Let's return to your senses. You can control touch now, right?"

I think about it and nod.

"If you can control touch, you can also decide whether your muscles and nerves feel pain. You can turn it down—or off entirely."

I gasp. "I can do that?"

"Of course!" she exclaims, excitement lighting her face. "Nature has its own balance, and that's yours. You shouldn't feel pain when you shift. It should be as seamless as blinking. Rather than experiencing bones breaking and ligaments stretching, you will learn to use both types of magic. Your shifter magic will nullify the pain, while your mage magic will speed up the process. With practice, you will be able to shift in seconds—just like that." She snaps her fingers, clearly pleased by my wide-eyed reaction.

"I really could do that?"

"Absolutely! You will also be able to shift specific parts of your body at will. Let's start small." She glances at my hands. "Try a single fingernail. Once you master that, the rest will follow naturally. I don't expect instant success," she adds with a teasing glint in her eye, "but by the end of today or tomorrow, you should manage to shift that one digit. Then we will move on to the entire body."

"Why are you helping me with my shifter magic?" I ask, curiosity lacing my words.

Mary pats my hand gently. "Because, my dear, your mage magic is already beautifully refined—we only need to show you what is possible. For you, that might be anything. You have been focusing without a wand, and that's rare. Even I need one for channelling my spells. That's your sigma nature shining through—you have always been a sigma, Lark. Becoming a wolf simply brought it fully to the surface."

I blink, trying to absorb her words.

"Now, let's try something simple," she continues. "Place your hand on the table and wiggle your index finger."

I obey, giving my finger a small wiggle.

"Good. Now focus on your nail. Make it thicker."

I raise an eyebrow, feeling slightly sceptical.

"This is basic shifter training," Mary says with a confident smile. "You have got this."

Suppressing a sigh, I concentrate, directing my magic

carefully at the cuticle, imagining it growing thicker. Slowly, millimetre by millimetre, the nail extends.

"Excellent!" Mary exclaims, her enthusiasm breaking my concentration. The nail snaps back to its usual form.

She grimaces. "Oops! My fault for interrupting. But that was remarkable for a first attempt. Over the next few hours—and tomorrow—keep practising. I'm proud of you, Lark. You really are talented."

Standing, she moves to a tall shelf lined with books.

"Now, this," Mary says, reverence in her voice, "is a very special book. Many magic users, if powerful enough, have wands. But the truly exceptional also receive grimoires. I believe this one's been waiting for you."

She shuffles back to the table, cradling the volume as if it were priceless treasure, then places it gently before me.

"This grimoire contains a piece of my grandmother's soul," she explains, her hand lingering on the cover. "Hatty didn't want her knowledge passed on to just anyone. When she died, she willed this book to find its way to another technomancer. And here you are."

Mary pats the book fondly before sliding it towards me. My hand hovers over its surface, sensing the magic radiating from within. There's no malice, no hidden threat—only a steady, welcoming hum.

"May I pick it up?" I ask, glancing at Mary.

Her eyes sparkle with approval as she nods.

Carefully, I lift the book. It's heavier than I expected, but the weight is reassuring. The magic tingles up my arm, stirring my technomancer magic in response, as though they are greeting each other.

As I hold it, the weight shifts, becoming lighter in my

grasp. A sudden urge to set it on the table overtakes me, so I do. The moment it touches the surface, the cover flips open on its own, and words begin to form on the first blank page:

Hello, Lark.
It's a pleasure to meet you. I'm so excited for us to work together.

Your friend always,
Hatty.

"Oh," I breathe, staring in awe. "Thank you, Hatty. I'm excited too."

Mary's face breaks into a delighted smile. "Indeed. This is wonderful. I knew you were the one. Now, when you return home and you have questions about magic, my grandmother Hatty—and her grimoire—will be there to help you."

Chapter Forty-Three

AFTER THE REVELATION of the grimoire, Mary—looking a little pale and tired—escorts me to my room.

"You will find it tricky to navigate this place. Even I get lost if I'm not paying attention," she says with a warm smile as we turn down another corridor that looks exactly like the last one. "So please don't wander off. I will be back tomorrow, and we can have breakfast together. You have earned a good night's sleep—it's been quite a day. It's been a pleasure teaching you, Lark. I've enjoyed myself immensely."

"Thank you, Mary. You have changed my view of magic for the better. I can't believe how much I've learned. And the grimoire..." I clutch it to my chest, it's a comforting weight in my arms. "It's amazing. I promise to take good care of her."

"I know you will."

On impulse, I lean in and give her a gentle hug. She stiffens slightly in surprise, then relaxes, patting my back with a quiet chuckle.

"All your things should be in there," she says, pulling away and pointing to a door. "Your mate was very insistent on you having everything you need. Now I must go and take a nap myself." She covers a yawn with the back of her hand. "Oh, I'm so tired. It's awful getting old. Don't do it," she laughs, her eyes twinkling with residual amusement.

"Good night, Mary."

"Good night, my dear."

I watch her shuffle down the corridor, worry tugging at me. The spark she'd had earlier is gone, replaced by exhaustion. I hope she will be okay.

Maybe I shouldn't have asked for her help. But then again, I don't regret it.

Mary is a marvel.

Stepping into the room, the door closes and locks behind me with a firm click.

The space is lovely, far nicer than I expected. It's on the ground floor, with French doors opening onto a small courtyard where a trickling fountain provides a soothing soundtrack. I glance at it and immediately feel the urge to find the bathroom.

"They have really committed to their monochrome aesthetic," I mutter, taking in the black-and-white décor.

A kettle sits on a small counter, surrounded by an assortment of tea bags, hot chocolate, and instant coffee sachets. A mini-fridge hums quietly, stocked with sandwiches, chocolate, and crisps. It's oddly comforting to know I won't starve, even though I'm still full from the lasagne.

The bathroom is a pleasant surprise. A deep bathtub beckons, and I waste no time filling it with hot water and a generous dollop of whatever bath products I can find. Placing the grimoire on the centre of the dressing table— safely away from the steam—I also remove my necklace, setting it gently beside the book.

As the tub fills, I grab my phone to message Merrick, checking in to make sure he and the others are safe. Talking is out of the question—we can't risk eavesdroppers—but texting is secure. I tell him about my day, the training, the flawed sensory bands, and Mary's promise to teach me how to craft better ones tomorrow.

After some thought, I take the necklace with me. I refuse to be vulnerable in a bath in this place. No, thank you.

I sink into the hot water with a sigh, the heat soothing muscles that have been tense all day. Between sitting stiff-backed in the council chamber and enduring the building's oppressive magic, my body has been through the wringer. But after working with Mary, the atmosphere feels less stifling, almost as if the building has decided I'm not a threat.

It's strange how much I've learned in one day. It's opened my eyes to the power magic users wield—and to what I could become if I wanted. But I don't want power. I want safety. I want Merrick. I want a simple life, where I can finally be myself.

Eventually, the water cools, and I reluctantly climb out, drying off and pulling on a comfortable lounging outfit—

jogging bottoms, a sports bra, and a loose T-shirt. Vulnerability isn't an option here, not even for pyjamas.

After drinking a few glasses of water, the room still feels warm, so I crack open the French doors to let in the night breeze. It does not help much, but it's better than nothing.

I settle on the sofa, phone in hand, and exchange more messages with Merrick. His replies arrive quickly, his words offering a steady warmth that eases the tension in my chest.

Still, the ache of missing him gnaws at me, sharper with each text. The way he signs off with a simple 'I love you' makes it even harder to ignore the empty space beside me.

I glance at the grimoire, but a faint headache makes me decide to delay looking at it. Instead, I lift my hand, wiggling my index finger.

Mary expects progress tomorrow, and I don't want to disappoint her. I focus, drawing on the shifter magic she taught me to control. Slowly, my nail thickens, elongates, and darkens, its edge turning predatory. A flicker of pride warms my chest.

Then, in my peripheral vision, a blur of movement catches my attention.

My heart stutters, unease trickling down my spine. I lower my hand, sitting up straighter.

The blur solidifies into a figure, and suddenly, I'm staring into a pair of blood-red eyes.

CHAPTER FORTY-FOUR

I YELP, my pulse thundering, as I leap from the sofa, placing it between me and the vampire. My hand flies to my bare throat.

Oh no.

My head was so full of magic, I didn't think to grab the necklace from next to the bath. *Stupid. So stupid, Lark.*

"How have you been, little birdie?" Leonidas purrs as he steps over the threshold, bypassing the Ministry of Magic's ward. His smile is cold and sharp, fangs gleaming like ivory daggers. "I've missed you."

My fingers twitch, subtly summoning magic to open the messaging app on my phone. As the text goes through, my magic pings, and relief flares.

"How did you... how did you find me?" My voice is

steadier than I'd have thought, but my body betrays me, trembling as I speak.

How the heck did he get past the wards? Who bloody told him I was here?

He always appears where he shouldn't. How does he know so much? Someone—a shifter or a mage—must be feeding him information, and it's disturbingly accurate. My thoughts churn like a storm. He knew my name, found me at the Facility, tracked down Human First when only my magic could locate them, and now he is here, in the heart of the Magic Sector. He can't possibly be that skilled a hunter...

Can he?

"You are wondering who told me, aren't you?" Leonidas tilts his head, crimson eyes gleaming with predatory delight. "There is a mole—someone who gave me every delicious detail about you. She was incredibly helpful."

"She?" My stomach clenches. Damn it! A shifter or a mage sold me out? Hannah? No, she'd never...

"Oh, no, no, no," Leonidas interrupts my spiralling thoughts, wagging an elegant finger. "Poor, poor Lark. You misunderstand. When I say 'she was helpful,' I meant *you* were helpful."

"Me?" My voice catches. "What? How?"

He chuckles, a low, menacing sound that fills the room like smoke. "Oh, how delightful. You truly have no idea. Let me enlighten you. You, Lark, are the gift that keeps on giving."

He strolls closer, his movements unnervingly fluid, as if he has all the time in the world to savour my horror.

"Your blood," he says, as though it's obvious. "It's

always been about your blood. I'm an ancient vampire, little one. Once I've tasted someone, I can track them anywhere. Sometimes... I can do more."

"What do you mean?" My voice barely rises above a whisper.

"Oh, Lark," he says with mock exasperation, leaning lazily against the sofa. "Powerful blood lets me *see*. I can see through your eyes, hear your thoughts. And my, my, you do think so loudly. You have been my unwitting messenger this entire time."

"No..." I whisper, shaking my head in denial.

That can't be true. It can't be.

"Oh, yes," he says, his grin widening to expose more of those gleaming fangs. "Talk, talk, talk," he mocks, puppeteering his hand near his ear. *"Will Merrick love me? Will Merrick hate me? Will he kiss me? Oh, Human First deserves punishment, but I do not want to see them die."*

The way he mimics me, mocking my life his tone high and taunting, makes my stomach churn. I want to throw up.

The ancient vampire rolls his eyes. "Let's be honest. I got rid of them just so you would shut the fuck up."

"No. You are lying," I croak.

Leonidas steps closer, his presence suffocating. "Oh, little one," he murmurs, almost tenderly, "I do not need to lie. You have been screaming your thoughts at me since the moment I licked your blood off the ground like a dog. This is your punishment. This is your fault. You are the mole, little birdie, and you sing so sweetly. You have been guiding me right to you all along."

His words strike me like a blow, the room tilts. I struggle to breathe as he takes another step.

"This game has been fun," he says, his voice a velvet caress. "But now, it is time to finish the hunt."

No.

I'm not dying here.

I can do this. I can do this. I can. I'm strong enough to deal with this man.

Leonidas laughs, the sound echoing like a death knell. "Oh, little birdie," he sneers, "you can't do this. You are already dead—you just haven't realised it yet."

Merrick will come for me.

"He won't reach you in time," Leonidas mocks. "Your Merrick left you here unprotected, like a suckling pig on a platter. All that's missing is an apple in your mouth. They don't care about you—some human-raised mage. You are an abomination. You would have made a beautiful vampire, truly wasted on the animals."

I edge toward the bathroom, pulse pounding in my ears, but I keep my gaze fixed on his, refusing to break eye contact.

"I'm telling you the truth," Leonidas continues. "This place? A fortress? And yet, here I am." He spreads his arms wide. "You even left the door open for me, and still, you have no idea you have been played. It's quite remarkable."

He tilts his head. "Ah, and now you are thinking of Paul. Your husband... ex-husband... the poor little man." He smacks his lips. "Paul tasted very bitter. You will never find his body. Just like"—he steps closer, voice lowering—"they will never find yours."

His hands morph, fingers lengthening into razor-sharp obsidian claws.

Nausea rises, but I force it down. Calling on every shred of courage, I channel shifter magic into my nails, pushing the change. My fingers tingle as my nails sharpen into vicious claws. My jaw aches, wolf teeth filling my mouth, the fangs pressing against my lips.

"You are not the only one who can bite," I say, my words thick and lisping around the new canines. My fangs are strong, built for shredding flesh.

A growl boils up from my chest, low and primal. "Come on, then, vampire," I challenge, sinking into a fighting stance. My muscles coil, ready to spring.

Leonidas hisses, red eyes aflame with fury. He moves faster than I can track, launching himself through the air with claws outstretched and aimed for my throat.

Chapter Forty-Five

I THROW MYSELF BACKWARDS, twisting just enough to feel the whisper of air as his razor-sharp claws slice past my face.

Too close.

He's too fast.

I'm going to die.

Leonidas laughs and lunges, his snarling face filling my vision. His claws are mere centimetres from my throat when a surge of magic explodes through the room. The force is violent, slamming into the vampire. His red eyes widen in shock as he freezes mid-strike, locked in place by the spell.

He is solid.

Frozen.

I crash onto the floor, pain shooting up my spine from

the jarring impact. My breath comes in short, frantic gasps as I scramble backwards, my shoulders hitting the wall.

That wasn't me. That was not my magic. I didn't even think of using it.

Powerful energy crackles in the air, buzzing across my skin like static. Whatever spell holds Leonidas is potent, thrumming like a live wire. Yet it didn't touch me, even though I was right there.

"What the heck just happened?" I whisper, pressing a trembling hand to my chest. Was it the building's magic?

The answer strides through the French doors, calm and unhurried. Lander's wand spins lazily between his fingers as he gives me a wave, his smug smile broadening as he surveys the immobilised vampire.

Before I can process his presence, the main door bursts open. Merrick and Riker charge in, their expressions feral.

I blink, my body still shaking so violently that my vision blurs. Merrick crosses the room in three swift strides and scoops me into his arms, his hands roaming over me in a frantic search for injuries.

He's here. He came for me.

This is all my fault.

"Are you hurt?"

"I'm okay," I rasp, my throat raw.

Merrick came for me just like he promised.

He pulls me close, his lips grazing my forehead. "I've got you," he murmurs. "You are safe now. We got him."

A sob breaks free, and I collapse against his chest, clinging to him as though he might vanish. Everything feels too raw—too much—but he is here.

That was too close. Far too close.

"Merrick!" Lander's sharp voice cuts through the moment.

Merrick pulls back reluctantly, his thumb skimming my cheek. His expression is shadowed with guilt and something darker—something I can't quite name. "I need to handle this," he says quietly. "I will be right there."

I nod, unable to form words.

"Stay here. You are safe now."

Riker offers me a small, reassuring smile and a quick wink as he follows Merrick. "Nice chompers," he teases, tapping his teeth.

Chompers? My hand flies to my mouth, and I realise my teeth are still wolfed out. Mortified, I focus on pulling the shifter magic back. Slowly, my teeth and claws shrink, returning to normal.

My knees threaten to buckle, but I force myself to move. I grab my necklace from the bathroom, fumbling to secure it around my neck. The cool weight offers a thin veneer of security. Back in the main room, I shove my feet into my boots, craving something solid beneath me.

Still shaking, I edge closer to the group. I need to see what they do with the vampire—and I need to tell Merrick the truth, that Leonidas has been in my head, pillaging my thoughts.

I'm the mole.

And Paul—Paul's dead.

My stomach twists, but I shove down the sob that threatens to erupt.

One thing at a time, Lark. One thing at a time.

"We got him, then," Lander says, voice aggravatingly

casual. He claps Merrick on the back, grin widening. "Great plan, pal."

Plan? What plan?

I clear my throat, my voice small as I ask, "Can you tell me what is going on?"

But my question is lost under Merrick's vicious growl. The frozen ancient vampire and the Alpha Prime lock eyes, both radiating raw fury as they size each other up. Leonidas's red gaze burns, but behind that mad arrogance, I see a flicker of unease.

"I know about the blood-borne link," Merrick snarls.

I flinch, dread curling in my stomach.

"I knew for certain you were in Lark's head after the Human First stunt," he continues. "There was no way you could have found those men without inside help. I spoke to Lander, and together, we arranged the Council meeting here in the Magic Sector." His voice hardens. "We knew you wouldn't be able to resist hunting Lark here. Every single step to trap you was meticulously planned."

Oh no.

"In your arrogance," Merrick growls, "you walked right into it."

"Here's the daylight spell," Lander says, tossing a bright yellow vial.

Merrick catches it without breaking eye contact with the vampire. A cruel smile reveals the sharp edges of his teeth. "Once you knew she was mine," he says, his voice low and dangerous, "you should've stayed far away. Hunting my fated mate? This was never going to end well for you."

With no hesitation, Merrick plunges his hand into the

frozen barrier around Leonidas. The second their skin meets, the vial's magic activates in a blinding flash of light.

I shield my eyes, heart pounding, every nerve on fire.

When the light fades, and I look again, the vampire is gone. Nothing remains but a dark pile of ash scattered across the floor.

It's over. Leonidas is dead.

I sway on my feet, lightheaded, and my head spins as Merrick's words echo in my mind, louder and sharper with every beat of my heart:

"I know about the blood-borne link."

"I knew for certain you were in Lark's head after the Human First stunt."

They knew.

They knew the vampire was in my mind, violating my thoughts, stealing every private moment.

They didn't stop him.

They used me.

I. Was. Bait.

The realisation hits like a hammer to my chest, knocking the breath from my lungs. An ache swells in my throat. My legs threaten to give way beneath the weight of it.

They planned this.

And my heart... my heart shatters.

Chapter Forty-Six

I WRAP my arms around my waist, hunch my shoulders, and lower my gaze to the gleaming chequered tiles beneath my feet. It's all so obvious now. They played me for a fool. On that, the vampire was right—I was being played by everyone, even those I trusted.

Was all the animosity between Merrick and Lander an act? No wonder Lander knew everything about the shit-show of my life. Merrick must have told him. At least when I was an unwitting mole, I had no idea what was happening. Merrick, though, knew exactly what he was doing.

I'm so tired—tired of men refusing to see me as their equal, tired of being treated like a pawn in someone else's game. I can see why he did it, why it all unfolded this way, but understanding doesn't mean I forgive him. This isn't how a new relationship should start—especially not one built on trust.

We have walked through fire together, yet I've been burned to ash. It's always *me* burning.

The broken pieces of my trust feel beyond repair. Merrick stomped on my feelings as though they were nothing. One man already did that to me; I vowed it wouldn't happen again.

I drift over to the dresser, pick up the grimoire, and clutch it to my chest like a shield. Around me, the room seethes with activity as shifters and magic users hurry in and out, dealing with the aftermath of the vampire's attack. It all feels distant, as though I'm watching through frosted glass.

Tears threaten, but I refuse to let them fall. Instead, a slow, simmering anger rises in my chest. For twenty agonising minutes, I was drowning in guilt, believing I'd let Merrick—and everyone else—down. Meanwhile, he knew the truth and never told me. Days of planning went on behind my back.

I shake my head, closing my eyes. A lone tear escapes anyway, and I swipe it away, furious with myself.

No. None of that, Lark. None of that.

"Are you all right?"

His voice makes me flinch. When did he get so close?

I open my eyes to find Merrick watching me, concern etched into his features. "We couldn't tell you," he says quietly. "If you had known, it wouldn't have worked. You were never really in danger. If we'd stopped him reading your thoughts, he would have suspected something, and we would have lost control of the situation. This way, we set the terms. Everything stayed contained."

"Did Mary know?" My voice sounds hollow, drained of feeling.

"No," he replies. "She didn't. Most of the council didn't either—just Lander. He is Chief of Security; this was his operation. It was kept on a need-to-know basis. It was a well-executed plan."

"Well-executed," I echo dully. "Yeah. You got him."

"You are safe," he says, his tone gentle, as if that alone could fix everything.

"Safe." The word tastes bitter. I nod mechanically, then turn away. "Thanks for keeping me safe."

"Little mate—"

"Don't call me that." My voice snaps like a whip. "I thought we were a team, Merrick—that we'd talk things through, make decisions together. But we're not, are we? I'm just a convenient pawn."

"You are not a convenience, and you are not a pawn," he says, his voice cracking. "I love you, Lark. I'd do anything to protect you."

"Even if it means keeping me in the dark?"

"Yes," he says without hesitation.

His admission slices through me like a blade. I press my hand to my chest, trying to ease the ache. "Fine," I say softly. "Can we talk about this later?"

"Lark, we need to talk now." He growls, a low note of warning in his voice.

I snap. "Don't you dare growl at me, Merrick Winters." My voice rises, thick with anger. "You want to do this here? Fine." I gesture at the crowded room. "Safe, you say? I had a *fascinating* conversation with the vampire—for at least ten minutes, Merrick. *Ten minutes.* While he gloated about how much fun it was to rummage through my head. He was *this* close to ripping my throat out before the magic finally kicked in and stopped him. What were you waiting for, exactly?"

His face pales, horror spreading across his features. "What?"

"Oh yeah, did your buddy Lander fail to mention that?" My hands shake with rage.

From the corner of my eye, I see Riker slam Lander against the glass doors, rattling them. He jabs a finger in Lander's face, while Lander holds up his hands defensively. Whatever excuses he's making drip with enough smugness to stoke Riker's temper further.

I shake my head. It's too late; the damage has already been done. "I'm tired of everyone steamrolling over my choices," I say, my voice trembling. "Don't you understand? I feel violated. And I'm heartbroken—"

My throat closes once again around the surge of emotion, but I press on. "The last time I felt like this was when I was fifteen, and the human government sterilised me for not being 'good enough.' Do you understand what that does to a person? And then, years later, I found the man I chose to spend my life with—buried inside my big sister."

Yet stupid me still trusted Merrick.

"Another few seconds tonight, and I'd be dead. I'm sorry Lander's timing wasn't perfect—really, I am. Then you could have walked away without the burden of a fated mate."

"Lark—" he begins, but I cut him off.

"I'm a sigma," I say, my tone rigid and cold as I lift my chin, "a lone wolf according to your own laws. I don't want a pack, nor do I need a fated mate. I can't return to the Human Sector, so, Alpha Prime, I'm formally requesting to live and work in the Enterprise Zone. Unless that's been taken from me too. Do I still have a job, an apartment? Or should I stay here in the Magic Sector?"

I refuse to look at him. I can't face the pain in his eyes, the silent anguish I know is there. It would only weaken my resolve.

"You can go back to your job and your home in the Enterprise Zone," he whispers.

"Thank you," I reply sharply, allowing myself the briefest glance at him. "Now leave me the fuck alone."

CHAPTER FORTY-SEVEN

I'VE BEEN STAYING LATE at work, grasping at any excuse to avoid going home, but the inevitable can't be postponed forever. As I walk past security, the guards give me odd looks, their gazes lingering like I've grown a second head. Their disapproval is almost tangible.

I ignore them, my trainers squeaking on the polished floor as I push through the doors into the stormy evening. The summer sky churns above, dark and brooding. The wind carries the scent of rain, tangling my hair and biting through my coat. I pull the fabric tighter and hunch my shoulders as I walk.

Paws echo softly behind me.

In my spare time, I've been designing better sensory bands. The Ministry of Magic has already introduced replacements after the old ones were exposed as dangerously flawed—a scandal that caused quite an uproar.

I quicken my pace, passing the oak tree and the empty plot where the wizard's house once stood. The residual magic hums faintly against my senses.

When I reach my building, the grey wolf trailing me watches me go inside.

Because I refused to speak to Merrick, he decided the best way to handle my rejection was by following me everywhere in his wolf form.

He won't let me go.

I give Matthew a quick wave as I pass the security desk. He waves back, his gaze flicking briefly to the wolf before pretending he sees nothing. The lift dings softly, and I step inside.

If I ignore the steady presence of the wolf shadowing me, it's almost as though my life has returned to normal, as if I've never had an epic adventure that upended everything.

I avoid the blond, nosy neighbour—Riker—who conveniently moved in across the hall.

Inside my apartment, I set Hatty on her book stand and make a half-hearted attempt at dinner, more from habit than hunger. Then I settle on the sofa, flipping through television channels until I land on an apocalypse film. I've developed a strange fascination with them—there's something grimly satisfying about watching worlds crumble while people fight to survive. It puts my problems into perspective. They feel smaller by comparison.

Hours pass in a blur of explosions, desperate protagonists, and collapsing cities, but eventually, I find myself drawn to the window. It's foolish, I know. My heart tugs before my feet can argue. I sigh, wander over, and lift the curtain a few centimetres.

There he is on the grass below the balcony, curled into a ball with his head resting on his paws, gazing right back at me.

It's raining.

For two weeks, this has been his routine—trailing me to work, following me home, then spending the nights outside my building, staring at my window. He is my big furry shadow.

The weather was decent until now, but as July settles in, the heavens have opened.

Using my shifter magic, I focus on him. Raindrops cling to his fur and drip off his nose.

"Bloody wolf," I mutter under my breath. "Why won't he just get lost?"

It's easier to stay angry than admit how much I miss him, but after two weeks, my hurt is wearing thin.

What will he do when winter arrives? The cold will be brutal. Yes, his coat will keep him warm, but he is not just a wolf—he is a man. A man reduced to this. I wonder if people are laughing at him, and I worry what this will do to his reputation.

He looks so sad.

I turn away, yank the curtains closed, and flop onto the sofa. The television is still on, but I can't concentrate.

My fated mate is outside in the rain, and I'm just sitting here. This is bloody ridiculous.

With a frustrated growl, I snatch a fluffy towel from the airing cupboard, stomp down the hall, and grab my keys and building pass. After putting on my trainers, I head downstairs and outside.

"Get in here!" I snap at the wolf.

His head is lowered, tail tucked, the drenched wolf tries to make himself smaller. He is soaked through as he follows me inside.

Matthew watches with wide eyes. I ignore him, throw the towel over Merrick, and dry him off with more vigour than necessary.

"You can't leave water everywhere—someone might slip. Your stinky fur is dripping," I grumble, rubbing harder than I need to.

Merrick, of course, does not smell. His coat is glossy and clean, but I don't want to acknowledge it. He stands patiently, fixing me with those big blue eyes as I work from head to tail.

His tongue lolls out when I dry his belly.

"Shut up," I mutter.

"Alpha Prime," Matthew says quietly, bowing his head in respect.

I roll my eyes and step into the lift, Merrick padding beside me. He sits obediently by my leg as we ride up, the damp towel dripping in my hand.

When we reach my apartment, I open the door, and he follows me inside.

"Don't you dare shift," I warn, tossing the towel into the washing machine.

I fill a bowl with water and take a couple of raw steaks from the fridge. He has been losing weight, and I can't stand seeing his ribs show. Placing the steaks on the floor next to the water bowl, I turn on my heel and march to my bedroom, slamming the door behind me.

In my dressing room, I change into pyjamas, then slam myself onto the bed, fluffing the pillow with more force than necessary.

With the covers pulled up to my chin, I listen to the rain and the soft tap-tap-tap of Merrick's claws pacing the hallway. At last, I hear the door creak as he settles, leaning against it.

I growl under my breath and close my eyes, but sleep does not come.

I'm being childish and cruel.

I've never been one to use the silent treatment—it's such an arsehole move, an awful tactic. Yet here I am, doing exactly that. It wasn't my intention. I broke up with him; that should've been the end.

But getting rid of a shifter, a fated mate, is harder than it sounds.

He has decided to be my self-appointed bodyguard.

I don't know who's running his empire while he's out here playing the world's saddest stalker. Perhaps he is secretly working when I'm not looking.

What do I do with him?

I miss him. I... I love him. I wouldn't be so hurt by his plan to catch Leonidas if I didn't love him. But can I forgive him?

Chapter Forty-Eight

UNABLE TO BEAR the weight of my thoughts, I get up and creep to the door. I crack it open, and his ears perk up as he lifts his head to look at me. His eyes brim with longing and something that looks suspiciously like guilt.

"How long are you going to do this?" I whisper, exasperated. "You are driving me mad."

He whines, then rolls onto his back, offering his belly in complete submission.

"Don't do that," I say, folding my arms. "You are making me feel bad, and this is your fault. You're the one who used me as bait to trap a psychotic vampire."

He rolls over and whines again, quieter this time.

I sigh, feeling my resolve begin to crack. "Would you like to set a time to talk?" I ask tentatively.

He nods at once, his tail giving a small wag.

"All right," I say. "We can talk. Maybe have breakfast—"

He shifts in an instant, so seamless and smooth it's as if magic itself holds its breath. Suddenly, he is standing there —gloriously, infuriatingly naked. All sculpted muscle, golden skin, and blatant confidence.

I roll my eyes. "I didn't mean now," I huff, keeping my gaze firmly above his neck.

He is so impossibly handsome. I once thought clean-shaven Merrick was the pinnacle of masculine beauty, but now, seeing him with stubble, I realise I was wrong. The roughness of his facial hair gives him a raw, primal quality that somehow makes him even more breathtaking.

And his eyes.

Bloody hell, his eyes. They are achingly sad, and the sight of them sends a keen ache straight to my chest.

My heart hurts.

I want to launch myself into his arms, to lose myself in his warmth and strength—but I can't.

I can't...

Can I?

Sometimes you have to stand your ground, be true to yourself.

Sometimes you have to admit you were wrong.

If he had hurt me deliberately, there would be no question—he could spend ten years following me, and my resolve wouldn't budge. But he didn't hurt me on purpose. He trusted the wrong person, yet did he truly have a choice?

What would I have done if our roles were reversed?

I'd want him to forgive me.

He messed up.

He did it out of love. And he will make mistakes again

—maybe even big ones, just as I will. Can I be cruel enough to deny us both a chance at happiness?

His eyes search mine, soft and brimming with something that steals my breath. They move over my face, slow and deliberate, as though he is studying something precious, he can't bear to lose.

He is looking at me as if I'm precious.

When I look at him, I see forever. My happiness is right there, within reach—all I have to do is take a leap.

My vision blurs as tears well in my eyes. I sniff, tilting my head back to stare at the ceiling, desperate to hold them at bay. But my whole body trembles, struggling to stay composed. When I finally exhale, it's a shaky breath that escapes as a small, wounded sound. I sense him stir.

A tear slides down the side of my nose. I swipe it away with the heel of my hand.

Then suddenly, he is there.

His hand cups my face, warm and steady, his thumb gently clearing the tear's path. Another tear falls, but he catches that too, his touch unwavering and patient. A low, soft rumble resonates in his chest—something I've never heard before. It takes me a moment to realise he's purring.

Wolf shifters can purr?

He steps closer, wrapping his arms around me. My cheek settles against his bare chest, and I'm enveloped in his warmth and comforting scent. The purr deepens, and the bass hums through me, soothing the tangled mass of hurt and stress, melting the tension in my muscles, and stilling the storm raging in my head.

Merrick feels safe.

For the first time in weeks, I feel safe.

Leaning against him, it's as though the broken pieces inside me finally begin to slot back into place.

"I love you, Lark," he murmurs, his voice thick with emotion. "I will always love you. And if you decide you can't forgive me, I will still love you. I will protect you for the rest of my life, because my world does not make sense without you. My life means nothing if I don't have you."

I lift my head, and his eyes—those beautiful, piercing eyes—glisten with unshed tears. Seeing this strong, steadfast man laid bare before me twists something deep inside.

Guilt and shame bubble up, knowing I've pushed him to this point.

Yet love follows, overwhelming and undeniable love.

"You lit up my world like the sun breaking through a storm," he goes on quietly. "You made me realise how lost I was. Because when I'm not near you, I feel it—sharp, unbearable. Missing you hurts, Lark. It's like a physical pain."

He pauses, resting his forehead gently against mine. His breath is warm and steady, yet electric with unspoken feeling.

"Losing you because I misjudged things was the worst moment of my life. The vampire used magic to breach the wards, disrupting Lander's freezing spell—it didn't trigger until that magic was displaced. When he attacked you, the spell finally activated, but it was too close. Too damn close. I should've planned for everything. I should have known."

His jaw tightens, and he exhales in frustration. "I hate myself for risking you. I hate that I failed you. I don't ever want you to feel that fear again. Not from me, not from anyone."

"You didn't fail me," I whisper.

He shakes his head, his voice raw. "I did. But I won't fail you again. As long as I'm breathing, I will protect you. Always."

His hand brushes my cheek, his thumb tracing a gentle path over my skin. "Please, Lark," he says, voice cracking. "Forgive me?"

The desperation in his gaze is nearly unbearable.

"Okay," I whisper, the word slipping out before I can think.

I see my own surprise echoed in his eyes, but he keeps me close.

"You are it for me, Lark. I will never stop fighting for us."

"I'm sorry," I manage, choking on the words. "I was terrified—so much was happening, and I didn't know how to cope. That's why I was so angry with you. It was all too much. I'm so sorry."

His fingers slide into my hair, massaging my scalp with disarming gentleness.

"I love you," I say, my voice quiet but laden with everything I've held back.

Merrick's arms tighten around me, his breath catching as he holds me. Each unspoken vow hums between us in every heartbeat.

I once thought the breakdown of my marriage was the worst thing that could ever happen to me. But now I see it was only the beginning—a painful shove toward a destiny I'd never imagined, a fate waiting for me all along.

It didn't break me; it transformed me.

Like a butterfly, I emerged from the wreckage stronger,

freer, and finally ready to embrace the life I was meant to have.

"The storm's passed. Would you like to go for a run?" Merrick asks softly.

"A run?"

"As wolves," he clarifies, a teasing smile curving his lips.

Before I can reply, a muffled voice calls through the front door. "I can drive. I will get the car."

I groan, pinching the bridge of my nose. "Was he eavesdropping this whole time?" I whisper, mortified.

Merrick does not bother hiding his amusement. "Probably."

"I've got you some clothes, Alpha," Riker's voice chimes in. "I will leave them at the door. Don't want your bare arse on the leather."

"Bloody nosy bear," I mutter, drawing a deep chuckle from Merrick.

"But if you two are keeping this 'fated mate' thing going," Riker continues, "you might want to invest in soundproofing. The whole Sector doesn't need to hear how much you lo—"

"Riker," Merrick growls, voice low and warning. "Not tonight."

Riker laughs, evidently undeterred. "All right, all right. I will meet you by the car."

Chapter Forty-Nine

Bonus Scene 1 - The Hotel
Merrick's point of view

The moment I step into the hotel lobby, a faint thrumming prickles beneath my skin, like an itch I can't scratch. My gaze sweeps the room, instincts sharpening before I consciously assess the space. It's clean, quiet, and entirely unremarkable.

Except for her.

My eyes lock on the woman sitting on the lobby sofa, a laptop at her side. Her scent strikes me before I fully register her presence—warm and faintly sweet, like strawberries, vanilla, and sunshine. The realisation hits like a blow to my chest, and my beast stirs.

No. Not possible.

I freeze mid-stride. From her profile, she seems ordinary enough—casual, comfortable, a hint of weariness in her posture. She adjusts the cheap jumper she is wearing, tugging at the sleeves as though shielding herself from the world. Nothing about her matches what I expected from the Ministry's newest IT recruit. Certainly not this.

Mine.

I shove the thought away and keep moving, each step deliberate and steady, though my instincts scream otherwise. I didn't come here to claim a mate. I came to deliver documents, vet a new hire with Human First ties, and discreetly investigate a potential security breach near the border. Routine.

Routine for anyone else, perhaps, but not for me. I don't play courier, and I've never vetted a new hire in person—especially not a human. Yet here I am, staring at my mate while fate conspires to upend my carefully constructed plans. I can't afford distractions, especially not pretty ones like her.

Still, a flicker of satisfaction sparks when her eyes lift to meet mine. They widen, surprise and vulnerability flickering across her face before she glances away, flustered. She is trying to compose herself, but I notice the signs—her quickened pulse, the subtle shift in her scent, attraction and nervousness laced with a sharper edge of defiance.

Interesting.

I approach, movements controlled and presence deliberate. She looks up, meeting my gaze with a challenge in her beautiful brown eyes. It's so hard not to smile. This human, barely half my size, is staring me down. Feisty. Brave. Possibly foolish, but the primal part of me appreciates it.

I stop in front of her, and for a moment, everything else fades. Her lips part slightly, as though she wants to speak but hesitates. The urge to lean closer—close the space between us—drums dangerously in my chest.

She is extraordinary.

"Mrs Emerson," I say, letting the name linger like a bitter taste. Restraint burns in my chest, holding back the simmering fire. If I dwell on what that name implies—on the man who tied her to it—I might tear this entire place apart.

"Yes, that's me." Her voice is polite and professional, but there's a steely edge beneath it. "Are you the courier for the Ministry?"

"Something like that." A faint twitch at the corner of my mouth betrays my amusement. It's not a lie, but hardly the whole truth.

Her brow furrows momentarily, doubt glimmering in her expression. She suspects I'm mocking her. I extend my hand. "May I see some identification?"

"Yeah, sure." She fumbles in the pocket of her oversized jogging bottoms, pulling out a plastic card. The motion is ungraceful but somehow endearing, entirely unguarded.

My fated mate is captivating—naturally beautiful, no matter what she wears. Her baggy clothes don't hide her curves.

When our fingers almost brush, I sense the tiniest tremor. She is anxious but trying to hide it.

I take the card, studying it longer than necessary—not to confirm her identity but to absorb her name. Significant. Important.

My mate.

Lark.

Lark Emerson.

Lark Winters, my wolf growls.

I flick the card back to her, the gesture casual.

"Okay, well, thank you," she says, accepting both the ID and the envelope of documents. She balances the hefty package on her knees. "Thank you for coming and dropping this off." Her wave towards the exit is almost dismissive, as though to usher me away. My beast rumbles, amused.

There is so much fire in her, hidden beneath nerves and exhaustion.

"No, Mrs Emerson. I must wait for you to review the documents and, if necessary, sign them."

Her brows shoot up. "I thought it was just paperwork for me to look over." She frowns at the envelope. "That's... unconventional."

"It might take some time," she warns, glancing at me uncertainly. "Would you like to take a seat?"

"No, I'm fine." I clasp my hands behind my back, forcing a parade-rest posture. The effort not to close the distance—to comfort her—burns through me.

Her gaze flicks around, unsure what to make of me.

Good. Let her wonder.

She examines the wax seal, humming softly. My wolf stirs, unsettled and intrigued. She is so unaware of the world she is entering, yet her scent reveals a hidden strength.

And she is *mine*.

I bite back the possessive growl clawing at my throat. Not here. Not now. Maybe not ever.

Her fingers brush the enchanted parchment as she

draws out the documents. The spell embedded within them activates, its faint magical aura rippling through my senses.

She flinches, shaking the paper as though it burned her. "Ouch! Stop that," she mutters.

A hint of a smile tugs at my lips. She is entirely endearing, utterly adorable. But I can't have her think I'm laughing at her expense. Schooling my features into a neutral mask, I let my gaze drift toward the glass doors, feigning disinterest.

CHAPTER FIFTY

BONUS SCENE 2 - THE MEETING
MERRICK'S POINT OF VIEW

THE AIR in the room grows heavy as I step inside. Paul, in the middle of a tantrum, freezes at the sight of me. His narrow shoulders square, a futile attempt at appearing intimidating. He is already lost, and he knows it.

He looks like hell.

Dove—the sister—straightens abruptly, her talon-like grip on Paul's arm vanishing as though I've caught her in the act. Her gaze snaps to me, pupils dilating as she sizes me up. She flicks out her tongue to wet her lips, tossing her hair over one shoulder in a practised move meant to be alluring.

Then comes the laugh—a high-pitched, grating sound drenched in insincerity. It's the kind of laugh meant to bait, to spark interest in a mate. But it misses its mark entirely and only sets my teeth on edge.

Her scent shifts, a cloying mixture of nerves and misdirected bravado. I resist the urge to wrinkle my nose. It's not just unappealing; it's the stench of desperation.

Pathetic.

I keep my expression impassive. The last thing I want is to encourage her—or hurt Lark.

How could anyone choose this woman over my mate? Someone so weak. My eyes narrow as I glance at Paul. A fool. Only a fool.

Behind me, Barry—Lark's solicitor—enters, juggling his files with a slight smile. Lark's sad eyes flick to mine for a brief moment, her composure unwavering despite the stench of desperation wafting from the two across the table.

I'm sorry, little mate. This farce of a meeting will be over soon.

Barry speaks first, cutting through the brittle hush. "Apologies for the delay. I had to complete some additional revisions pertaining to this case." He sits beside Lark and offers her a kind smile, lowering his voice so the humans won't overhear. "How are you holding up?"

"I'm managing," she replies softly, her silver eyes drifting to the sensory band on her wrist.

"Good to see you have got a band. That'll help immensely," Barry says, patting his files. "Let's get this done quickly."

I move to the head of the table and pour myself a glass of water, taking my time. I allow the silence to drag on, long enough to unsettle them, then fix my gaze on the Fool.

"Mr Emerson."

Paul responds immediately, slamming his hand on the table. "Who the hell are you?" he demands. His whiny voice slices through the tension and puts my bodyguards on edge.

I'm unimpressed.

Ignoring his outburst, I open the top folder, skimming its contents. "What can I do for you, Mr Emerson?"

He hits the table again. "I'm here to get my wife!"

I tilt my head. "Are you now? Did you lose her?"

I know what you did, you pathetic little man. And if you slam your hand once more, I will rip your arm off.

"Don't play games, you filthy beast," he snarls, leaning forward as if proximity might intimidate me. "I told you on the phone—we had a disagreement, and now she's taken a job with the Ministry. I want to talk to her. I want her to come home. Whatever contract she has with you animals is null and void. She's human. She doesn't belong here."

My stare does not waver. "Mrs Emerson is an adult and perfectly capable of making her own decisions. Can you tell me why she left?"

Paul's face darkens. "That's none of your business."

I shift my focus to Lark. "But I'd like to know."

Before the Fool can retort, Dove jumps in, her voice sickly sweet. "It was just a little misunderstanding. A tiny quarrel, nothing major."

I raise a brow in disbelief. "A small misunderstanding? She moved to an entirely different sector to get away from her husband. That's quite the disagreement. And you are?"

"I'm her sister, Dove," she says, flashing a practised smile that's too eager, too contrived. She is desperate for attention. "We have been so worried about her. She's not well, you see. It runs in the family—on *her* father's side."

Lark's father's side, right... "That sounds serious."

"It is," Dove confides, as though imparting some dreadful secret. Her little act is pitiful.

Standing at the back of the room, Riker remains the picture of professional detachment—except for the finger he sticks in his mouth as he pretends to gag. Subtle as ever, my second-in-command and best friend. At least someone else appreciates how absurd this all is.

He gets it.

Paul changes tack, his tone becoming plaintive. "Look, I love my wife. I'd never hurt her intentionally. This whole divorce thing is ridiculous. She can't just leave me!"

He calls what he did to her *love*. The Fool is seething. Lark leaving him has not just bruised his pride—it's shattered it. His fragile ego lies in ruins, and it's clear he has no idea how to handle the fallout.

Without her, he is left with nothing.

Only now, in the wreckage of her absence, does he grasp the magnitude of what he's done—what he has lost. The best thing that could have ever happened to him has slipped through his fingers, all because of his selfishness.

I've had enough of his lies and excuses. Lark is mine. The audacity—coming here together, unwashed and stinking of each other, is beyond galling. "You both reek of each other. Do you and Mrs Emerson have an open relationship?"

Paul sputters, his face flushing an angry red.

Dove freezes, her sickly, desperate smile faltering.

A glint of satisfaction flashes in Lark's eyes as she leans back.

Good.

I'm going to rip these two fool's little lives apart. Paul's arrogance, Dove's vomit-inducing attempts at seduction—they are like midges buzzing at my ears. I'm more than ready to swat them.

"Mrs Emerson recorded a home video before she left you." My tone is measured, but the weight of the words shifts the air in the room. Paul stiffens; Dove blinks, failing to grasp the gravity of the situation.

"If you would," I say, gesturing for Lark to proceed. I make sure not to use her name.

Lark slides the laptop to the centre of the table. Her motions are precise, her expression neutral, but I can see the strain in her shoulders and sense how much effort it costs. This moment is tearing her apart more than anyone else realises.

She presses play, and the room resonates with muted sounds and betrayal.

Paul reacts instantly. His chair screeches violently as he bolts to his feet, his face twisted with fury. He lunges for the laptop like a cornered animal, but Riker is faster. My second-in-command snatches the device and tucks it under his arm with a grin full of teeth.

Riker likes my feisty mate, and I bet he hates this prick.

"Now, now," he drawls lazily. "No destroying Ministry property, Mr Emerson. Did you have that temper with your wife?" He takes a step back, daring Paul to make a move. The guards close ranks beside him, a silent wall of muscle.

Paul puffs up, red-faced, like a rooster preparing to fight. "I would never lay a hand on her!" he shouts, clenching his fists.

"No, you wouldn't," I agree lightly. "But you would have awful sex with her sister."

Dove's cheeks darken scarlet. "Awful?" she squeaks. "It wasn't awful!"

"It *looked* awful," Riker mutters, enjoying himself. "Like you were having some sort of episode."

The room is stunned into silence, and I capitalise on it. "Let's try this again, shall we? With the truth this time. Your wife, Mrs Emerson, caught you in the act with her sister. She recorded it because she knew you would deny it —as you have done repeatedly."

Barry, the consummate professional, shakes his head and jots notes in his file.

Paul's fists tremble, his face darkening.

Dove, apparently unaware of the need for self-preservation, blurts, "We didn't think she'd be home! Paul said she'd be working late, that she had a big project. We didn't think it would hurt anyone."

I lean forward, my voice slicing through her excuses and lies like a knife. "You didn't think it would hurt anyone? Did it never occur to you, even for a second, how deeply it would shatter Lark to find out you were sneaking around with her husband? You didn't think she'd notice her sheets reeking of the two of you?"

Dove looks honestly offended. "I'd have changed the sheets," she says, as though that's a valid defence. Then, with unmitigated gall, she adds, "Lark needs to come home, and we can continue as we were. I mean, we need her salary to keep the house!"

I blink, letting her words hang in the air. "Charming," I say flatly.

I can't kill them—Lark would be upset. But in a few years, perhaps I could arrange a little *accident*.

Time to wrap this up. I motion to Barry, who slides a document across the table to Paul's solicitor. The man skims it briefly, then stands to gather his things.

"We're done here," the solicitor announces briskly, not sparing Paul so much as a glance.

Paul's face twists in fury. "Where the hell do you think you're going?" he snaps. "I paid you a fortune to be here!"

"There's not enough money in the world to fix *this*," the man replies, straightening his tie. "Your wife is no longer your problem. The marriage has been annulled."

"Annulled?" Paul's voice cracks, disbelief and outrage warring for dominance. "That's bullshit! You can't annul nearly thirty years of marriage!"

Barry taps the papers in front of him. "The law says otherwise," he remarks simply. "Here's your copy for reference."

Paul snatches the documents, scanning them furiously. "It says here she was mauled by a shifter. What the hell does that mean? Is she dead?"

Dove gasps in theatrical horror, grabbing his arm like she is auditioning for a soap opera. "Lark's dead? Oh my God, my poor sister! A shifter killed her? Who's going to help me with—"

"WILL YOU SHUT UP!" Paul roars, silencing her. He glares at me, his face a mask of rage. "What does this *mean*?"

"It means your wife is no longer human," I explain calmly. "She is a ward of the Shifter Sector now. Her marriage to you is void, as she is legally considered deceased in the human world. All her property is being transferred to the Ministry."

I watch the words sink in—or fail to. Paul's anger clouds his limited comprehension. His expression contorts, unable to accept the truth. It has not registered yet that I've stripped him of everything.

Not yet.

The Fool's anger overrides any shred of logic. By the time it sinks in, he will be lucky to own a pair of socks, let alone crawl back to whatever semblance of life he had before.

"She's turned into a monster," Paul spits, his tone dripping venom.

A growl rumbles in my chest. *You want to see a monster? I will gladly show you one, you pathetic excuse for a man.*

"Did she agree to this? Was this part of her job?"

"No," I say evenly. "Unfortunately, Lark was attacked while saving a colleague from harm. She is an incredibly brave woman."

The words bounce off his thick skull. He's not listening.

"That's everything you will need for your records. If you can move out tonight, the Ministry will be selling the house and all joint assets. You will receive your share once the process is complete."

"They're selling the house?" Dove whines. "But how can you?" Her nails dig into Paul's arm, her desperation palpable. I wonder if he even notices—or if he is too used to the pain by now.

She is disgusting. Always grasping, always clawing for what she believes is hers.

"It's all legally binding," Barry interjects with a casual shrug.

Paul's hand trembles as he stabs a finger at the papers. "What's this name here?" His voice rises, thick with jealousy and confusion. "This isn't her maiden name! Who is this Winters? Why has her surname changed?"

I glance at Lark, meeting her confused frown with a calm, deliberate expression.

"Lark, do you have anything to add?" I ask gently.

Her expression flickers with horror, but she quickly shakes her head. "Uh... no, I'm fine. Thank you."

Paul's head snaps toward her at the sound of her voice. His eyes widen, and for the first time, he truly *looks*. He stares at her in shock. "Lark?" he croaks. "Lark?"

Dove's shrill voice slices through the tension. "But... but you're *beautiful*!" she cries, eyeing Lark with mingled confusion and envy.

She has always been beautiful, you fake bitch. My teeth grind, but I maintain my composure.

"What on earth happened to you?" Dove demands, suspicion darkening her gaze as jealousy seeps through. "You look like... our great-grandmother. Is that what happens when someone becomes a shifter?"

My smile is cold and sharp. "Well, your marriage is annulled, and this meeting is over. You can both leave now."

I catch Riker's eye and give him a subtle nod. He responds with a grin full of teeth, feral and eager. Behind him, the guards shift into position, ready to ensure these two are escorted out swiftly and without incident.

"Why Winters?" Paul persists.

"Oh, isn't it obvious in the documents?" I reply, letting my smile sharpen. "Section four, paragraph seven. Lark *Winters* has taken her mate's name."

"Mate?" Paul and Dove echo, their voices overlapping in disbelief.

I meet Lark's wide eyes, then turn back to the unhappy pair. "Oh yes. Lark will soon be mated to the Alpha Prime."

"The *Alpha Prime*?" Dove screeches, her grip on Paul tightening as if he is her only lifeline.

"Yes." My grin widens, wolfish and unapologetic. "*Me*."

Their reactions are priceless—Paul's fury, Dove's shock, and Lark's dawning realisation.

I meet her gaze and hold it. She does not fully understand yet. But she will.

Her life isn't just about to change—it's about to transform the world.

And I will be there, every step of the way.

I will fight for her. Protect her. She is mine—now and always.

BITTEN VAMPIRE

THE BITTEN CHRONICLES

BROGAN THOMAS

The wizard's house groans as it settles onto the rubbish-strewn plot of land at the edge of the Vampire Sector.

Dear Reader,

Thank you for taking a chance on my book! I can't believe I've done it again. I hope you enjoyed the story as much as I loved writing it. If you did, I would be incredibly grateful if you could take a moment to leave a review or give it a rating.

Every single review makes a big difference—it helps other readers discover my work and supports me as an author.

Your kind words might even inspire me to keep writing more stories like this one. Who knows? Your review could even be featured in one of my marketing campaigns—how exciting would that be?

Thanks a million!

Love,
Brogan x

P.S. DON'T FORGET! Sign up on my VIP email list! You will get early access to all sorts of goodies, including: signed copies, private giveaways, advance notice of future projects and free stuff! The link is on my website at **www.brogan-thomas.com** your email will be kept 100% private, and you can unsubscribe at any time, with zero spam.

ABOUT THE AUTHOR

Brogan lives in Ireland with her husband and their eleven furry children: five furry minions of darkness (aka the cats), four hellhounds (the dogs), and two traditional unicorns (fat, hairy Irish cobs).

In 2019 she decided to embrace her craziness by writing about the imaginary people that live in her head. Her first love is her husband, followed by her number-one favourite furry child Bob the cob, then reading. When not reading or writing, she can be found knee-deep in horse poo and fur while blissfully ignoring all adult responsibilities.

amazon.com/author/broganthomas

facebook.com/BroganThomasBooks

instagram.com/broganthomasbooks

goodreads.com/Brogan_Thomas

bookbub.com/authors/brogan-thomas

Also by Brogan Thomas

Creatures of the Otherworld series

Cursed Wolf (Forrest)

Cursed Demon (Emma)

Cursed Vampire (Tru)

Cursed Witch (Tuesday)

Cursed Fae (Pepper)

Cursed Dragon (Kricket)

Rebel of the Otherworld series

Rebel Unicorn (Tru)

Rebel Vampire (Tru)

The Bitten Chronicles

Bitten Shifter (Lark)

Bitten Vampire (Winifred)

Made in the USA
Middletown, DE
22 March 2025